For Jason: this book would never have happened
without you.

And for my mother and those nights playing hangman in
the living room with a child who wouldn't sleep.

Sleepless

LOUISE MUMFORD

ONE PLACE. MANY STORIES

HQ
An imprint of HarperCollins*Publishers* Ltd
1 London Bridge Street
London SE1 9GF

HarperCollins*Publishers*
1st Floor, Watermarque Building, Ringsend Road
Dublin 4, Ireland

www.harpercollins.co.uk

This paperback edition 2020
2
This edition published in Great Britain by
HQ, an imprint of HarperCollins*Publishers* Ltd 2020

ISBN: 9780008412241

MIX
Paper from
responsible sources
FSC
www.fsc.org   FSC® C007454

This book is produced from independently certified FSC™ paper
to ensure responsible forest management.

For more information visit: www.harpercollins.co.uk/green

Printed and bound by
CPI Group (UK) Ltd, Croydon, CR0 4YY

Chapter 1

There was already a gridlock of cars stretching away behind the accident. *Her* accident. Thea felt a weird ownership over it, like a cat licking at her poor dead kitten.

Her fault – no doubt.

It had to be. In total, she'd probably only slept for four hours … that week.

Behind her was the three-vehicle sandwich in which her car was the crushed metal filling. She staggered back and tried to close the mangled door.

Someone pulled at her elbow: a man, dragging her back from the road where she stood gazing into the traffic. He was uninjured but shouting something, and Thea couldn't focus, her mind slipping off him in the same way his glasses slid down his sweaty nose.

The actual moment of impact had been strangely soothing. Thea couldn't remember any sound really, so there had just been this lovely, pillowy-white cushioning as the airbag deployed and then – whoosh! – like a fairground ride, she was spun around.

She hadn't done it on purpose. She'd thought about things like that quite a few times, in those dead, red-eye hours of the night when she felt like the only person left on earth who was still awake.

Ironically, as her car smashed into the one in front, she had actually been congratulating herself that she'd got through the day, that she could do this living thing, even without any sleep, with just a cold sponge for a brain and sandpaper balls for eyes.

She could do it.

But clearly, she couldn't.

How many years of sleeplessness? Too many. Too many achingly long nights that then smudged themselves into joyless, grey, listless days before lights out and another eight hours of frantic panicking. Too many nights etched into the bloodshot spiderwebs in the whites of her eyes.

There was a woman with the man now and Thea looked for blood on her, expecting broken limbs and jagged wounds, but there was nothing, not even a torn blouse. Both of them worked their mouths madly, like gulping fish, expectantly looking at her and then the cars and then back to her again. She should respond, she thought, but she didn't know what to say. The words were there, but they were busy dancing in her brain, enjoying themselves – shaken loose by the impact and free to partner up however they chose.

Her car was concertinaed. It was a shock, how impressively the whole thing could crumple, yet keep her whole as a seed inside its tattered fruit.

But, if she was fruit, then she was the rotten kind, she realized with a gulp that turned into a choking gasp. She could have hurt that man and woman staring at her now. She could have *killed* them. Up until that point, the only damage her insomnia had done had been to herself – her social life, her concentration, mood, skin, memory and general joy in living. It had never affected someone else, never nearly crushed them in a smoking metal box.

There was pain now. Her nose, a tender, pulsating blob, her knees suddenly shakier than they had been, blood on her collarbone where her seatbelt had taken a bite.

2

Abruptly, she sank to the cold ground at the roadside. Soon there would be flaring emergency lights and sirens; there would be gentle fingers prodding at her and questions asked and, dimly, she realized she would have to get herself together for all of that. More people gathered, but from her viewpoint sat on the ground, they were just feet, their voices so far above her they may as well have been stars.

There would be so much to do after something like this, Thea thought: the forms and phone calls, appointments and claims. The effort. She didn't have it in her. She felt so light there was nothing left of her and dealing with all of this needed solidity; it needed heft, a person who felt like they left a footprint when they walked. If someone blew on her she would simply dissipate, like dust on the wind.

Idly, she watched liquid seep from under her car and with the same blankness with which she'd thought of everything else, she wondered if the liquid was flammable, or if it was merely water.

She should have cared, one way or the other.

At that moment her hand buzzed. She blinked. Maybe it was an injury of some kind, she thought slowly. She would probably need to get it checked out, once she got up from this really rather comfortable bit of damp ground. It buzzed again and this time her eyes managed to get the message over to her brain that she was still clutching her phone. Looking down at it, a notification flashed up, some advert from one of her apps, something she'd probably seen a thousand times before. At first, she thought it was the universe's idea of a cruel joke. But then, as she sat there amongst the twisted metal and shattered glass, she came to think of it more as salvation:

Morpheus. Dream your way to a better you – one sleep at a time.

3

Chapter 2

Thea stared at the frog.

She had successfully risen from the dead for yet another day.

It was one week after the car crash. Thea had removed all clocks from her bedroom to prevent feeling anxious at night about the hours passing. However, this now meant she spent the time feeling anxious about *not knowing* how many hours were passing, which she wasn't sure was an improvement. Last night she had certainly spent many hours in bed, a lot of them with her eyes shut kidding herself she was dozing. The sky had been a watery blue when she finally did drop off.

Waking to the alarm was like dragging herself out of a deep grave.

She did the usual estimation again: an hour or so of sleep, tops. That was pretty much classed as sleep deprivation, wasn't it? Some dictatorships used that as torture. By rights, after years of sleeping like this, she shouldn't have been walking, talking, working … driving. She should have been huddled in a corner, hollow-eyed and drooling.

Mornings were finely tuned. As adrenaline kicked at brain cells that only wanted sleep, she had discovered that mornings were not a time for decision-making. She washed, dressed in the clothes laid out ready the night before, grabbed her pre-prepared breakfast and lunch and got out of the door, her head beginning to pound.

She was a bruise and the rest of the world was a poking finger. The frog looked at her.

Instead of work, this morning Thea found herself at the Car Recovery Centre, picking her way through the graveyard of other people's vehicles with an overly cheerful assistant. She clutched a cardboard box to her chest. It was filled with the belongings that had been rescued from her car. The bright green frog sprawled on top, a present from her mother when she had bought her first car. He had a red kerchief around his neck and a button in his middle that, when pressed, played a selection of children's songs. His green was clean, his kerchief still tied neatly, his button still working. It was as if the crash had never happened. She, on the other hand, felt as if her own stuffing was showing.

'We clear out the cars ourselves, but just wanna check that there's nothing we missed.' The man edged his stomach past the hulk of an estate car.

'Umm … I'm okay. You seem to have it all here. I don't need to see the—'

'There you go.' He pointed.

The thing in front of her still had some of the essential features of a car, but they were in all the wrong places: wheels squashed too close together, windscreen crumpled, half the bonnet missing. Suddenly, the car park around her shifted and fell away and she was back in the driver's seat, the airbags a cushion around her, smoke in her hair.

She took a deep breath.

Someone else could have ended up as twisted and shattered as the lump of metal and glass in front of her.

And then, within twenty minutes, she really was back in the driver's seat. A different car provided by her insurance, the inside smelling of polish and air freshener.

All she had to do was turn the ignition key.

A woman with a clipboard stood expectantly by the car, waiting for her to drive away, smile frozen.

It was now 10 a.m. and the world had come into pulsing, throbbing focus. Thea popped a paracetamol for her eternal headache, stared at the dashboard and blinked a few times, hoping that would make her eyelids lighter.

The woman waited expectantly.

All she had to do was turn the key.

Her hand hovered near the ignition, but, in her head, she could hear the grinding squeal of metal against metal and the noise was so loud it made her fingers shake.

People as twisted and shattered as that lump of metal and glass.

She fumbled for the door handle and lurched out of the car, grabbing her box of belongings.

'Umm … Miss Mackenzie?' She heard the woman call out after her, but the voice was an echo and Thea walked fast, away, out of the car park, not looking back.

'I'm sorry!' She shouted behind her. 'Can you just—? Look, I'll pick it up later …'

And she kept walking until the whole place was out of sight and she was out of breath, her eyes stinging with tears she hadn't realized she'd cried. The frog stared at her as she got out her phone to call a taxi, and, once again, the notification popped up on her screen:

Morpheus. Dream your way to a better you – one sleep at a time.

Thea blamed the frog and the broken carcass of her car as the reasons why she found herself that evening in the local pub, squashed between her desk-mate, Lisa, and a man from a different department with a thin face and thinner hair.

The office where she spent her days moving numbers from one spreadsheet to another was a grey, open-plan box. It always smelled of microwave-ready meals from the encrusted kitchen in the corner, had carpet the consistency of Velcro and an air-conditioning system that had a poor grasp of the seasons. She didn't even have a desk of her own but shared one with Lisa, a middle-aged woman who filled her workspace with so many photographs, paperweights and cute figures that they often made attempts to colonize Thea's territory. She spent probably too much of her day pushing back googly-eyed unicorns with a pencil. One cuddly car-frog was more than enough for her.

But, this time, when Lisa had asked her to the pub for after-work drinks, Thea had said yes.

She deserved a night out. She deserved the kind of night other people had regularly. One without worrying about how late it could get and that she wouldn't have time for her wind-down routine and it was Thursday and she had work the next morning and she couldn't get up late but she wouldn't get any sleep at all and that car crash would be nothing compared to the mistakes she could make if she was utterly, utterly sleepless—

'See? Aren't you glad you came out? You should do it more often.' Lisa's nails had tiny daisies painted on them.

It was Margaret's leaving drinks. Thea hadn't really known that Margaret had ever arrived in the first place.

'Too good for the likes of us, eh?' The thin man smiled.

Thea thought about trying to explain it. She didn't feel like she was better than them at all; in fact they were all quite clearly better than her – better at being human and sociable and remembering each other's birthdays and the ages of their children. Thea didn't have the energy for any of that. She tried sleeping later at the weekends in the hope that would tide her over for the coming week, but it never did. Sleep debt, it was called, and her debt was the kind that got loan sharks circling. She would never be able to repay it.

But that was going to stop, Thea thought, taking a swig of her wine. She couldn't let insomnia continue to ruin her days as well as her nights. A life – that's what she was going to have. Starting now.

'Cheers, Mark,' she said, raising her glass with a hand that continued to shake.

'It's Mike.'

Luckily, her 7 p.m. boost of brief energy kicked in and she listened, laughed in the right places, bought drinks, admired photos of holidays and children and did it all despite the fact that her brain began to whirl and the noise and heat of the pub began to close in on her.

'And so, Mark, what do you like to do in your free time?'

He had a weak chin and there was a strange smell to him, as if he'd been out in the rain and left to dry too slowly, but he seemed pleasant enough. Thea smiled.

'It's Mike.'

More photos, more drinks, more laughing, more brain swirling, more noise and heat. But the noise was welcome; it drowned out the sound of grinding metal that she couldn't get out of her head. Lisa's perfume masked the acrid smell of burnt rubber.

People as twisted and shattered as that lump of metal and glass.

'Another, Mark?' She forced the corners of her mouth back up into a smile and motioned with her empty wine glass.

'Mike.'

'Shit! Sorry! Really I'm—'

But he had already turned away to the woman on his other side. She couldn't blame him. It seemed that she could do everything except remember this man's name. It slipped out of her grasp every time she opened her mouth. The wine churned in her empty stomach and suddenly she wanted to leave, before Mark – Mike! – told everyone how stupid she was, before she threw up the wine, before her exhausted brain refused to tell her equally exhausted body what to do and she had to be carried out of the pub like an invalid.

Using every last bit of willpower, she heaved herself up from her seat and shuffled past Lisa who tried to grab her hand and slur something incomprehensible. Then she was out of the door,

8

the air hitting her like an open palm. She wasn't sure if it was alcohol or exhaustion that made her steps wobble.

Of course, back at home, after a bath and a ready meal, she was wide awake. This state continued until early the next morning, and, at some point during one of those red-eyed hours, she looked once more at the notifications on her phone, emboldened by the wine still fizzing in her blood.

Morpheus. Dream your way to a better you – one sleep at a time. She clicked on it.

Chapter 3

'Well, it's probably a cult, isn't it, darling?'

It was a week after Thea's unsuccessful trip to the pub and her mother was eating haloumi salad, her silk scarf nearly trailing in the food. Luckily, you had to get really close to see that the scarf was printed with tiny little vaginas.

'You'll get there and then, give it a few weeks, you'll be having orgies and giving blow jobs. Constantly. Mark my words. Cult.'

Sometimes Thea wished she didn't have a mother who said things like "orgies" and "blow jobs" in the middle of a crowded restaurant where the tables were so close you could practically breathe on someone else's food.

'A cult might be good for you.' Vivian speared an asparagus tip thoughtfully. 'More sex.'

Thea could feel her face burning. She wasn't sure how much more of this she could stand.

Vivian lowered her voice to a dramatic stage whisper, but couldn't hide the glint in her eyes: '*I think I have more sex than you!*'

She probably did. Thea had to admit it.

'Mum! I swear I will leave if you carry on!' Thea tried to keep her voice stern as Vivian smiled at the few furtive glances she was getting, like a queen amongst her courtiers.

'Sorry, teapot. Can't help myself. Winding you up is too much fun. Will be good.'

Thea hated being called "teapot" too. Her mother had started it when she was little because, 'You had such a sweet little rounded tummy and these skinny arms and legs.' Vivian thought it cute. Thea disagreed.

'Right. It's not a cult. It's a trial for a new sleep app and they'll pay for me to be a part of it. All I have to do is apply for an interview. Thing is, it'll last for six weeks, and obviously the office won't give me leave for that long so' – Thea momentarily found her ham panini fascinating – 'umm … if I'm accepted, I'll just leave my job.'

That was all it had ever been – a job. Not a career, not a vocation, not a calling. Hers was one desk among many in an office with strip lighting that buzzed. It paid the bills. Of course, those bills would still need to be paid, even if she left that desk …

Unhinged, that's how she felt. It was as if the car accident had snapped a vital part of her and it was now flapping wildly in the wind, loose from its fixings, hanging in there by not very much at all.

Vivian stopped eating and reached across the table, laying her hand over Thea's. She stared intensely into her daughter's eyes and, when she spoke, it was with a deliberate solemnity. 'That, my love, is the best news I've heard this year. I'm delighted! You're wasted in … whatever it is that you do in that little office. Come help us out at HQ. We always need someone to paint the placards.'

HQ was a living room. The Menopausal Army ('Probably best to call us Post-Menopausal now, darling!') had had many names over the years but always the same goal: change. Vivian Mackenzie had spent nearly thirty fervent, bright-eyed years protesting, marching, arguing and educating on anything and everything that needed it. A lot of things needed it. They still did, but Vivian had, over the last few years, taken a step back from leading it all. Thea was banned from calling this retirement.

'You are a creative soul, anyway – I've always thought it,' Vivian continued. 'We can find you another job.' She gripped Thea's hand tighter. 'I blame myself, you know, for this inability of yours to sleep properly. We moved around so much when you were little, there was no routine, no stability. You were so well behaved, but it's left its mark. I see that now.' She emphasized the next words. '*I own it.*'

There it was. There was the pause, which Thea was meant to fill with the reassurance that Vivian's chaotic lifestyle when she was little had not irrevocably scarred her in any way. Old age was making her mother sentimental.

'Mum, it's not your fault—'

'Is it dangerous? How does it work? You hear such stories these days. These big companies, they have no morals, no sense of responsibility …'

'I don't know. I'm being sent an introductory pack. I can back out if it doesn't sound right. There are loads of these kinds of sleep apps around. It'll probably turn out to be crap and I'll be back at square one.'

Vivian sighed, frowned and fiddled with the huge turquoise bangle on her wrist. Today she was dressed in a bright red tunic top and a necklace in the shape of bats joined together at the wing, even though Hallowe'en was weeks away. Thea wished she'd worn better-fitting jeans, and that maybe she hadn't decided to cut her own fringe this month. But both jeans and hair were clean, and on some bleak mornings, after only an hour's sleep, that was all she could manage.

'I don't like it,' Vivian finally proclaimed. 'But I raised you to know your own mind. So do it if you want to. But you call me the minute anything feels off and I will come and get you wherever you are. And, darling … remember the keys.'

Ah yes, the old key trick: Vivian's idea of teaching Thea self-defence when she turned thirteen. 'When out late at night, teapot, hold your keys in your hand like this … yes, that's it, with the points sticking out between your fingers, like a knuckleduster. Okay, then if any man makes a grab at you, just swipe … yes, like that … mind the cat, teapot … swipe up and nearly blind the bugger.' She hadn't yet had a chance to try it out.

'Okay, Mum.'

Vivian unwound her scarf, shaking it out so anyone left in the café who hadn't yet seen its print got an eyeful. 'I suppose you could make some new friends at least, and anyway – you might not even get accepted for this interview, hmm?'

That was the thing, Thea thought as she avoided her mother's eye. She already had been.

Chapter 4

The male voice was deep, rich and warm:

'It suddenly seems like everyone is talking about sleep.

'You already know how vital it is, otherwise you wouldn't be listening to this. Experts are still not sure exactly what the sleeping brain does. They know it orders and organizes itself ready for the next day, much like a parent picking up after their children. The brain dreams and tries to make sense of the world.

'You know the scare stories. People who consistently don't get enough sleep have a higher risk of health issues from cancer to heart disease; they are more likely to suffer from dementia when they get older. They get angry more quickly, feel more stupid, react more slowly.

'Modern society is caffeine-fuelled and overstimulated. You've probably tried all the sleep aids. Your bedroom is a lavender-scented, cool, dark, silk-sheeted, mood-music oasis, right?

'And yet you still don't sleep.

'This is why you have reached out to us.

'We are different. Brainchild of revered internet guru Moses Ing, this technology has been decades in research and development, combining the best of recent sleep theory to help you fall into a peaceful, restorative, long slumber.

'But this technology promises even more. With continued use, you can use the app and the hardware to actually reprogramme your brain. Want to lose weight? Manage stress? Stop smoking? Have more confidence? The only limit is you.

'Intrigued? We hope you are. Be the first to experience the new sleep technology that will change the world – one sleep at a time.

'Morpheus.

'Dream your way to a better you.'

The envelope from Ing Enterprises held only two slim cards. On one was the link to the audio file she had just listened to with the words 'One-time use only' printed underneath.

The other card simply said:

Preliminary Meeting
Your Sleep Guru is: Harriet Stowe
Venue: Home address
Time: Saturday 16th Sept, 11 a.m.

Chapter 5

Thea felt much the same about people visiting her house as she did about splinters – she wanted them out.

Her house was tiny for a start: the stairs were in the living room and the living room was nearly in the kitchen, with the dining room as merely a cramped corner. She liked it like that. It was her small safe space where she could crawl and hide after an exhausting day spent trying to seem human.

Two people in it seemed too much.

'So,' Harriet Stowe said, sat at Thea's dining table and glancing at an open folder in front of her. 'I hope you understand the slightly clandestine route we have had to take. Our competitors are ruthless, and we cannot let any significant information out into the public domain, certainly not until we have launched.'

Harriet had put her voluminous, purple-lined coat on the newel post of the stairs. Thea's fingers itched to move it to the coat hook, where coats were expected to be.

She had no other choice but to be strict about the house. It had to have the right lighting and temperature, it had to have candles and a scent diffuser constantly puffing out clouds of lavender mist. It had to be quiet and clean and peaceful, because that's what every article about sleep had impressed upon her: you had to create the right environment for it to come, blinking into sight, like a shy, rare animal.

'I always find, in circumstances such as these, it's best to be led by the client,' Harriet continued, pushing her cat's-eye reading glasses down her nose so she could peer at her paperwork. 'Please feel free to ask me any questions about the trial that may be on your mind.'

Moving into her kitchen, which was the size of a postage stamp, Thea attempted to remember how much instant coffee a normal person put in their mug. Two tablespoons of it was definitely too much.

'Thea?' Harriet steepled her fingers together and rested her little pointed chin on them.

Thea came out of the kitchen, carrying the coffees, which were definitely not the right colour. Her mind, rather unhelpfully, went as blank as a badly loaded webpage.

'Umm … My mother thinks you're a cult.'

Harriet raised a carefully shaded eyebrow.

Thea put the coffees down. 'That wasn't my question! Umm … what risks are there?'

Harriet considered her coffee with a distinct air of trepidation. 'Ah, good question.'

Thea suspected that was what she always said, regardless of the actual first question offered. Harriet's stiletto heels sank into the carpet, jabbing deep holes into the pile. She had already left a trail of little woodworm pocks from the front door to the chair.

'Shall I tell you a bit more about the process first? So you understand, yes?'

Thea nodded and Harriet's hand hovered near the cup. She was in her forties – older than Thea who was twenty-seven – and dressed in the kind of well-made pencil skirt and blouse that could not be picked up in the supermarket as part of a weekly shop.

'The six-week trial is made up of three phases and each phase lasts two weeks. Phase One is orientation, where we get to know you. Phase Two is where we start with the tech, fine-tuning it as appropriate, with sleep as our goal. Phase Three is where we then use the tech to help you become the best that you can be.'

Best? Thea would gladly have settled for merely better. Even a bit.

Harriet's delivery was smooth and expressive, and Thea got the distinct impression that this was a script she had gone through many times before. She still hadn't picked up the mug.

'The tech itself comprises two parts, the part you download onto your phone as an app, and the incredibly small discs that fix, completely harmlessly and without pain, to your temples. They work in tandem using a variety of technologies, some well-known, some new, to help you drift into the best sleep of your life.'

A diffuser puffed wheezily.

'I am assuming you have exhausted all other possible options – therapy? Medication?' Harriet picked up a pen as sleek and shiny as a bullet.

'Yes,' Thea said.

It wasn't a complete lie – she had at least attended the therapy sessions a few times. And she'd tried medication, which, despite her misgivings, had worked. During the day. The office hadn't been keen on her napping her working hours away.

'And how do you think a lack of sleep is affecting you? Relationships and so on? Would you say you've got to a critical point?' Harriet's eyes ranged around the room, taking in the distinct lack of any happy couple or girl squad photos amongst the candles.

Thea rubbed at her eyes. It would have been a relief every so often if she could have just taken out her eyeballs and dunked them in cold water. The gunk and grit of sleeplessness would float off down the plughole and she could then pop the eyeballs back in, totally refreshed.

'Critical point?' Thea went over and hung up Harriet's coat. 'Yeah, I think it's been reached.'

People as twisted and shattered as that lump of metal and glass.

Harriet paused in her writing, 'I'm sorry to hear that,' she said as she considered her over the top of her glasses. It sounded genuine. All of a sudden, Thea's eyes began to sting. Harriet pushed her glasses up a little and considered the papers in front of her. Instinctively, she reached out once more for the coffee mug, looked in it, paused, and set it back down again.

Harriet picked up a framed photo. 'But your mother, Vivian Mackenzie. You spend a lot of time with her?'

Did Harriet mean "too much time"? Thea couldn't tell.

'Some. Not much. I have friends.'

She was getting good at lying.

'And your mother's … activism? She founded … let me see, The Menopausal Army, no?' Harriet couldn't stop the flicker of a smile at the name. 'At Ing Enterprises we are not so sure this would be such a good fit for us.'

Thea's coffee sloshed over the side of the mug as she put it down too heavily. *Not a good fit.* What did that mean? Would she be blacklisted from the trial because her mother had morals and an insane need to march every single weekend, no matter what the weather was like?

'Oh – that? She's retired now. Completely.'

The lie came out so easily. But it wasn't completely untrue – her mother had stopped doing the on-camera stuff and organizing campaigns. She'd definitely taken a step back … just not quite as far back as Thea would have Harriet believe.

Harriet jotted down notes. Thea fiddled with a loose thread on her jumper, wanting the woman gone, and the skin of her safe little house to close back over after the splinter had been tweezered out.

Safe little house.

Thea realized with a cold, sick feeling in her stomach that, in about four months' time, if she gave up her job and her savings ran out, she would no longer be able to afford this safe little house. That flapping, unhinged part of her mind creaked.

'Anyhow. We are getting a little ahead of ourselves.' Harriet smiled. 'It's not yet guaranteed that you are the type of candidate we are looking for. May we now move on to the second part of this little chat?'

It was much like delicate dentistry. Harriet magnified and examined, jabbing and poking, blowing air on corners of Thea's mind that Thea hadn't really known existed, manoeuvring around any white-hot patches where a nerve throbbed. Questions and topics ranged from her childhood to what perfume she wore, the future of robotics to what type of tea she drank. Thea didn't know what the "correct" answers were, so had no clue as to whether she was doing well – or not.

She liked to do well.

After about half an hour, Harriet sighed happily and stretched her shoulders.

'Well, it's been lovely meeting you. We'll be in touch to let you know if you have been selected for preliminary testing.'

Once again, she grasped the handle of her mug, a natural move to finish the drink before she left. Before she could stop herself, she had taken a large gulp and that was when Thea knew that Harriet's foundation was worth the money: it hid the shade of puce she must have turned when she finally tasted the coffee.

Only later, when she was vacuuming the stiletto pocks from the carpet, did Thea realize that she'd never told anyone from Ing Enterprises about The Menopausal Army, or even her mother's name.

Chapter 6

A beard spoke to her.

'My name is Rory. I'll be looking after you tonight,' it explained. There was a face amongst the hair but, mired in grogginess, Thea couldn't focus on it.

A door slid open with a sigh.

'This is your preliminary sleep assessment. You passed the interview stage – well done. We have a few questions to get through first, just some routine paperwork, and then we can begin. You will spend the night here, and we'll monitor your sleep. As you know, this is the final stage. If we approve you here, that's it – you're in. You have your overnight bag?'

The building she'd arrived at was nothing special and, frankly, special was what Thea had been expecting. The clinic room had made up for that a little with its white surfaces like shiny icing on a cake. It was small but more expensively fitted out than the whole of her own house. The bed had a reassuringly plump mattress. At least she'd be comfortable whilst lying awake in the dark for the whole night.

'I can watch TV?' Thea asked.

Rory smiled, but it was hard to see under the beard. His eyes were kind though. He was the only slightly scruffy thing about the room with his saggy trousers and a faded T-shirt that had once probably had a superhero reference on it.

'Of course,' he said. 'You're not in prison, Miss Mackenzie.'

Sleep was a demanding god who required silk pillowcases and expensive room sprays, hypnotherapy and the soundtrack of a gentle river flowing through a forest. She'd tried everything.

Except *this*.

'Ready?' Rory asked.

Six hours later, the high-pitched wail of an alarm didn't wake her up because she hadn't yet fallen asleep.

Her mind didn't *race* at night, because that would suggest that it could eventually tire itself out – no, her mind *fizzed* like nuclear fusion, something with an infinite capacity to continue fizzing no matter how late, or early, it got.

The overhead light blazed into life, nearly blinding her. Squinting and disorientated by the sound, Thea scrambled out of bed, not sure what was going on, but pretty certain she didn't want to be in bed to greet it. Rory appeared as she was fumbling with her slippers. She felt herself blush under the bright light, awkward in her sensible pyjamas. He yelled something she couldn't hear above the pounding, painful sound of the alarm.

Rolling his eyes, he came into the room and took her arm, leaning in close. For some reason, she was acutely aware that her pyjamas had penguins on them. In scarves.

'SO SORRY! FIRE ALARM! WE HAVE TO GO!'

A few minutes later, Thea was standing in the clinic car park in her fluffy slippers, damp spreading into them from the wet ground. The building itself was a drab blot of grey behind them and the street lights turned the puddles to gold.

Rory had unplugged her but there had been no time to unstick all the patches and wires, making her look like the unfinished science experiment that she was. Other members of the sleep trial and their attendants milled around, making polite small talk and exchanging sympathetic glances.

'So. *Do you come here often?*' A man in shorts and a T-shirt nudged her, his feet bare and turning a mottled purple from the cold. Varicose veins bulged up on his skinny legs like inquisitive worms. He was obviously pleased with his wit.

Thea didn't like being nudged.

She tried to avoid eye contact with him, but he moved in front of her, an expectant grin on his face. Thea turned to stare at the chain-link fence.

She heard the man sigh. 'It don't cost anything to be pleasant. Cheer up, love.'

Thea took a deep breath.

Heat whooshed, not over but *through* her. She felt as if it could shoot out of her eyes like she'd seen in superhero films. If she looked at him, she could turn him to ash.

Cheer up, love. Be pleasant, even if your brain feels as if it could ooze through your nose. Smile, even if this might be your last chance to get help and you are wasting it out here in the car park wearing soggy slippers. The nice man wants a pleasant conversation. *Be nice to the man.*

It was a well-known side effect of poor sleep, wasn't it? Recklessness. She'd read that somewhere.

What happened next, therefore, wasn't strictly her fault.

She took a step closer and brought her knee up hard, aiming for his crotch. But he, seeing the intention in her stare, angled away just in time and she ended up kneeing him in the thigh instead.

'So sorry!' Rory hurriedly appeared between them, leading Thea away and calling back over his shoulder, 'She's deeply disturbed. Shouldn't be unsupervised.'

'She tried to knee me in the balls!' the man shouted after them.

'No, no, that was just … an uncontrollable leg twitch …' Rory interjected before Thea could say anything.

He plonked her on a low wall. 'What are you doing?'

'He was a creep!' she said, crossing her arms.

'The world is full of them.' Rory sighed. 'Can't knee them all in the balls.'

Thea watched the man shiver as he walked away, his shoulders beginning to hunch. He looked older and thinner than she'd thought, now that he was further away. It was easy to call him a creep, she found herself thinking, when in fact, he'd maybe just been another exhausted human being like her, trying, in his own ham-fisted way, to make a connection with someone, anyone, because it was cold and dark and wide-awake nights lasted a very long time.

'Look, I'm sorry but we've just been told that this session will be called off for tonight.' Rory looked down at his clipboard, a plastic ink stamp dangling from it on a piece of string: surprisingly low-tech for such a cutting-edge company. 'Can't really get any useful data after this. It's a shame because this was the last round of tests before the trial begins. You were so close.'

And, to her complete surprise and shame, Thea felt hot tears forming. 'You mean – that's it?'

In that moment, she felt the weight of all the years she still had left – all those sleepless years – and that weight crushed her.

Rory considered her. There were little lines fanning out from his eyes and, Thea thought, he was probably one of those people who had a proper, hearty, throw-your-head-back laugh.

'It's – what? Around four in the morning,' he said. 'You've been awake the whole time. And you've lived like this for …'

… too long …

'… pretty much all your adult life. Whoa …' He exhaled.

Rory gazed at her thoughtfully. Thea imagined him in some sort of flat-share where they all got takeaways and lounged around on cushions on the floor. It was the kind of place where there were always dirty dishes in the sink and a permanent message on a chalkboard in the kitchen: 'BUY MILK!!!!'

Thea never ran out of milk; she had her groceries delivered every week.

'Look. I wouldn't normally do this.'

What? For a crazy moment, Thea thought he was going to ask her out on a date. Would she want to go on a date with him? He was nice-enough looking, under the beard, and he'd been kind to her. But it was dark and she couldn't see him properly, and beards gave you a rash, didn't they?

He angled away from her for a few seconds, fumbling with his clipboard, then he glanced to see if anyone was near. It was done so quickly. One moment he'd bent towards her and Thea hadn't known what to think; the next he was gone.

There was a piece of paper in her hand.

Thea took a closer look. It was all about her: weight, height, sleep history, some graphs and numerical data that she couldn't decipher. But, more importantly, the form had been stamped:

CLIENT APPROVED.

Chapter 7

It was the kind of place where hitchhikers got chopped up by axe-wielding maniacs. Brown, bare hills, a lonely road, a few run-down houses, clearly abandoned – just sky and grass and a low-level sense of fear at an animal level.

'One room, one night. You're the last of 'em,' the man muttered from behind the reception desk whilst writing in a book as yellowed as his fingers. He looked as weathered and grey as ancient stone, his face pitted as if it had endured centuries of unrelenting rain.

The pub was called "Sanity's End" with thick walls, mullioned windows and empty hooks where pretty hanging baskets had once swung. Now they were just hooks, as if the pub had armoured itself, porcupine-style. How was it still in business? There was no one else around and the whole area was too grim and stark to be a tourist spot.

'Busy lately?' Thea ventured.

The man looked up and put the pen he'd been using behind his ear. A few flakes of dandruff dislodged and fell gently to be reunited with their friends on his shoulder.

'What do you think?' he said harshly.

Thea took a look around at the ghost-bar, the stools still stacked on the tabletops, the unravelling carpet and the heavy curtains that had once been red but were now so covered in dust they'd paled to a rusty pink. There was a sticky wood veneer on the reception desk, which held a dusty stand of local brochures and a cardboard charity box in the shape of a lifeboat. Thea put in all the change she had left – after all, she was unlikely to need it in the next six weeks.

'See there?' A grimy fingernail pointed to a group of framed photographs on a nearby wall. 'Used to be a lifeboat man. She were mine.'

Thea dutifully peered at the picture, what she could see of it under a thick layer of dust on the glass that made the boat look as if it was nosing out of a fog.

'Your lot keeps us going since the tourists stopped.' He sniffed and turned to consider the three large brass keys hanging behind him. When he moved one, it left a brighter key-shaped spot on the wall. 'When the monastery closed down over on the island in the Eighties, there was still the lighthouse for people to go and see. But that dried up too, eventually, taking the village 'ere on the mainland with it. No one needed the boat trip over, see? That's how it goes.' His bushy brows drew together for a moment. 'But then you lot came and bought the whole place. Like I said, you're the last of 'em. They's been arriving all week cos I've only got a few rooms, see? Some of you what comes late in the day, you can't go out in the boat at night and 'ave to stay over.'

The sleep trial itself was to take place on a small island in a purpose-built Sleep Centre, just a fifteen-minute boat ride away. Privacy was vital, she had been told.

'Don't look like that!' Harriet had remonstrated via Skype. 'There is a regular boat service, specially constructed, state-of-the-art buildings, living quarters and all the facilities you could want. Think of it as a luxury hotel stay. It's certainly not Alcatraz!'

Harriet hadn't mentioned that she'd have to stay in the pub at the end of the world the night before, however. Not quite as hi-tech. The man put the heavy room key, rough with rust, into her hand.

'Kitchen's closed because it's late,' he continued.

It was 5 p.m.

'But I could make you a sandwich.' He shuffled off through another tattered curtain behind him. Thea heard some clunking noises and he emerged with a can.

'Tuna,' he said, reading from the label. 'I can make you a tuna sandwich.'

Thea wasn't quite so keen on the idea of a tuna and dandruff sandwich.

'That's kind but I'm not hungry, thank you,' she said hastily. 'Probably have an early night.'

'Suit yourself. No loud music, no animals, no extra guests permitted in your room. There's a TV but we don't get much of a reception up here. Breakfast is paid for so I have to serve it. At eight o'clock, it'll be. They order it in – fancy stuff, half of it looks like kitty litter.'

He thumped a card down onto the desk in front of her, wrinkling his nose at it as if it smelled.

'They say I also got to get feedback from you. The guests. You gotta fill in that form. About your stay. Apparently the last ones said I could offer a' – he stopped and shuffled through the other cards he had in his hand – '*more sophisticated range of amenities.* I mean, what else do they want? They gotta kettle and them little fancy soaps … Anyway. They made me watch a video about it. So, there you go.' He passed her a snapped-off chunk of chocolate.

Then he stuffed some dry leaves into her hand, 'Couldn't get rose petals. Sorry.'

Thea studied the melting, leaf-studded chocolate in her palm.

'Umm … I think you're meant to put those on the bed? The chocolate and the … petals?' she managed.

He stared at her with his arms crossed, a face of stone.

'I know.'

The next afternoon Thea stood on the deserted dock, feeling queasy.

A seagull screeched above her and she felt the sound in her teeth. There was a rhythmic slapping of waves against concrete and the sky was the colour of stewed tea.

Harriet had said she could opt out after Phase One, no matter what. And Phase One was just orientation, a "getting to know you", probably some sleep tracking and questionnaires. This was the social media age! Everyone was now accountable for everything! What could they do? The worst was that any information gained on her sleep would then be passed on to some big data company and for years afterwards businesses would try to sell her mattresses and herbal tablets any time she searched the web.

So, all she had to do was buckle up, get through a few weeks and then go home, dignity, data and brain intact.

The queasiness remained.

That morning she had filled in her accommodation feedback form with the comment "Couldn't have asked for more". She had found herself kind of admiring the pub owner for his resistance to hospitality even though that was his actual business.

A plate with a bacon roll on it had appeared by her elbow at breakfast. She had glanced up at him as he had left the room, but his face remained a mask of pitted granite. Maybe the feedback card had softened him up. There had even been a sprinkling of flour on top of the roll – at least she had *hoped* it was flour and not just more dandruff. She had eaten it anyway. It had smelled delicious and he had been right, the breakfast provided had been kitty litter.

Her thoughts about bacon and anti-social pub owners were interrupted by the confident tap-tapping of someone walking determinedly in heels towards her.

It could only be Harriet. She was the only woman who would wear stilettos to get on a boat.

'Thea! Early. Nice to see. Raring to go?'

Harriet flicked the end of her scarf back over her shoulder. Thea tugged at her bobble hat and nudged the hem of her jeans over her old trainers, feeling dowdy in comparison, a bedraggled stray next to a sleek house cat.

'Is it just me?'

'Oh … yes. You're the last, you see. We had to wait for the weather to clear to make the crossing again for you. Not that I'll overwhelm you with introductions tonight. Plenty of time for that.'

Thea felt she should fill the pause.

'What did you do before—?'

But Harriet interrupted her, standing on tiptoe to wave.

'Boat's here!'

Thea gingerly stepped on, steadied by the skipper, trying to avoid the slippery bits while Harriet strode through as if she was on a New York catwalk and immediately joined the skipper at the front, which was sectioned off by glass; whether this was to intentionally discourage any more questions, Thea couldn't be sure.

She kept her eyes on the mainland receding behind her. The queasiness settled as sour bile in her throat. She watched as the coastline became a blocky shape, and then finally impressionist splodges of muted colour. Thea was leaving behind all of that; instead she was out here, in the grey waves, free, released from job, routine, her whole life, such as it was.

'You okay, Thea?' Harriet called back towards her.

'Fine!'

'Because if you're seasick—'

'No! I'm fine!'

She was fine, even though she'd never learned to swim, had never even put her head under the water in the bath and the boat rocked around alarmingly like a fairground ride – except those rides went through safety checks, didn't they? The sea didn't.

Not for the first time, she cursed her mother for spending

30

hours and hours trying to save the oceans but no time at all teaching her own daughter how to swim.

What had Harriet said? Think of it like a luxury hotel stay.

Okay, so this was a luxury hotel stay. She could go for bracing coastal walks along the clifftops, read books by an open fire, meet new people … meet *some* new people … okay only a *few* new people. She wasn't great at people. A holiday.

As a lab rat.

'Look!' Harriet pointed ahead of them.

Out of the gloom rose sheer cliff walls, black and slick, the waves whirling and churning against them. Dragons. The cliffs looked as if they should have dragons perched on top of them, waiting for one to shrug its wings open and send a scorching arc of fire across the rocks. As the boat got closer, these cliffs blocked out the sky and the world turned to shadow.

Suddenly Thea felt very small.

Chapter 8

'Good morning, Thea Mackenzie.'

Thea stuck her head out from under the duvet and rubbed her eyes, looking for whoever had just come in. 'Huh? Good morn—'

'Your schedule for today is being displayed.'

Thea was talking to the room. She blinked sleepily and her schedule appeared on one wall.

8 a.m.: breakfast, cafeteria, main hall
9 a.m.: welcome address
9.10 a.m.: yoga and meditation, lawn
10 a.m.: health assessment, lab 7
Noon: lunch, cafeteria, main hall
1 p.m.: Sleep School, lecture theatre
3 p.m.: break, free time
3.30 p.m.: cardio, gym studio 2
4.30 p.m.: shower, own room
5 p.m.: health assessment, lab 4
6 p.m.: dinner, cafeteria, main hall
7 p.m.: fitting of sleep monitoring equipment, own room
10 p.m.: recommended wind-down time

Sleep School sounded horrendous. For some reason, Thea

could only imagine this being a room full of prone bodies and the sound of chanting as someone yelled 'SLEEP!' in the face of anyone who dared to open their eyes.

She'd probably got about one hour of sleep. She couldn't blame the room: there was a bed so plush it threatened to swallow her whole as soon as she got into it. She ran a hand over the surface of her bedside table, almost expecting her fingers to sink in, so glossy was the material – *too* glossy – it was starting to remind her of a sick, sweaty fever sheen. The only thing in the space that wasn't cream or white was Thea. She had her penguin pyjamas to thank for that.

As she cleaned her teeth after showering, a towel wrapped around her, she wandered over to the door. Last night, Harriet had closed the door after her as she'd left. Thea hadn't thought about it since. But, looking at it now, the edges of it merely a pencil sketch, she couldn't even work out how it opened – let alone try to lock the damn thing. As she was peering closely at it, it slid open smoothly and Thea found herself nearly nose-to-nose with Harriet.

Harriet stepped back sharply, her startled expression quickly replaced once again by a smile.

'Ah, good morning, Thea. I see you are already up and awake. Perhaps … put on some clothes?' She held out a stack of neatly folded material.

Thea reddened and clutched at her wet towel.

'I was trying to work out how the door opened.'

'There is a biometric sensor – just there.' Harriet pointed to a spot on the wall that looked exactly the same as the rest. 'Just look at it and the door opens.'

'How does it lock?'

'Lock?' A crease appeared between Harriet's perfectly symmetrical brows. 'A lock isn't needed, Thea. The same biometric device is on the outside of your door. Only those with clearance have access to your room. Completely safe.'

The smile intensified.

'Now, the clothes?'

There was a flowing tunic top and trousers in a soft, stretchy material accompanied by a pair of fur-lined moccasins. Her mother would feel vindicated, Thea thought, because there was no way around it – they were cult clothes.

Harriet led her to a cathedral. This cathedral, like every cathedral before it, was built to stun the masses into greater belief. Thea did feel a bit stunned: it was probably all the glossy whiteness everywhere. A glass roof curved over them.

A reverential hush of voices swelled into the space, which consisted of the main hall and the cafeteria. The Sleep Centre was comprised of two large spherical buildings, or "bubbles" as Harriet called them, and currently Thea was in the Client Bubble. Three storeys high, the upper floors were accessed by a gleaming stainless-steel lift in the middle, walkways radiating out from it to the higher floors like rays from the sun.

Out of habit, Thea avoided eye contact as she made her way through the tables.

'How many people are on this trial?' she asked Harriet.

'Fifty.'

And there they all were, choosing food and chatting to each other. It was already making the small of her back sweat. When talking to new people, Thea became an overinflated balloon, stretching out, out, out, until her rubber couldn't stretch anymore and eventually burst, scattering disjointed small talk. Luckily, Harriet guided her to a table on their own. It hadn't escaped Thea that Harriet still got to wear her own clothes: today a silky jumpsuit, the kind that didn't suit Thea because it highlighted the fact that she had too little leg – and too much middle.

'Until the system gets to know you and your dietary needs, you have a pretty standard breakfast. Hope that's okay?'

The plate of food was so wholesomely healthy it looked as if it should have been artfully placed next to a bunch of flowers, or a sunset, and then posted on Instagram. Usually, Thea sploshed milk on some muesli in a Tupperware container when she arrived at work. The most important thing in her mornings was to make sure she got out of the house on time, preferably washed, as she was always still half-asleep. Food was way down on her list of morning priorities.

'So? Excited for today?' Harriet stirred at some purple sludge in her glass. She didn't wait for a response. 'I'll be with you for most of it, unless you're having a health assessment, or you're in a lecture. You're going to love Sleep School: *so* informative. Sleep is fascinating, don't you think?'

'I don't know. I don't get much of it.' The drink in front of her looked like coffee. She sipped at it. It was definitely *not* coffee.

'Made from mushrooms! Amazingly good for you. You'll get used to it. I swear I've lost about a stone working here and I just feel so energized. All the time. It's crazy!'

It was as if someone had turned Harriet up a few notches. Her smile was wider, her voice chummier, her eyes warmer. She was altogether more … everything … compared to the woman who had come to her house a month or so ago. Maybe someone had slipped something into her sludge. Maybe they all had drugs in their food and, in six weeks' time, Thea would wake up to find this had all been a mushroom dream.

'Fellow pioneers!'

A voice rang out. People looked around, confused, trying to locate the person speaking, until others who had worked it out nudged them and pointed upwards.

There on one of the second-floor walkways, a woman stood looking down on them. She had incredibly long, incredibly straight, incredibly red hair.

'Is that Moses Ing?' someone whispered loudly near Thea. 'Thought he was a man?'

Harriet frowned at the whisperer, a young woman with a pencil securing her dark, frizzy hair who smiled widely at Harriet and gave Thea a little wave. The woman on the walkway continued.

'My name is Delores. On behalf of Ing Enterprises I welcome you here today and wish you a happy and healthy stay with us. We are on the cusp of an exciting future.'

Harriet looked up at Delores with the bright-eyed face of someone who has seen God.

'A human being sleeps for roughly eight hours every night. Until very recently, those eight hours have been an unknowable land for scientists. Technology is now allowing us to take a peek at that land, to map and explore it. Getting you to sleep will not be a problem; I guarantee it. Give us a week or so to allow the systems to get to know you and we will then be able to facilitate you into the best sleep of your life. But better than that, we will then be able to help you start building the person you have always wanted to be. How? Through the untapped power of your sleep, and your dreams. You lovely people here before me' – she gestured down to the upturned faces below her, smiling warmly – 'you are the beginning of something that will help humanity take the next evolutionary leap.'

Harriet started to clap enthusiastically, and others joined in. The way she felt today, Thea would not be able to help evolution make a leap so much as a stumbling sprawl. Her eyes felt as if they'd been put in the oven for too long.

'One last bit of housekeeping before I leave you all to it,' Delores said. 'Those of you who have been here for a few days already know that, for clients, there is no internet coverage nor mobile signal.' There was a very slight murmuring and Delores raised her hand for quiet, smiling widely. 'I know, I know – we are all addicted to our phones, myself included.' She waved her own smartphone at them. 'But the studies all agree: these gadgets of ours affect our sleep, not only its duration, but also its quality. If we are here to try and fix your sleep issues, it seems foolish to start off with the biggest problem still lurking in our pockets. Of course, landline phones are available free of charge to allow you to keep in touch with friends and family.'

Thea didn't have a pocket in her cult clothes, but she'd shoved her phone into the waistband of her trousers and she pressed a hand to her middle, feeling the outline of what was now essentially a lump of useless plastic, glass and metal.

'Enjoy today!' The woman raised her voice. 'Enjoy every moment but, best of all, enjoy the new and improved you that is just around the corner!'

At that she stepped out of view. Harriet turned back to Thea and sighed happily.

'Shall we begin?'

Chapter 9

'Kiddy fiddlers,' a man in downward dog whispered to Thea.

'Huh?' It was only a few hours after Delores's inaugural speech and Thea was contemplating her knees very closely.

'The monks here. The monastery was closed down by the Catholic Church years ago. Kiddy fiddlers. Until then it was quite a nice spot. The monks made fudge.'

Thea wasn't sure what the expected response would be to that, and they were now in cat pose so she went with a vague 'Right?'

The monastery itself was up on the hill, not quite at one with the cutesy ducks-and-ice-cream vibe of the green below it where they were currently doing yoga. It was an eyeless, austere blot: a retinal detachment of a place with a bell tower bleeding rust down one wall.

'Why did people want to visit that?' she wondered aloud.

Everyone was attempting a back bend. Thea lay and looked at the sky. The man was more successful, his upside-down face turning purple as he gazed at her, a shark-tooth necklace dangling the wrong way up his nose.

'Beats me,' he wheezed. 'Now, the lighthouse – round the other side of the island? That's where I'd go.'

Maybe one day, Thea thought, people might come to take

pictures of the Sleep Centre. It was an awkward cuckoo amongst the rest of the island's structures, two huge white golf balls separated by a blocky middle bit.

'Bit phallic, no?' her mother had observed when Thea had described it to her via landline after breakfast. 'And in which testicle do you live?'

Thea had smiled. 'The left one. It's called the Client Bubble. The other one is the Staff Bubble where the staff live and there are labs and everything.'

'So, you live in the left testicle. Just making that clear.'

'Yes, thank you, Mother.'

She hadn't been able to see it properly when she'd arrived last night, but now, in the daylight, she could fully take in its clean, sci-fi strangeness. If there were any ghost monks floating around the place, she wondered what they would have made of the Centre: crossed themselves and muttered about the devil?

Meditation ended the session. She took a breath in and then let it out …

One …

Two …

Three …

A warm, wrapped chocolate was pushed into her hand. Thea opened her eyes and found the frizzy-haired woman with pencils in her hair from earlier sitting next to her. The woman pressed a finger to her lips and smiled, then she glanced around at everyone else with their eyes closed and carefully reached into her shoe once more, bringing out more chocolate for herself.

The Centre frowned upon caffeine, refined sugar, processed foods and alcohol.

Foot chocolate was still chocolate. Thea ate it and smiled back.

It was the walls.

Perhaps it was their fever-sheen gleam, or the way they swallowed noise, but after only her first day, Thea felt that they just

39

might swallow her up too. One second there she'd be in her beige clothes, the next she would wander too close to the equally beige walls and they would liquidly close over her and she would be like fruit sinking in cream, never to be seen again.

It was late afternoon and she had half an hour to shower after her gym session. The shower had taken her precisely five minutes and now the walls of her room pressed in on her. She had lived on her own for years and had never experienced a problem with walls before. She liked them. The walls of her house had kept the world out and given her a cocoon in which she'd tried to burrow deep and sleep. Walls were fine.

She wandered into a corridor, smiling politely at the people she passed. Maybe that was it. Maybe it wasn't the walls. Maybe it was the people. In her sleep-deprived experience, people were exhausting, with their egos and subtexts and hints and emotions and needs. She'd always tried to limit people. And now, here she was – surrounded by them.

And the walls.

Her steps quickened.

She had to get out. There was a lighthouse to see, after all, and out in the fields with the empty sky around her, perhaps she would have a chance to think.

Despite half expecting shouts and alarms to go off as soon as she set foot on the gravel, the doors opened without a sound and Thea stepped through. The air was the kind of cold that woke a person up, but politely, without the bite of winter just yet. It was exactly what she needed. There were a few people sitting on the green so she skirted it and took the uphill path that would lead her to the coast.

Her first session at Sleep School had taught her there were two stages of sleep. The first half of the night was ruled more by NREM sleep where the muscles relaxed, but then in the second half, it switched to a dominance of REM sleep, which locked the muscles and allowed the brain to safely dream.

If she'd taken anything away from the lesson, it was that she was obviously not getting enough REM sleep. She wasn't sure she wanted to know what a lack of it could do to a person – maybe she'd skip that lecture.

Thea's thought process was interrupted. She hadn't really ever done much rambling and she was discovering that, as it was the middle of October, the polite cold was actually becoming pretty sharp, especially as she hadn't been issued with a coat and was only wearing her thin cult clothes. Worse than that, nature, at that moment, had turned into a stony path, which she wasn't sure her stupid soft-soled moccasins could handle.

Thea had to stop. She was more out of breath than she was going to admit and, so far, she hadn't seen any sign of a light-house. The moccasins were not going to make it, she could feel sharp little stones gouging into the butter-soft leather with every step and she wasn't keen on destroying them on her first day. She resolved to ask for outdoor shoes.

The path, however, had taken her somewhat closer to the monastery. A small field of scratchy-looking plants separated her from its stone walls, mottled with moss and pockmarked like diseased skin. Nasty things had happened here, and walls remembered.

She gazed up at the empty glassless windows, the wind blowing her hair in her face, so she wasn't sure later, when she thought about it, whether the slight movement at one shadowy aperture had been her own hair, or something within. It flicked across her vision with the speed of a snake's tongue.

Her hair.

Probably.

Or a bird.

Though, for the briefest second, she could have sworn she saw the pale blob of a face.

Chapter 10

Rory's beard, and the rest of him, was waiting for her at her health assessment the next day.

'Hello, Miss Mackenzie. Tried to knee anyone in the balls lately?'

His colleague looked rather startled and a deep blush spread across his acne as he scuttled from the room. Thea hopped up onto the bed and swung her legs back and forth, feeling at ease for the first time since she arrived, even with the pale blob of a face at the monastery window still lingering in her mind.

'Haven't had to. Don't give me a reason.'

He chuckled at that and started flicking through the papers on his clipboard.

'I'll do my best. Pretty straightforward. We've done all the baseline tests so now this is it: the big day. Time for the tech.'

Thea waggled her feet. The walls seemed to have less of that sticky sheen in Rory's lab, not that she could see that much of them – the Centre's sleek simplicity had been elbowed out of the way by monitors, wires, coffee mugs and little action figures posed mid battle.

'You didn't say you'd be working here too,' she said.

Rory turned to consult a computer screen. 'Didn't know at the time. A place came up.' He faced her again. 'Weird how things work out, eh?'

'I'm perhaps not the best judge of weird right now.'

She could have asked him about the monastery then, and the face that was probably not a face but something else completely. Maybe there were more staff quarters over there. That was probably the explanation, Thea thought – steadfastly ignoring the fact that the place was clearly a ruin and uninhabitable.

Just as she was about to open her mouth, Rory brought a box over to her and they both stared inside, Thea acutely aware just how close his arm was next to hers. He was wearing a chunky black watch that looked as if it had had a hard life so far and today's T-shirt was as baffling to Thea as the last one: a logo for a university that was probably some hip television reference. She returned her attention to the box, not knowing what to expect.

Inside were two five-pence-size metal discs.

'This is such *amazing* tech,' Rory whispered as if he didn't want to disturb the discs. 'Eventually, when it's gone public, each person will need these little beauties and an app in order for it all to work properly. But there's already rumours that they're working on a completely hardware-free version.'

'No discs? How?' Thea lowered her voice too, in case she woke the disc-babies.

'If I knew that I wouldn't be here, would I?' He carefully lifted one out and held it balanced on the tip of his finger. 'I don't know how it works – that's not my pay level. I just read the data as it's fed to my computer. So, welcome to Phase One.' He gave an elaborate bow. 'The discs will get to know you for the next two weeks and find out your sleep patterns. Then it'll know what to do with you.'

He gently placed a disc on each temple, so gently that Thea didn't think they would stick. She touched one gingerly and it felt rock solid. There was no pain.

'How?'

'Magic.'

Thea made a face.

'How do I get the bloody things off again?' she said, shaking her head to see if she could loosen them.

'Well, you don't have to worry about that right now. They're perfectly safe and you can't accidentally knock them off in your sleep. They slide right off when we're done.'

He tapped away on the tablet computer he was holding. Thea imagined electric signals needling their way into her brain, meeting her blinking, beleaguered neurons and fizzing life into them, making them judder and dance.

'So have you met him? Moses Ing?' She poked at the discs on her temples.

Rory didn't look up from his swiping, the screen bathing his face in a frigid glow. 'Not yet. Won't hold my breath. Not sure I'm important enough.'

'I thought it would have been him greeting us on the first day, y'know, doing the speech. Not whatsername.'

'Delores.'

'Hmm. Seeing as it's his invention.'

'She's top level at Ing Enterprises, though. Everyone's heard of her. Scarily clever. And, y'know … scary.'

She could have said it at that point. Rory would have listened. The pale blob of a face in the monastery window where no face should be.

'And …' she smiled '… it's not going to end up brainwashing me to … I don't know … want to kill the prime minister when I hear an ABBA song?'

Rory laughed out loud at that and his laugh was just as she thought it would be, deep and rich, the sonic equivalent of a chocolate mousse.

'No brainwashing. I'm pretty sure of it.' He rummaged amongst the printouts and tiny action-figure battles on his desk, his back to her. 'I spotted you yesterday, by the way. Thought you'd got away with it?'

Thea stopped swinging her legs. How had he seen her? He must have followed her from the Centre, all the way to the monastery—

'Here.' He grabbed something from the desk and offered it to her.

Blinking, Thea saw a chocolate bar in his hand.

He smiled. 'There's no staff restriction on chocolate – that's just for the clients, y'know, to keep you healthy. So, technically this is contraband. But I won't tell if you won't.'

Tell. There it was: her chance again. Tell him, she thought, as she looked at the chocolate bar and up into his kind eyes. But she'd probably imagined it, hadn't she? It had been a bit of plastic fluttering in the wind, a bird, an old bit of paper, a trick of the eye.

Not a face.

Chapter 11

'The white-crowned sparrow, when it is migrating and has to be in flight constantly, can go pretty much completely without sleep. Nifty little trick, right? But, get this, the bird does this *with nearly no side effects.*'

Weirdly for a lecturer specializing in sleep, it didn't look as if he got much: he was twitchy and hollow-eyed. He stopped here to let his words sink in, smoothing back his threadbare hair.

Thea had been attending these Sleep School lectures for a few days now. Sometimes, she realized during those lectures, she was so busy *looking* thoughtful and attentive that she forgot to *listen* to what the lecturer was actually saying. She quickly corrected that now and tuned back into him.

'Imagine you are that bird, hmm?' the lecturer continued. Thea wrote down notes; there might be some sort of test on all of this and she didn't like to fail at things. Failing at sleep was enough. 'Every spring and autumn, tens of thousands of white-crowned sparrows (*Zonotrichia leucophrys*) migrate the 4,000 kilometres between Alaska and Southern California. They fly day and night with little chance for rest. Imagine it: flapping away constantly, on the move to your winter home, you can't fall asleep because you'd plummet from the sky and die. You've also got to keep an eye out for predators and keep yourself fed. Solution? Stay awake, of course! Scientists are currently trying to understand what is going on in the bird's brain at that time, especially … *and this is the key part* … especially as these birds sleep *two-thirds less than normal* yet, in certain tests conducted, performed *no worse* than other sparrows on tasks of learning and memory.'

He paused for a moment.

The man a seat away from Thea was drawing a bird in his notebook; it had angry, bloodshot eyes and a coffee cup held between two wings. The speech bubble coming from it said, *'Caffeine! I need more caffeine!'*

'Imagine it, hmm? Imagine not having to waste all that time asleep … *and for it to have absolutely no effect on your physical and mental wellbeing.* Well, Morpheus is already imagining that.'

Surreptitiously, Thea glanced at her phone. Without internet connection or a mobile signal, it was now nothing more than an ornament. She didn't know why she continued to carry it around with her, much less why she couldn't help but glance at it throughout the day, checking for notifications that would never appear. The landline phones meant Thea had got a few calls in with her mother:

'So, teapot. Cured yet?'

'Mum, you are aware that you've asked that every time I've phoned you? And I phone you every day!'

'Well, clever company like them, they should have got it sorted by now. Are you?'

'NO!'

'I'd be thinking about getting my money back, if I were you.'

'It doesn't work like that.'

'Oh. Well, that's disappointing. Are you eating?'

'Yes, Mum. You'd love it, it's all avocado and mung beans. Actually, you wouldn't like the coffee. They call it that but really it's some kind of evil concoction made of—'

'I heard of a drug trial once. They gave them all something

for the common cold and it made their hair fall out. All of their hair, even, y'know, the hair on their—'

'My hair hasn't fallen out, so we're okay.'

'Made any friends?'

Thea rolled her eyes. 'Not yet, we've only been here a few days. And I'm not six, thanks, Mother. Want to also check I'm wearing clean knickers and eating my breakfast? Look, I have to dash—'

'Wait! Before you go, I've thought of a safe phrase you can say if it turns out to be a cult and they start to listen in – that is, if they're not already.'

'Mum!'

'So this is it okay? *I'm really missing the cat.* That's the phrase.'

Thea hadn't even known that they still made phone handsets like those – chunky, curved white things that people used to have fixed to their walls in Nineties sitcoms. The room had been big enough to fit a side table and a comfortable chair, one of a few similar places scattered around the Client Bubble that had to be booked before use. Thea had thought it would be tricky to get a slot with fifty people trying to phone home at the same time like a bunch of lemming ETs – but she hadn't had a problem so far.

'Unfortunately, we are not little white-crowned sparrows,' the lecturer continued. 'Well, not yet anyway—' Cue some polite laughter. 'There are some people who can actually survive on only a few hours' sleep, say two or three, and who don't seem to have any ill effects. The Sleepless Elite, we jokingly call them. Let these people not be mistaken for some celebrities who *insist* they do fine on such shortened sleep, but their erratic, ill-judged behaviour would suggest otherwise. Name no names, eh?' More laughter. The lecturer brightened up.

In front of her was the frizzy-haired woman who had given Thea chocolate during yoga. She had used her name badge as a hair clip and stabbed pencils into her hair, arranging them so they stuck out like a spiky tiara. Rosie, the badge told Thea. There

48

was a heart drawn over the letter i. One pencil drooped and fell onto Thea's desk with a clatter that made heads turn. Rosie tried to pull the other pencils out, but one snagged and hung precariously, dangling over Thea's notes until she reached out, carefully unwound the hair where it had caught on the metal part of the eraser and tapped Rosie on the shoulder.

'Thanks,' Rosie whispered, taking the pencil from her. She smiled.

Thea was somewhat startled when she felt her desk tremble as a scuffed boot came into view. The woman calmly climbed over the desk, apologizing as she sent other people's notebooks and pens sliding to the floor, and plonked herself down next to Thea.

'Hi!' She smiled brightly. 'I'm Rosie.'

Heads turned again. Thea felt the heat in her cheeks, but the lecturer continued, oblivious.

'The technology each of you is currently wearing is light years ahead of any rival company. The leaps we are making …' The lecturer glanced sideways as if someone was watching from the wings. He coughed.

Rosie spoke to herself, 'Hello, Rosie, nice to meet you. My name's' – she took a look at Thea's badge – 'Thea – ooh, nice name.'

This time, Thea was almost sure the lecturer frowned at her. She slouched in her seat. Rosie yawned dramatically, 'Are you bored yet?'

The lecturer raised his voice. 'But, hey, I am jumping ahead of myself a bit here, aren't I? Let's get back to the here and now, hmm? As a society we are now realizing that sleep, once denigrated and dismissed as a weakness almost, could actually hold the key for mankind's next evolutionary leap.'

Thea yawned and black blobs drifted across her vision. Eye floaters. An optician had explained that the jelly substance in some people's eyes could become more liquid and then bits of it

49

could clump together to do laps across their vision. 'No need to worry,' her optician had reassured her. It had certainly sounded worrying. Her eyeballs were literally melting and bits of them were indulging in a spot of synchronized swimming but that, apparently, was okay.

She yawned again and tried to hide it this time in case she offended the lecturer. The first few nights in a new place were always tough: pillow too soft, then too hard, duvet too warm, then too cold and there was always a light blinking somewhere. It made holidays such a joy.

Thea glanced around at the others near her, all of them with their little silver dots attached to their temples. She wondered how many hours each one of them had slept that night. One man called Richard with a scrawny neck and a thin-lipped tortoise head was already nodding off, his head dipping to a rhythm of its own. Head jerking too low, he woke himself up, caught Thea's eye and gave her a sheepish smile.

'We're not even allowed coffee, y'know,' Rosie stage-whispered again. 'Well, they call it coffee, what they serve, but it's made from mushrooms or something. Not magic ones either. Not that I've tried magic mushrooms, have you?'

Thea wasn't sure Rosie was trying her best at the whole whispering thing.

'Shush,' Thea gently admonished, stifling a smile.

'Sorry.'

'And no. I haven't tried magic mushrooms.'

Rosie took a look around at everyone else and then raised her voice just that little bit more. 'Do you want to?'

Thea couldn't help but laugh. Someone shushed them and that made her want to laugh even more. She didn't think she'd ever been shushed in her entire life.

The lecturer coughed. 'Luckily, you are here, at the heart of cutting-edge research into the science of sleep. But that is only a start. Wait until you find out the kind of learning the brain can do whilst you sleep – you will be astounded. And that will be the focus of our next lecture. Thank you for …'

A bell rang. Rosie gave a little fist pump. People began to move, gathering pads of paper and pens. The lecturer had to shout the end of his sentence.

'… listening.'

'So – I've decided. You're going to be my friend during all of this. Sorry but you don't get a choice, okay?'

Outside the lecture theatre, Rosie linked her arm through Thea's and gave her a little lopsided smile.

'What if I turn out to be a nightmare?' Thea asked, trying to keep up with Rosie's pace.

'Well, the best friendships are those you have to work at – or some such bollocks. Don't be a nightmare. Simple!'

Thea laughed. Rosie was wearing her cult top knotted at the middle and had tied a bright green ribbon around the waistband of her trousers. One of her pencils fell out of her hair and clattered to the floor. She rushed to rescue it. Thea tried to think of something to say, but luckily Rosie had enough to say for the both of them.

'Look at us all,' Rosie gestured to the other clients coming out of the hall. 'So, you have now officially joined The Desperados, the worst-dressed bunch of people ever – with added head jewellery!' She tapped at her disc. Around hers she'd drawn a heart. 'I would ask you what you're doing later, y'know, small talk – but we all know that this afternoon will be another round of torture in the gym and more prodding by the lab nerds.'

'Did someone say lab nerd?' Rory appeared so suddenly at Rosie's side she jumped and lost another pencil from her hair. 'I do like to appear when summoned.'

Thea laughed and stopped Rosie's pencil from rolling away with her foot. 'Rosie, this is Rory. He works here.'

'And obviously by lab nerd, I meant highly intelligent and

well-respected member of staff, yeah?' She regrouped, grabbed the pencil and twirled it as if it was a mini baton.

'Ah, I'm okay with nerd, don't worry.' He surreptitiously slid a chocolate bar out of the inside pocket of his white coat and passed it to Thea, looking around to see who was watching in an exaggerated way, whilst she slid it up her sleeve. 'See ya later. Got to practise my prodding.'

Rosie snorted.

'No! Wait!' Rory backed away. 'That came out wrong. Let's all just believe I said something witty and cool, yeah?' And he walked off.

Rosie raised her eyebrows meaningfully at Thea. 'Well, I see you've already been busy making a *friend*.'

'Do you want some of the chocolate or not?'

Rosie began to sing quietly, 'Thea and Rory sitting in a tree. K-I-S-S-I-N—'

But she never got to G because Thea flicked the pencil out of her fingers and they both headed towards the doorway, laughing.

Perhaps this would work, Thea thought, as she walked through the double doors, arm safely linked in Rosie's, Rory's chocolate bar nestled against her wrist. Perhaps, despite the fever-sheen walls and cult clothes, the glimpse of white in the monastery window and the cold metal at her temples ... perhaps this was exactly what she needed.

Chapter 12

A week later and, for Thea, the world around her, which had been grey and flat like a broken pop-up book, suddenly sprang open.

There was no doubt about it: she was getting more sleep.

Not much. She fell asleep at around 7 a.m., but now she was waking later, nearer 10 a.m. The usual one hour of sleep had blossomed into nearly three. Those hours were a cool aloe vera gel smoothed onto her brain and eyes.

Odd hours though. She couldn't get away from that. It was as if her body was fighting sleep the whole night and then, like a stubborn toddler, gave in just as the day started for everyone else. If this was her normal sleep pattern then she would be seriously out of step with … well, the world.

Sleep therapy took place in a room with one curved white wall and a view of the old monastery. Seeing its streaked stone and ravaged eyes reminded Thea of that twilit walk she'd taken over a week ago. She turned away.

It was a bit of plastic fluttering in the wind, a bird, an old bit of paper, a trick of the light.

Not a face.

Rosie patted the empty seat next to her and Thea sat down.

When was the last time someone other than her mother had saved a chair for her? Thea wondered. It took her far too long to come up with an answer.

They had been put into 'families' for most group sessions, each one overseen by a sleep guru. Thea's family consisted of about ten people and she only knew the names of a handful.

'I used to have an Action Ken to go with my Barbie when I was little.' Rosie stared dreamily at one of their group, Ethan, over her cup of mushroom coffee as they waited for the session to start. 'And that guy over there is exactly like a walking Action Ken! You would, wouldn't you?' She angled Thea's face towards him. 'Wouldn't you? You would.'

She wouldn't let go of Thea's face until she'd agreed that yes, she would. Which she did because Rosie holding her chin and staring at her intently was starting to catch people's attention. Including Ethan's.

'I wonder what he's in for?' Rosie continued. 'I'd like to see one of those people who just fall asleep anywhere. I saw it on a documentary once. They, like, sneeze, and then just collapse to the ground, completely asleep. It's amazing. I get these night terrors, right? Like, awful, awful night terrors. I wake up screaming, then the dog starts howling and I'm sweating like I've run a marathon. It's just wrong. I mean, I'm single at the mo, but that could change, you know, any day now, and I can't be waking him up every night like a banshee, can I? It'd put him off. What's your thing?'

Rosie made it sound a bit like a superpower.

'I just don't sleep much,' Thea replied, a little dazed because talking to Rosie was like being on permanent fast-forward. 'Don't get to sleep until it's time to wake up for work in the morning.'

'Whoa. Weird.'

On one side of the room there were little canapé trays of vegetables masquerading as something more enticing. Rosie got up and filled a plate, thoughtfully picking through the selection before returning to her seat.

'Being awake for so long on your own must be boring though, no?' she said, unwinding a carrot concoction. 'What do you *do* with all that time?'

'Read.'

Rosie blinked.

'Think.'

Rosie blinked again.

'Watch television sometimes …'

Rosie's face lit up. 'I love a good box set! But not those nature docs – they're brutal. I do not want to see another baby seal being mutilated while I'm eating my Pot Noodle.'

But Thea was hardly listening. In her mind she was back at the monastery walls as the daylight slunk away, looking up at a flicker of movement in the window.

Harriet tapped on her tablet a few more times and then stood up, clapping her hands once for order.

'Okay, everyone. Let's make a start.'

Thea saw Ethan mutter something to himself. Harriet turned and smiled at him.

'Let's start with you, Ethan,' she said brightly, flicking her ponytail over her shoulder with slightly more vehemence than was needed. 'Everyone, this is Ethan's space. Ethan, tell us why you're here.'

'Because you're paying me.' He crossed one ankle over a knee and studied a fingernail. Rosie's description of him as a Ken doll wasn't so far off the mark, Thea thought, except a Ken doll had a happy smile painted on his chiselled face.

'Yes. How droll.' Harriet narrowed her eyes. 'I meant, why can't you sleep? You have nightmares, yes?'

'*Ooh! We have something in common!*' Rosie whispered excitedly to Thea.

Ethan switched his concentration to something on the sole of his shoe.

'You have no trouble going to sleep but then are woken up

by the nightmares and can't fall asleep again. Am I correct?'

Ethan put his foot back down and, for a moment, just sat there with his hands on his knees, staring at the floor. Then he stood, quickly fixing Harriet with a challenging stare.

'Sorry, Harriet. Got to go to the bathroom. You'll have to start with someone else.'

He walked off and Harriet pressed her lips together firmly, as if trying to stop herself from saying something. She took a deep breath and then switched her smile back on.

'So? Anyone else like to start?'

Luckily, hands went up. Thea couldn't remember many of the others' names apart from a couple. One of them was Moira, a middle-aged woman with thick, round, owlish glasses. She went sleepwalking almost every night. 'Which is scary because I live alone and what happens if I manage to get the front door open? Once I even made myself a peanut butter and jam sandwich, completely asleep!' She yawned. 'And I don't even like peanut butter and jam! But at least I know why I can't ever lose any damn weight …'

Thea recognized tortoise-Richard from the lecture – the man who had nodded off. There were big dark smudges under his eyes and he was so softly spoken that everyone had to lean in a little to hear him properly.

'I wake up and I can't move. I'm paralyzed, as if something is pinning me down and I'm petrified because then it feels like I'm choking.'

His hand went to his neck.

'And I'm trying to move and I'm trying to breathe and it all just gets worse and worse. It's over in a few minutes but I can do that a couple of times a night. Lucky I have no one to wake up, eh?'

He lowered his voice even further to a sad little whisper. 'I'm too scared to go to sleep.'

His head drooped.

There was a pause and Harriet looked up from her tablet. 'Right! Lovely!' she said and Thea got the distinct impression that she hadn't been listening. 'Now, next. Please think of a dream or nightmare that has stuck in your head and share it with your partner.'

If she'd had nightmares, which she didn't, nor dreams either really – but if she did, Thea would have had nightmares about the monastery. The rust staining the tower wall, spires like needle teeth and the blank dark windows where the blackness inside the old place came seeping out …

If she had nightmares, she would have had them about the pale blob of a face, only half-glimpsed.

'I was in a cuckoo clock,' Rosie said in a soft voice. 'It must have come from my grandparents, right, because they had this cuckoo clock I was absolutely fascinated with as a child. Huge old thing. Anyway. I'm in the cuckoo clock having scones and tea with the cuckoo and it's great. It's all warm and cosy and the cuckoo is telling me how much she loves her job. She's wearing a shawl and she's got little glasses perched on her beak, even though her eyes are totally on the side of her head, right, so they'd be useless. Every so often she gets up and shoots out of the door to call the time, but she always comes back and we carry on having tea. I loved it in that cuckoo clock and I was really sad when I woke up.'

'Have you still got the clock?' Thea asked.

'Nah. I was too little when they died. My mother sold all their stuff, used up the money. She's a peach, my mum.' Rosie's smile didn't quite convince. 'Was. She was …' She sniffed.

Thea started to say something but was interrupted by Ethan marching back into the main hall holding his mobile phone aloft as if it was lighting his way.

'This is bollocks!' He tossed the phone onto the little table they were clustered around and crossed his arms, those much-appreciated-by-Rosie biceps bulging. 'We should be able to use our phones, like normal people. I didn't sign up for this!'

Eye contact was carefully avoided.

Harriet massaged the bridge of her nose for a moment and clenched her jaw before going over to him, stilettos stabbing the floor. She whispered something to him that the rest of them couldn't hear.

'It's not bloody good enough!' He continued in the same loud tone. 'You're a bunch of tech geniuses who don't approve of Wi-Fi?'

There were a few sniggers. Harriet sighed and turned to them all.

'Respectfully – yes, you did sign up for this. No one reads the small print, do they? And you can use a phone; there are plenty provided, they're just not yours.' Harriet paused and smiled kindly at the group. 'And a bit of a tech detox doesn't seem to have done anyone any harm. Now, are there any other issues people want to raise, or may we proceed?'

To her own surprise as much as Harriet's, Thea raised her hand.

Chapter 13

She didn't know why she'd done it.

Harriet had asked and up had gone her hand, seemingly of its own accord.

She blamed the extra sleep.

They were now sat on the green. Nearby, the monastery gift shop was meant to look like a picturesque cottage with its peaked red-tiled hat. But there was nothing picturesque about it. Its wooden front door, warped by damp, bowed out slightly as if the whole place was a pus-filled spot, holding its wrongness inside, the outside skin stretched so tight it could pop and ooze at any moment.

It wasn't forbidden to spend their lunch and breaktimes outside, but it was late October and, invariably, Rosie and Thea found themselves alone on blanket-covered wet grass even though the weather wasn't too cold.

Normally, in her sleepless world, the hours after lunch were a dirty water stain on the day: grey, shapeless, ever spreading. Today, however, Thea gazed around her with a new clarity: eyesight sharp, brain sharper.

'What's the big deal about outdoor shoes anyway?' Rosie asked.

How could Thea explain it to Rosie? That sometimes, when she was in the Centre, she felt that the walls would suck her in, the glossy cream closing over her completely, sealing over her mouth when she tried to scream?

The face in the monastery window.

'I just like getting some fresh air,' was all she could articulate. She'd thought about telling Rosie what she'd seen but, however she played it in her mind, it just sounded silly. No one was there. A few carefully worded questions to Rory one day had confirmed that the monastery was abandoned and had been since the last monk had shuffled out in the 1980s.

'Yep, well, it is certainly fresh today.' Rosie pulled another blanket tighter across her shoulders. The sky didn't look fresh at all; it looked grimy, like over-handled dough. 'I'll come though, if you want to go for a walk. Could use the exercise.'

'Ladies.' Rory sat down next to them.

He rustled the bag invitingly.

'What is it today?' Rosie sat up and made a swipe for it.

She was too slow and Rory hid it behind his back.

'Today, my fellow connoisseurs' – there was more rustling as he fumbled with the bag behind him – 'we have a veritable feast, a delight … a *delectation* … of cocoa and milky goodness!'

With a flourish he produced a bunch of chocolate bars and laid them reverently on the grass, fanning them out like cards.

Rosie pounced on one and tore the wrapper off immediately.

'God, I love you, Rory Thirwood,' she said, her mouth full of chocolate bar. 'Seriously, I will have your babies. My stash ran out a week ago. Bloody inhuman, not letting us have chocolate.'

'I aim to please,' he said modestly, unpacking a sandwich and an apple for himself. 'But I'm not in the mood for procreation right now, thanks all the same.'

Thea rolled her eyes and chose a chocolate bar.

'So, I hear you've been making a name for yourself.' Rory turned to Thea.

'It's just shoes! God! What is the big deal? Why do we have to wear these stupid slippers all the time anyway?'

'I think in therapy you might want to consider "talking through" your problem with moccasins.' Rory ducked as Thea threw his apple at him. 'And your anger issues.'

Thea leant back on her elbows and stretched her legs out in front of her, wiggling her feet. She'd been awake for most of the previous night, the dark hours a staircase and her mind a small ball gathering speed down its stairs. Usually the stairs were unending, but again last night, the ball had finally come to rest. She had slept longer.

'Bring on Phase Two,' Rosie said, never one to let a silence linger. 'I am done with my night terrors. I woke up so sweaty last night, I had to have a shower at one in the morning.'

'What was the nightmare?' Thea asked.

'Rats. They were gnawing my toes off.' She licked the wrapper clean and then flopped back onto the grass. 'It's going to work, right? The tech?'

Rory rubbed his apple on his trousers. He was wearing baggy cords and a T-shirt over a long-sleeved top. This time the T-shirt had a print of zombie mermaids eating sailors.

'Well, there's a lot of tech. And a lot of clever people doing a lot with that tech, so yeah, hopefully, it'll work.'

Thea wasn't listening. She was marvelling at how fast she could think, and how she didn't feel like her joints were gummed up with sludge. There was so much space in her brain, now she wasn't always obsessing about how tired she felt, or how she'd get through the day, or whether she'd had enough coffee to attempt driving. But there was another kind of space opening up too: it was picnic-blanket-sized and big enough to fit jokes and gossip and random chat that went nowhere. It was big enough for Rosie and Rory.

Thea clenched her fists. 'Look. I think I saw something. Up at the monastery. I went for a walk up there when I first arrived and I saw … something at one of the windows.' She picked up pace. 'And I know it's stupid but I can't get it out of my head and I need proper outdoor shoes to get up there again and, no, I don't believe in ghosts and, yes, I totally understand if you think I'm crazy—'

She gasped for breath. It was probably the most she'd said in one go since she'd arrived. Rory and Rosie stared at her.

'Ghosts?' Rosie said hopefully.

Someone cleared their throat behind them. 'It was you, wasn't it – you're the one who asked for shoes?'

Thea twisted to see Ethan stood behind her, feet planted wide, arms crossed like a bouncer in a nightclub doorway. Rosie hurriedly smoothed her hair and swiped chocolate stains from her mouth.

'Yes,' Thea said. 'I did.' She hoped he hadn't heard her rant about ghosts and faces in windows.

He nodded and frowned. 'This phone thing ...'

'Chocolate?' Rosie offered.

Ethan ignored her and stared off into the distance, as if the trees were doing something he disapproved of.

'Sometimes you sniff the milk and it smells okay, but you know – despite the smell – that it's about to turn,' Ethan said, still staring.

Rory turned to get a better look at him. 'Are you okay, mate? Look, there really isn't anything to worry about. Studies show that smartphones—'

'Thea!' Harriet called to her as she teetered over the grass towards them, the wet earth sucking at her heels. 'Thea, so this is where you are! Really? In this weather? You'll catch a chill. Anyway ... 'She stopped at the small group of people and inspected the damage to her shoes. 'Delores would like a little word with you.'

She began to wobble back to the Centre, calling behind her, 'Come on then!'

Thea got up, clutching her blanket to her, feeling a bit light-headed. 'Wait! Why—?'

But Harriet was too far away. Was this about the shoes? Was Thea about to be reprimanded by the headteacher for a stupid pair of stupid shoes? It seemed so ridiculous.

Ethan caught her eye and muttered softly, 'Yep. You can't smell it yet but, the milk's about to go bad.'

Maybe it was some kind of prickle in her soul that made her look up, past the windows on the first few floors of the Sleep Centre, higher, to a window at the top of the Staff Bubble, where someone stood, probably watching over the green. To Thea though, it really seemed like she was watching her and her alone.

Delores.

Chapter 14

"Striking" was the perfect word to describe Delores; it had just the right edge of violence lingering in it. Beautiful, but also really fucking intimidating.

She was sitting on a low, deep, half-moon windowsill in an office at the very top of the Staff Bubble. It had high curved walls and a ceiling made completely of glass. Light flooded in: too much, too bright, weaponized. It slanted so as to miss Delores's desk but fell squarely on the seat opposite, so any guest would have to squint and sweat uncomfortably through their meeting.

'Thea Mackenzie.'

It wasn't a question, so Thea didn't reply. Despite her best efforts, her heart was thumping loudly and she felt as if she had done something wrong. She *hadn't* done anything wrong. She'd asked for shoes, for God's sake!

Rory had taken her in the lift in the middle of the building, the walkways to each floor radiating from it. He'd given her hand a squeeze before leaving her at the office door.

Delores continued to gaze down at the scene below her, whatever it was. From Thea's angle all she could see was the dough-coloured sky.

'How are you finding everything?' Delores didn't turn to look at her.

Thea couldn't stop herself. 'Is this about the shoes?'

'Hmm?'

For the first time, Delores wrenched her eyes away from the window and swivelled a little to face Thea. She was wearing a dress the colour of newly sharpened knives.

'The shoes? I asked for outdoor shoes …'

Delores cocked her head to one side. 'Did you?' She smiled a little. 'You wish to explore?'

And there was the opportunity to tell Delores the truth, that she wanted to hunt for phantom faces in ruined monastery windows but the sunlight on her face was so bright and hot it melted the words in her throat.

'There's a lighthouse. Apparently. It's why people used to come and visit the island. Boat-trippers, you know? I thought it might be … nice … to go and see it.'

'*Nice*. Yes.' Delores sounded as if she couldn't agree, despite her words. 'But no, this isn't about the shoes. Though I'm sure they can be arranged.'

She moved from the windowsill to stand behind her desk. It was a huge monolith of concrete that reminded Thea uncomfortably of a sacrificial altar. With her long red hair and pale Celtic skin, Delores would have fitted the high priestess role perfectly.

'What this is about, however, is *you*, Thea Mackenzie. You have shown some … interesting … results in your sleep data.'

'I have?'

'You were interesting from the start. It's why we accepted you on the trial and why I fought to keep your place, even after we found out about your mother's troublemaking past.'

'She's retired!'

'No matter. She is a very small fish. You are the one who is important. You are … different to the others.'

'Different?'

'Yes. We haven't even begun Phase Two and yet, here you are. We allow you an average of just under three hours of sleep per night. *Three hours.* Most people would eventually crash. You, however, haven't. That is significant. Your skin and hair are healthier than before, you perform much better on the aptitude tests and you have become more sociable. You haven't merely avoided crashing; you have *thrived.*'

Delores smoothed the concrete top of her desk. It was empty apart from a laptop and a sinuous twist of ornamental stone.

'You have been disappointingly easy to fix.'

Thea almost felt ashamed, as if she'd been wasting everyone's time.

'If it was so easy, why did I feel so terrible all the time, y'know, before?'

'Technically, you are not an insomniac at all. You are a night owl. You work to a different sleep pattern to most of the world. Given freedom, you would naturally fall asleep around' – Delores glanced at her laptop – 'seven in the morning and wake around two and a half to three hours later. The problem is not your sleep, it is that your sleep pattern does not fit into modern working life. Turning up on time for your nine-to-five becomes tricky.'

Delores paused and came around the side of the desk so she could sit on the edge and look at Thea, a small crease appearing between her eyebrows. 'Just under three hours. Some people say they sleep only that amount, but in fact, get more without realizing it. However, you're the real thing. You know, I've never actually met one of you.'

Suddenly Thea remembered the lecture. 'The Sleepless Elite,' she whispered.

People who could live happily on a tiny amount of sleep. The word "elite" suggested private clubs, cocktail parties and carpet so thick you could lose a shoe. Thea glanced at her feet. She'd be happy to lose the moccasins.

'Well, that's just a silly name. But, who knows?' Delores crossed her legs. 'Sleeping less is, as I said, fascinating, but what I want you to now consider is, well, not sleeping *at all*. Successfully. With the help of Morpheus. You could be our white-crowned sparrow.'

Thea remembered the picture from the lecture: a speckled bird with a rather incongruous helmet of white and black that made it look as if it was about to go for a bike ride. She imagined it, its little chest heaving as it determinedly flew on, through the night, through sleep.

'I could go insane.'

'No. Morpheus could do it with no risk to you. Think of sleep as malleable, like plasticine, and Morpheus gently rolling and massaging it into the smallest ball it could be. It's still plasticine, hmm? It's just been squashed together. We would mould your sleep into the smallest ball possible – and you wouldn't even notice.'

'Until my brain began to ooze out of my ears.'

Delores sighed and uncrossed her legs. She placed her hands carefully together in a prayer position and tapped the two index fingers repeatedly.

'You are the perfect candidate for this. In a usual test subject, we would have to try and squeeze seven or eight hours sleep but with you it would only be three. Three! Morpheus could get rid of three hours, I'm sure.' She paused and stopped tapping her fingers. 'Of course, all of this would come with a certain ... remuneration.'

The pauses for effect were starting to annoy Thea. She wondered if Delores did this in real life, went into a café and said things like: 'I'll have the flat white, the bran muffin and a ... [cue dramatic pause] ... chocolate slice.' Though, of course, she would never go into cafés. Coffee would magically appear for a woman like her.

'How much money?'

'Twenty thousand.'

Thea narrowed her eyes. She was hoping that, by narrowing them, Delores wouldn't see her utter shock. Twenty thousand pounds! The warning light flashed around in her mind, illuminating corners where things like *consequences* lurked, but Thea was already too dazzled by that number.

Twenty thousand pounds!

Delores put her chin on the tips of her fingers.

Getting up, Thea wandered over to the window. Below was the village green with the forest looming behind, reeds rustling around the pond and her 'family' out doing star jumps for their afternoon exercise session. Rosie was at the front, star-jumping like a demented jack-in-the-box, going twice the speed of everyone else and still managing to hold a conversation with Ethan. Not a conversation, Thea noted: a monologue. Ethan was his usual grim self, looking stern even when jumping up and down.

It was ridiculous. She had barely coped on one hour's sleep, but Delores thought Morpheus could successfully get rid of even that? It wouldn't work. And would probably nearly kill her in the process.

But – the money. She needed it. She couldn't continue the way she had been – she saw that now. All of her energy had been going into just getting through each sleep-deprived day, and every day doing that dragged her down just a little more. The money would give her 7 a.m. to 10 a.m. every morning whilst she worked out what to do with her life; it would give her breathing space.

But she'd be a breathing guinea pig.

She turned to face Delores. 'I'd like those shoes, please, and I'd like to go out for a walk around the island to think it through. With Rosie. I think … I'd also like to phone my mother.'

Delores smiled coldly and nodded. 'I would need an answer by the end of the day.'

Suddenly her mother took control of Thea's mouth.

'And, I think ... it'll probably have to be more than twenty thousand ...'

Chapter 15

Thea had her own angel and devil, except they weren't sitting on her shoulders but walking beside her.

'I'd chew my own arm off for that kind of money!' Rosie panted up the hill, still dressed in her gym gear from earlier, the wind fluffing her crazy hair into even crazier shapes. 'Let them know that, yeah – if they have some more money lying round? Totally up for chewing my own arm off in the name of science!'

'It's danger money,' Ethan called back to them, waiting a little further up the path.

They hadn't been able to get hold of Rory, but, as Harriet had handed her the trainers with a look of puzzlement on her face, Thea had spotted Ethan hovering nearby trying to act as if he wasn't listening in. It had been easy enough to get another pair of trainers for him.

'It's a shame you couldn't get through to your mum, though.'

They'd tried. But mid-afternoon was peak plotting time for the women at HQ – and by "plotting" they often meant "napping". There was no answer.

Thea continued to plod, staring at her newly issued trainers, the same as Rosie and Ethan's. They had springy soles and she felt like she could walk for hours, at least twice around the small island. The cult clothes had been replaced by fleece-lined leggings and a puffy jacket that kept her warm despite the chill air.

'My mother would probably suspect this is all a patriarchal conspiracy of some sort,' Thea said.

Rosie nodded seriously. 'Well, most things are,' she said.

Thea wasn't sure if Rosie actually knew what a patriarchal conspiracy was.

'You could talk about it to Harriet,' Rosie said.

'Yeah, you *could*.' Ethan cracked his knuckles together. 'But you wouldn't get a straight answer.'

'Oh, she's not so bad.' Rosie stopped as if to admire the view stretching out below them, but really trying to catch her breath. 'Fierce shoes! Gave me a lipstick a few days ago, just cos I complimented her on the colour. Bet she's got a great Insta page.'

'It's a science experiment, that's all,' Thea pondered. 'It's what scientists do, isn't it? Try to push things a bit further?'

'Yeah!' Rosie grinned. 'Like Frankenstein, right? Make a new human being.'

Thea stopped and there was a pause as Rosie's brain caught up with what she'd just said, ''Cept of course it was a monster, wasn't it? Not that you'll—' Rosie's eyes went wide in dismay, slow-loris-style.

'Turn into a monster?'

'You might.' Ethan laughed, just briefly, but it was an actual laugh. He looked as surprised at it as they did.

'Why do they want to do it, though?' Rosie frowned. 'I thought they were helping us to get *more* sleep, not less. I don't understand.'

Ethan called over his shoulder as he marched on ahead of them, 'Bet the MOD have been trying to do something like this for years. A soldier who doesn't sleep? An *army* that doesn't sleep?'

'Or a doctor,' Thea added, both women walking quicker to keep up with him. 'Think of all the lives that could be saved if there were no sleep-deprived doctors.'

71

'Or the lives that could be *taken* by those wide-awake soldiers.'

Rosie's eyes became bigger still. 'What? People who never sleep? But that's just … *unnatural.*'

The monastery was close now, and though Thea had been thinking of sleepless soldiers and twenty thousand pounds, she had also been thinking of this place. They were standing at the side of it, between them and its walls a stretch of spiky weeds. Clouds had started to roll in while they had been walking: fat and heavy and grey, squatting in the sky like miserable buddhas. The walls of the monastery blended in, towering above them, the bell tower still wounded and bleeding rust.

'Grim place,' Ethan said softly.

'Is this where you were?' Rosie asked. 'Y'know when you saw it?'

'Saw what?' Ethan asked, fixing her with a glare.

Thea blushed. 'I don't know. Something. I couldn't tell what it was.'

A bird. A piece of plastic. A face.

'Ooh, I bet there are some juicy ghosts up there.' Rosie rubbed her hands together. 'I love a good ghost story. Don't believe them, but love watching all of that real ghost hunters' stuff; the psychics pretending like they're talking to the dead. It's hilarious!'

Ethan cracked his knuckles and sighed and Thea could tell by his expression that he thought they were a pair of impressionable idiots.

'Hellllooo!' Rosie threw her arms wide and twirled around. 'Heeelllllooooo, ghosties! Here we are! Come talk to us, ghosties!'

'Cut it out, Rosie.' Thea grabbed her arm, uncomfortable suddenly, as if they were prodding a sleeping predator that they really, *really* shouldn't wake. There had been abuse here, sadness, fear; there was a menace in those walls, *porous* walls that had sucked up every scream and drop of torment over the years.

'Come on, ghosties! Hellllllloooooooooooooooo!'

Rosie shrugged Thea off and picked her way through some of

the shallower bracken that formed a thick barricade around the monastery itself. Ethan sighed.

'I'm carrying on to the lighthouse,' he said to Thea. 'You deal with your weird friend.'

They both heard a sharp yelp and the sound of rustling.

'Rosie!' Thea yelled.

But Rosie had disappeared.

'*Rosie!*'

A patch of bracken moved in response.

'I'm okay!' a faint voice called back. 'I twisted my ankle … The ground's a bit uneven … I'm fine …'

A pause.

'Okay, maybe I'm not fine. I can't seem to put much weight on this ankle …'

Ethan muttered something under his breath, pushed past Thea and stomped into the undergrowth. A few moments later he came back out, supporting a limping Rosie, who looked quite ashen-faced but probably didn't need to cling to him as tightly as she was.

Thea raised an eyebrow.

'It was the ghosts!' Rosie defended herself. 'They got me. Don't mess with the supernatural, kids!'

She sank down onto the path and hauled herself over to lean against the nearest tree. Thea and Ethan continued to look unimpressed.

'Look, sorry for being an idiot, okay? You guys go on to the lighthouse without me. I don't want to go back yet – our time's not up. I'll just stay here, enjoy the view and wait for you to return.' She prodded her ankle gently and winced as she tried to move it.

Thea gazed at the monastery. It was just a ruin, another rotting place full of woodworm, mould and broken glass. Each window was a black hole with nothing in it. No flicker. No face. She had been wrong.

She hugged her jacket tighter to her.

Ethan hadn't even looked back but was already climbing further on up the path. Thea lingered near Rosie, unwilling to leave her on her own, but Rosie shooed her away, shouting after them, 'If you see a ghost, give me a yell!'

Chapter 16

Standing at the cliff edge, Thea wasn't afraid of falling; she was afraid of jumping.

Her leg muscles twitched as if they wanted to leap without permission. She'd lose control and hurl herself straight down onto the eager rocks below, the waves like a tongue licking its lips. She wouldn't have to worry about not being able to swim; her mangled body would be thrown against the rocks before she had time to try and take a breath.

Swimming looked so easy, so graceful. On television, she watched people dive, their bodies curving like commas and then they flicked through the water so fast. So little effort. For her, it had always been nothing *but* effort, which then quickly turned into panicked flailing, and chlorine water up her nose making her brain sting.

'See them?'

Thea could make out things that looked like smooth grey rocks, which ducked in and out of the water, as if playing whack-a-mole on their own. Maybe they were seals. Or maybe they were rocks being dunked by the waves.

'Yeah.'

Ethan looked at her. 'You don't, do you?'

Thea squinted. 'Not really.' She laughed. 'But that's probably my fault. I never seem to spot, y'know, nature stuff when people point it out. Y'know, they go "Oooh, look over there, at that lesser-spotted whatsit" and I look and I can never see it. Then it's gone. Sorry.'

'Ah well, it can be tricky sometimes.'

It was quite sweet that Ethan took the time to help her, trying to point out the seals. They stood companionably for a while, watching the gulls swoop as if rehearsing an aerial show, screeching to each other and squabbling on the cliffs. They had taken the path that climbed upwards. The wind had become stronger now, no more playful bumps and nudges. Its mood had darkened and it roared in Thea's ears, trying to get under her jacket, tangling her hair and whipping it into her eyes so they watered.

'Thanks for letting me come,' Ethan said, not making eye contact.

'That's okay.'

'I think I needed a break from the place, y'know. It was getting to me.'

'Really? I hadn't noticed.' Thea gave him a sly glance and for one terrible moment thought he hadn't got her joke. But then he smiled, the lines on his forehead smoothing out.

'So why are you here then?' Thea asked, emboldened.

He sniffed and hurled a pebble out to sea. 'I don't do the whole sharing thing, just so you know.' The smile disappeared.

'Oh! Right! Sorry!'

'Don't mean to be rude. Anyway, Harriet told everyone, didn't she? Nightmares. Leave it there.'

'Yes! Of course! Sorry! None of my business.' Thea blushed furiously.

Then suddenly, as they rounded the curve, there it was: the lighthouse.

It wasn't as tall as Thea had expected. In fact it was quite dumpy and stunted-looking, the runt of the lighthouse litter, its white paint looking rather dirty now. Unloved.

'People came to see that?' Thea said in a disdainful tone.

'I guess it looked better when it was properly maintained? I think they came because of the stained glass at the top. See the colours? I think it's quite unusual for a lighthouse. They're pictures, scenes or something …'

They dutifully stood and gazed at it because they had walked all that way to come and stare. So stare they did. Determinedly.

'Obviously, we'll tell Rosie that it was amazing,' Thea said.

'Best lighthouse ever.'

'Epic.'

They had no other choice but to make their way back. Thea had hoped that somehow making it to the lighthouse would magically give her the decision she needed to make, so it was with a sigh that she followed Ethan back to the path, noticing that he was shortening his stride so she could keep up.

'I could live on an island like this.' Ethan cracked his knuckles again. 'No people, with their constant bloody chatter: who did this? Why do that? What happened there? It drives me crazy, all the time, just talking for talking's sake. The noise of it.'

It only took him a few seconds for realization to dawn. 'Ah. Not you. Didn't mean you. You've been fine.'

He sounded like he meant it. Thea felt absurdly proud.

'It's okay,' she reassured him. 'I'm not great sometimes at the whole talking-to-people thing.'

He held a massive fern leaf aside for her to pass, the green of it glossy like a jungle plant.

'So … going to do it?' he asked.

Skidding a little on the loose gravel of the path, Thea steadied herself as sleepless soldiers and red-eyed guinea pigs danced together through her mind. The fern leaf sprang back against her shoulder, a soft green hand on her neck.

She shrugged. 'We'd better get back to Rosie.'

But, when they got to the monastery, Rosie was gone.

Chapter 17

Thea felt like the grey, hulking monastery at her back would unsheathe its claws at any moment and pounce on her, snapping her little rodent neck.

There was only silence.

'Rosie!' Ethan yelled, veins bulging in his throat.

'How could she not be here?' Thea went around the tree they'd left Rosie propped up against. 'She can't walk far – where would she go?'

'I know she's your friend and all, but the girl's a bloody idiot.'

Ethan strode a little way into the bracken, swiping at it as if it was attacking him, while Thea, at a loss, took to staring at the ground, as if she could track her, as if she knew what to look for. Which she didn't.

That's when they heard it.

From the monastery.

A low sound, weak.

A moaning. Something in pain. A wretched sound.

The pit of Thea's stomach went cold and her heart flopped sickly into her throat. The moaning continued and Ethan looked at her, eyes wide, both of them seemingly frozen by the sound.

'What is that?' he hissed.

'I don't know.'

He carefully backed away from the monastery. 'Do you think it's Rosie?'

Thea really hoped it wasn't because that tortured noise should never come from a human being. 'The last time I came here … I think I saw something … a face, at the window. I think it could have been a face. I don't know.'

'A face? Someone in the monastery?'

'I don't know.'

The moaning choked off. Silence oozed back over them, thick with menace. Then a voice came, mewling and shattered: 'H-h-help … *help me!*'

Watching in horror, Thea and Ethan stared at one of the lowest windows and kept on staring, not able to do anything else, as *something* began to move along the bottom edge. Something pale. Something unfurling.

Hard to tell at the distance but they looked like …

… *fingers* …

… spreading, one by one, clawing themselves upwards, clutching at the windowsill as if trying to drag the rest of – whatever it was – up behind them. Spidery, questing, pale … fingers.

'*Help me …*'

A face bobbed up.

'I'm just a ghostie …'

Ethan sighed. Rosie waved and laughed through the empty hole of the window, leaning on the sill for support and slapping it at intervals as she gasped with glee. Thea relaxed her shoulders, not even realizing that she had hunched them up. Ethan crossed his arms.

'The look on your faces!' Rosie yelled. 'That was so worth dragging myself over here! I knew I'd get you!'

'Hilarious,' said Ethan, stony-faced.

Thea cringed a little for Rosie, inwardly promising to take her aside and tell her to tone it down a bit if she was to have any chance with Ethan.

'How did you get in there? What about your ankle?' she called over.

'I went all Swiss Family Robinson! Made a crutch from a branch I found,' Rosie shouted proudly. 'Took it slow over here, then got in through this window. It's pretty low to the ground.'

'Well, stay there! I'll come and help you out.'

'I'm not.' Ethan walked back towards the path. 'Clearly she doesn't need any more help if she can do that. I'm going back. She does my head in. Nice meeting you again.'

He strode off. Thea couldn't really blame him.

She turned back to the monastery and set off through the prickly bushes, picking her way carefully. Rosie threw her crutch out of the window and onto the ground below, steadying herself with both hands as she tried to get her knee on the edge, tongue poking out of the side of her mouth, her frizzy curls bouncing over her eyes.

She didn't see it coming.

But Thea saw it; she saw it all.

It was over in a flash, so quickly it took her brain a few moments to catch up.

Something moved behind Rosie as she looked up and smiled at Thea.

Something pale

and fast

and strong.

One moment, Rosie was smiling at Thea and the next, her head slammed hard, sickeningly hard, into the thick stone wall and her body then slumped, doll-like, over the sill.

Thea had been close enough to hear the crunch of bone and teeth.

And close enough to see the face behind Rosie, its mouth stretched unnaturally wide in a howl of pure fury before it vanished back into the gloom.

Chapter 18

'Hello, you old rogue. I knew you'd be here. I need to pick your brains.'

The restaurant was softly lit and hushed. Vivian slid into a seat at a table for two, opposite a man who would cut himself if he was any more sharply suited. There was a silk triangle of pocket-handkerchief poking out of his breast pocket.

'Vivian.' He savoured the word and smiled, putting down his newspaper and signalling to a waiter. 'To what do I owe the pleasure?'

'I shouldn't be seen drinking with someone who renounced their ideals and plunged themselves into the clutches of rampant capitalism—' Vivian couldn't stop her lips twitching into a smile.

'Another glass of the sauvignon blanc, please,' he said to the waiter who disappeared as swiftly as he had materialized. 'I'll drink it if you won't.'

'I never refuse wine, Tristan. You know that.'

'Oh, yes. Yes, I do. Many an interesting evening has been the result.'

'Before you sold out.'

'Took over the family firm, I think you mean? Business isn't the devil. We can't all of us be activists forever, you know, Viv. Some of us can help in a different way.'

Vivian had to admit that capitalists did drink a better class of wine. And, like the wine, they aged well. Tristan still had his floppy hair, now white, and that boyish hint of mischief that she had so loved. She had not dressed up especially for this evening, having other more important things to concentrate on than the pain of the underwire in her bra as it tried its best to pierce her heart.

'So how may I be of service?' Tristan put down his glass.

'Ing Enterprises.'

'The technology firm?'

'Yes. You invest in stuff like that. Know anything about it?'

Music played softly, a tune Vivian was sure she knew but couldn't place. The cutlery glimmered in the candlelight and tapestries hung from the walls, the scenes they depicted lost in the shadows.

'Not really. It hasn't been on anyone's radar for years; it used to mostly specialize in hardware. It's not one I have shares in, unfortunately.'

'Unfortunately?'

'Well, there's been a bit of a buzz about it of late. The share price has gone up. It's the name as well: Moses Ing, bit of a legend. Why the interest, old girl?'

'Don't call me old girl. Makes me sound like a cow.'

'Apologies.'

Vivian leant in, her elbow accidentally tipping up a plate that clattered too loudly.

'I want to know more about them,' she said. 'Thought you might have someone I could chat with.'

Tristan ran his finger around the top of his wine glass. 'Might do. Might do. Is this work?'

'You could say that.'

'Because you've got that expression on your face. What's Ing Enterprises done to you?'

'Nothing yet. I want to keep it that way.'

He smiled to himself and straightened the newspaper at the side of his plate. Vivian remembered how he'd always been like that, even in the midst of a marijuana-infused protest camp site: he'd liked his space and bit of order.

'How's Thea?' he asked.

'She's amazing. Got her head screwed on. Don't know where she got that from.'

An image popped up in Vivian's mind. Thea at about six, arranging a doll business meeting, not a tea party. The meeting had been about how to give out the necessary chores in the shared house in which they had been staying that month. She had even made a list in wobbly handwriting for everyone to look at. Everyone had ignored it.

Tristan cleared his throat. 'You know …'

Vivian glanced up to find him looking at her rather more searchingly than she would have liked. It didn't suit him, she decided; it made him look old.

'I always wondered. I mean, you never said but—'

'Whose is she?' Vivian smiled at him. 'Mine. She's all mine. No one else's.'

He returned the smile with less conviction and thoughtfully swirled his wine. 'You never said. All those years.'

What was his expression now? The lighting was so ridiculously dim in restaurants these days and Vivian couldn't quite work it out. It couldn't be … disappointment, surely?

He shrugged. 'Those days, the marches, the protests, the shitty little bedsits. They seem so very far away now. Like a dream. I think I was high for most of it.'

They both gazed at each other. Their table was a white-clothed raft set adrift in a badly lit sea.

'So?' Vivian snapped open a menu, enjoying the sharp sound. 'Are we going to order? Or am I to get my own table?'

'Oh no. We can make an evening of it.'

Vivian smiled and took another sip of wine. 'Well, let's not get ahead of ourselves, Tristan …'

Vivian got back from her meal with Tristan later than planned, lit a joss stick, and unclasped her bra with a sigh of relief.

She reached for a nettle teabag, changed her mind and poured herself one last glass of wine. The living room floor was a trip hazard of paint pots and cardboard, leftovers from that day's protest preparation. They needed Thea. She always had such neat lettering and a way with colour.

The house was too quiet. During the day it was HQ: there was bustle and phones ringing, people coming and going with tea and paper and new problems to be solved. The website was new: MenopausalArmy.com, but, disappointingly, they were still trying to raise awareness on many of the same issues they'd been working on since the Seventies. And the menopause was long gone. It would be more apt to call themselves OldCronesCompany.com now.

At night, though, HQ returned to the pumpkin it was: an empty house. She could hear the pipes ticking.

Perhaps, in her next phone call, she wouldn't tell Thea that she had been trying to dig up information on a perfectly innocent technology company. But old habits were hard to break. Not that there was anything to worry about – she had spoken to Thea only the day before and had been delighted to hear that she was already sleeping better.

The wine disappeared rather too quickly and Vivian sighed – it was time to take her old bones to bed. But thinking of Thea reminded her to glance at the answerphone on her way upstairs. Thea would have nagged her to use her mobile, or at least switch it on, or maybe just find it. It had to be in her desk somewhere. Vivian was suspicious of carrying around something that was to all intents and purposes a glorified tracking device.

Old habits were hard to break.

A red light blinked in the hallway.

Vivian played the waiting message: 'Oh, hi Mum – no panic. Just wanted to run something past you. Catch you tomorrow. Love you, bye!'

Vivian knew her daughter's voice and there was a hectic edge to it that she'd rarely heard before. She played the message again, glad that the red light had switched itself off because it felt too much like "Stop!", "Don't!", "Beware!"

It felt like a warning.

Chapter 19

The monitor beeped. It was a strangely soothing sound.

Beep. Rosie's still alive.

Beep. Still alive.

Beep. Still alive.

Beep. Alive, alive, alive.

Thea sat in a chair next to the bed in the medical wing located in the Staff Bubble. It was evening. Had it all only happened a few hours ago? She felt dazed. She stared at Rosie, at the mess of her face, the swelling, the blood, one eye swaddled in bandages, the other mercifully closed. Her chest rose and fell gently, rhythmically, hypnotically. If Thea focused on that, she didn't have to think of anything else; her brain could just fill itself with the rhythm of it. And the beeping.

Beep.

Alive.

Beep.

Alive.

The door opened.

'Thea?' Rory's voice. She didn't turn around.

'I brought you some food. You need to eat something.'

She could hear him put a tray down and then he dragged a

chair over to sit next to her. Out of the side of her gaze she saw him rub at his beard.

'She's given us all a bit of a scare,' he said.

There was quiet.

Beep. *Thea's fault.*

Beep. *Thea's fault.*

'I …' Her voice caught. 'I thought she was—'

Head lolling to one side, blood-matted hair, pulpy flesh.

Rory nodded.

Rosie's chest rose and fell. The woman who had been constantly fidgeting, moving, smiling and gesticulating was gone and in her place was a quiet mechanical automaton. Near her undamaged eye, Thea could still see the heart she'd drawn around one of the discs on her temple.

'The doctor tells me she is stable, but they will have to wait and see if there has been any internal bleeding on the brain.'

Thea imagined blood like sticky cherry jam, spreading itself slowly across the crevices of Rosie's brain and oozing into the cracks.

'Her eye?'

'There's a lot of swelling. Hard to tell. They're optimistic she won't lose the sight.'

'If she wakes up.'

One of Rosie's hands lay above the covers, the nails neatly filed and rainbow-coloured. Thea willed a finger to twitch.

'She's young, healthy – she's got an excellent chance of recovery.'

Thea swivelled to fix him with a hard stare. She remembered the way Rosie's face had looked when she first got to her: squashed fruit with shards of bone poking through.

'Did the doctor actually tell you that?'

'Uh … no.'

Weirdly, it looked like Rory was the one out of the two of them who had had the least sleep. There was hardly any white left in his eyes, just angry red webs.

'I've brought some of Rosie's things. Just in case she needs them.' He put a plastic bag at her feet. It immediately sagged and toppled over.

She felt like the bag, the things she wanted to say just spilling out of her, even as she tried to hold her plastic handles together.

'There's someone in the monastery.' Thea instinctively lowered her voice, watching the bag slide once more.

'Huh?'

'There's someone in the monastery. They cracked Rosie's head into the wall. I saw it.'

Rory scratched at his beard again, his brow furrowing.

'But ... Rosie slipped and fell.'

Thea gripped the arm of his chair.

'What? No, that's not true. I saw it. There's someone in the monastery and they hurt Rosie.'

Behind them, a throat was very deliberately cleared.

'That will be all for now, Mr Thirwood,' said Delores.

Thea turned around. Delores was standing in the doorway, her red hair a shock of colour against the white of the wall next to her. She clasped her hands in front of her, an oddly demure pose, like a saint about to pray.

Rory got up so quickly that he pushed his chair back with his knees and the legs screeched against the floor. He didn't make eye contact with Thea as he quickly skirted around Delores. Thea stood in Ethan's classic pose: arms crossed and feet planted firmly.

She'd be damned if she spoke first.

Delores took a few steps into the room and, behind her, the door closed noiselessly.

Beep.

Rosie's alive.

Beep.

Alive.

'Miss Denestrio is a very lucky girl, wouldn't you say?'

Thea wasn't in the mood for dancing around the subject. 'You told people she fell. That's a lie. Someone is in the monastery.'

'So you've said. Many times. To the doctors, to Ms Stowe, to anyone who will listen to you.'

'Have you even called the police?'

'Miss Mackenzie, I fully understand your concern. This has been a blow to us all. Of course, accidents like this remind us why we discourage clients from leaving the safety of the Centre in the first place.'

'But it wasn't an accident, was it?' Thea deliberately raised her voice. 'Someone shoved her head into a wall so hard she's actually swallowed some of her teeth.'

'Yes, as you keep saying. *To everyone.* You've had an exhausting day—'

'No, no, no. Don't brush this off. I wasn't imagining it. It happened.'

Delores walked around Thea to the bedside where she hovered a hand over Rosie, not quite touching her, an odd gesture as if in blessing.

'And, at first light tomorrow, we will have a search party scour the monastery. If there is anyone to be found, we will find them. I don't mean to make you sound delusional. It's just, well, this is an *island*, Miss Mackenzie; it's hard for someone to just sneak in.'

'I don't care. I saw it.'

Delores pressed her lips together briefly.

'And what about Rosie's family?' Thea continued. 'Have they been told? When is she going to be moved to a proper hospital?'

'Miss Denestrio has no family. Her mother recently overdosed – cocaine, I believe. Of course, you probably knew that already. You two have become quite friendly lately.'

No, she hadn't known that. There was so much she didn't know and now may never get the chance to ask. Small talk. They had wasted their words on chocolate and strange cuckoo dreams when really their talk should have been much bigger, because one day they would be sat in a hospital wing realizing they didn't really know anything about each other.

'As for the hospital,' Delores continued, 'it is winter and it is to be expected that the boat service may be temporarily suspended due to weather. I believe snow is forecast. Our facilities here are world-class. Rest assured, Miss Denestrio will get better care here than in a grubby mainland hospital.'

Delores gave Rosie one last look and then she moved to the door. All the tins and jars of Thea's mind had now rolled loose from their shopping bag and she was just left with the floppy plastic, so thin you could poke a finger through it. Through her. Her shoulders sagged.

At the doorway, Delores turned to Thea. 'Naturally, due to the unusual circumstances today, we will not expect your answer until tomorrow. Take the time to, shall we say, *sleep* on it.'

For a few seconds, Thea was confused. Answer? Then she remembered: the sleep study. The Sleepless Elite. Of course, that was why Delores had come! To check on *her*. To check she still had her little guinea pig.

Not for Rosie.

Thea stood straighter, each beep of the machine behind her matched by the pulse throbbing in her temples. When she spoke, it was light and pleasant – but there was steel glinting under her words.

'Oh, I've already made up my mind, Delores,' she said. 'Thanks for the offer, but, once the boat starts operating again, I'll be leaving.'

Delores's face set, a stone expression with flinty eyes.

'With Rosie.'

Chapter 20

Nearly one week had passed since Thea had told Delores that she had decided to leave.

She had decidedly not left.

Snow had fallen. Waves had risen. Boats and search parties had been rescheduled. The machine kept beeping at Rosie's side, October turned to November and Phase Two had started without her.

It had been a week of sitting next to Rosie, the hours melting away in a sludge of time that lost meaning, so much so that she had to be dragged away for meals and only left willingly to try and phone her mother. Frustratingly, the telephone rooms were nearly always fully booked whenever she tried to use them and then there was a problem with the line so that, once the number was dialled, all Thea got was static. Due to the bad weather, so she was told.

'I have something of a treat for you.' Delores spoke to the crowd below her on the walkway at breakfast. 'A rather rare and special treat. There is someone here that I thought you would all like to meet.'

A murmuring rippled through the people gathered together in the morning light of the cafeteria. Harriet had marched Thea to breakfast, promising, yet again, that the telephone line was due to be fixed.

Delores continued, 'This is someone you may want to give a huge round of applause to, for creating the tech that has gone into helping you feel the way you do this morning—'

At this, Harriet gasped. 'No! It can't be! No one's seen him for decades—'

'May I introduce …' – here Delores stretched out her arm, beckoning someone – 'Moses Ing!'

There was a stunned silence as a man stepped forward. Next to Thea, Harriet gulped in a big breath and then started clapping, her bracelets jangling, as others quickly copied her. A swell of applause spread around the room and the man, dark-skinned with a dandelion-clock puff of grey hair, acknowledged it with a smile, holding his hands out in a classic pose of modesty.

Harriet put a palm to her chest, her eyes shining and wide. 'He's actually here!'

Moses continued to smile and nod and wave and Delores looked on like a proud mother at a school concert. It seemed Delores wasn't the real god, after all, just a disciple like the rest of them. The real god was wearing chinos and a button-down shirt.

Then, just as everyone's hands began to sting and a few calls of 'Speech!' could be heard … he was gone.

A final wave, and he turned and stepped back out of sight. Delores came forward again and the clapping petered out, disappointedly.

'I'd like to thank Moses for being here today. We know how much he values his privacy, and for him to come and see you here, well, that has been a huge privilege for us all; I'm sure you'd agree. Now, I won't disturb your breakfast any longer. Please enjoy the rest of your day.'

The cafeteria hummed with whispered excitement. Thea felt oddly deflated. She hadn't really imagined what Moses Ing would look like, but it had never occurred to her that he would look so ... normal. She'd expected charisma and some sort of rock-star quality, or the opposite, twitchy and awkward. Not like an uncle on a log cabin holiday. But if he had managed to get to the island ...

... then she could now leave. With Rosie.

Harriet grabbed her elbow and practically forced her into a seat at one of the tables. Today the older woman was wearing a cunningly draped dress that managed to look both informal and also absolutely killer, her blonde hair neatly scraped back into a golden shiny swirl of a ponytail.

She placed a mushroom coffee in front of Thea. 'Good news. Tomorrow it looks like the weather's going to briefly improve enough for a search party to the monastery, to find your ghost.'

Thea looked up from her coffee in shock. The search party was actually happening? She seriously considered hugging Harriet.

'You know, everyone thinks you've lost it.' Harriet glanced around to check who was listening. Thea reconsidered the hugging. 'This whole face in the window thing – really? You seemed so much more stable than that. I have to say, I'm a little disappointed.'

How to explain it: the mistrust that was creeping in like rust over old metal, so strong she could feel the tang of it in her mouth?

'I saw it. Him, her, whoever it was. It's at the monastery. I want to go with them.'

'What?'

'I want to go with the search party.'

Harriet leant back and crossed her legs, tweaking her cat's-eye glasses a little further down her nose so she could peer over them. Again, Thea tried to guess her age. She was one of those women who always looked around forty until a mannerism or slight tilt of the head gave them away.

'I'm afraid I think you're seeing monsters where there are only shadows, Thea; I really do. I've been with this company for a fair few years now and I can truly say that I don't know where I would be without them. It's not just a job. It's a way of life. Staff here are valued, cared about. They are looked after. A company like that is not the wolf at the door you think it is …' Thea opened her mouth, but Harriet held out her hand, palm up.

She pressed her lips together and smoothed at her hair, glancing around at the tables closest to them and then up at the walkway, like Delores could still be there, hanging from her ankles like a bat, listening in.

She sighed. 'But … *but* … if that's what you want. I'll do my best. I don't see the harm in it.'

Harriet had not been in that hospital room with Delores. She had not seen the way the woman had really only been interested in Thea's answer, not Rosie or her injuries, or how she'd got them.

'Do you think perhaps you have some trust issues?' Harriet continued to stare over her glasses.

'What?'

'Well, your file. You're twenty-seven. Father not a part of your life, no real relationships, yet you're actually quite a good-looking young woman, under that fringe. The only significant relationship you have is with your mother, and she's a conspiracy theorist—'

'She's not!' Thea thought for a minute. 'She's … retired …'

Something was worrying her, but it wasn't anything to do with trust issues. Over the past week as everyone around her had had their sleep gently massaged by Phase Two of the technology, allowing them to gain blissful extra hours of sleep – Thea hadn't.

Slept.

At all.

With a suddenness that unnerved her, she had gone from luxuriating in her nearly three hours of sleep only to have it snatched away. No sleep at all, for night after night after night. Her fingernails were sore from trying to prise the discs away from her temples. They hadn't budged. It was more likely she'd lose a fingernail before she got one of them to move.

Her mind kept trying to sing the same tune, a tra-la-la of 'everything's fine, everything's fine'. But underneath that was another deeper melody, a discordant chord.

They didn't need her permission to start the tests. The little bloody discs were already on her head and they could start experimenting on her whenever they wanted, even if she was no longer part of the trial.

A sleepless soldier.

By now, her eyes should have felt like Velcro and her brain should have been a claggy porridge of neurons. But this was the truly terrifying part:

She felt fine.

Delores's voice floated back to her. *'Think of sleep as malleable, like plasticine, and Morpheus gently rolling and massaging it into the smallest ball it could be. It's still plasticine, hmm? It's just been squashed together. We would mould your sleep into the smallest ball possible – and you wouldn't even notice.'*

Thea's brain was polished and buffed to a high shine. She felt better than she had ever felt before: alive, alert, awake.

Too awake.

Chapter 21

She shouldn't have been there.

It was late. But the beep of the machine was strangely soothing, and tomorrow she'd be with the search party and probably wouldn't be able to visit.

She did what she always did lately: she put the pack of chocolate buttons Rory smuggled for her on the bed by Rosie's hand, as if she could wake up, reach out and take one any time she chose.

And she talked.

'... so everyone seems to be getting a great night's sleep and I just stay awake, except I don't feel like a zombie the next day. I feel great, which I shouldn't because who should feel great after nights and nights of being awake? So that makes me think maybe they're trialling the Sleepless Elite thing on me regardless. Except that makes me sound paranoid, doesn't it? At least I'm getting through all the books I'd been wanting to read ...'

She popped a chocolate button into her mouth and watched Rosie's hand. It didn't twitch.

'We all miss you.' Her throat swelled around the chocolate and she blinked back tears. 'I miss you. I—'

That was when the screaming began.

Thea jolted upright. It wasn't the sound of someone screaming in fear, or an excited squeal – this was rage bundled and bound into one voice box, a pure howl of fury so intense it sounded like it could tear the person's throat in two.

Thea ran to the door of Rosie's room. There were other doorways in this corridor of the building, doors that Thea hadn't given much thought to. But what if they were all little hospital rooms like Rosie's?

And, more importantly, *why would you have so many?*

She kept to one side and peered through the glass window into the corridor beyond. There were a group of people not far from her, but she wouldn't have to worry about being seen. They were far too focused on the man being held between them.

Thea had seen evangelical healings on television, the way the afflicted would shake and judder under the priest's touch while the priest shouted something like: 'Satan! Be gone!' It always ended with the person cured and floppy, sagging gratefully into the arms of their family.

The man in the corridor flailed and jerked as if demon-possessed but no one near him was going to bother laying hands on his head. They were too busy trying to secure his arms and feet as he kicked and twisted and strained, all the while screaming in that terrible way. There were no words in what he yelled over and over again, or rather, if there had been they'd become so badly mangled together they could no longer be understood.

They shuffled with him as a group – a many-legged monster making its halting way along the corridor – and Thea shrank back as they passed her door, glancing at Rosie.

Another face swam into her memory: a pale blob in an arched window.

Had they found the person in the monastery?

She carefully opened the door and tiptoed into the corridor. All she had to do was follow the screaming – so she did. It brought her to a door not too far away from Rosie's, with a similar square pane of a window.

They had got the man closer to the bed but that was as far as he was going to let them. Thea managed to get a proper look at his face and realized with a jolt that it was Richard from her sleep therapy group, tortoise-Richard with his bald head, sad voice and sheepish smile. There was no smile now. Richard's voice was beginning to sound hoarse and ragged, but he continued to wrestle the others holding him, jerking his body so hard Thea feared one of his joints would pop.

Then his rolling, wide eyes caught hers. Thea froze. But she needn't have feared – his eyes may have been looking at her but what they were seeing was something else, something that made him cringe suddenly, his gaze never leaving her, the screaming turning wetly to a wild keening. He stilled.

He stood, chest heaving, limbs slack, all fight gone.

One of the men holding him must have been lulled into a false sense of security and loosened his grip as he tried to edge him towards the bed. It was all the chance Richard needed. With a roar that made the tendons in his neck bulge Richard wrenched one arm free with a strength that belied his skinny frame, grabbing the nearest thing to hand.

A chair.

Fast and hard, he shoved the chair at the man nearest him who tried to defend himself by holding out an arm as protection. Thea was pretty certain she saw that arm bend in a very unnatural way. And then it was chaos for a few seconds. Richard reared and bucked as the others tried to hold him, while in a corner another man looked as if he was preparing a syringe.

Just before the syringe punctured his arm and the rest of the men pinned him down, Richard turned his head again, looking at Thea, and this time he was Richard once more, the one she'd sat in a therapy room with and watched nod off in a lecture hall.

For a second she saw the horror dawn in his eyes.

An arm shot out of the nearby door as Thea hurried past on her way back to Rosie and, without giving her any time to react, pulled her into the room. She yelped.

It was dark.

'Shh!'

'Rory?'

'Shh!'

Thea lowered her voice to a whisper. 'What are you doing?'

Outside the closed door, voices floated past them. Thea felt like a small fish in the coral as the sharks swam past. She could feel her heart thudding in her throat and all she could think about was Richard and his crazed eyes.

The voices receded. She was getting used to the dark now though and could make out shelving to one side of the room. There were the shapes of mops, brooms and buckets in the corner, but what she was most aware of was just how close she was to Rory. Their noses were nearly touching. He smelled of coffee and something woody, his aftershave maybe, or the soap he used.

'What's happened to Richard?' she asked.

'Huh?'

'Richard? I just saw him. He was … I guess he was struggling, or … or really angry, maybe? And there were some guys holding him down and then they sedated him.'

'What? Look, I don't know anything about that and we don't have much time – I like you, right? And I feel kinda responsible for you being here because I approved your form.'

Her brain had snagged on him saying he liked her. In school, when she'd been a teenager, you went to the boiler room to make out, appearing ten minutes later looking a bit flushed, adjusting your jumper. She was suddenly fifteen again, too close in the dark with a boy, feeling like her hands and feet and lips and, well, *everything* about her was just too big, too clumsy, too awkward.

She moved her foot and it hit something in the dark, a something that clattered noisily to the floor.

They both froze.

Rory put his hand on her shoulder and she could just about see that he had put his finger to his lips.

They waited.

Nobody burst in demanding to know why two grown people were hiding in a broom closet.

Rory's shoulders relaxed. 'I thought it was just a sleep trial.'

He'd moved his hand from her shoulder but had now started gripping the tops of both her arms, like she might run away from him before he could finish.

'What do you mean? It *is* a sleep trial …'

He shoved his face closer to her, his beard tickling her chin.

'I … heard some stuff … from the other technicians. There's something else going on. The data we're collecting from you, how you sleep, when you dream, what you dream, all of that is being uploaded to another server. I don't know where. And they're really interested in REM sleep. Incredibly interested. Phase One and Two are just a cover; it's Phase Three that is important and it's something to do with your dreams. I don't know what. They told you that you could be your best you, right, in Phase Three? That they'd fix you. Smoking, lose weight, whatever. Well that's just a lie. I've heard them talk. They don't care about fixing you. There's something else they want.'

It was a lot for Thea to take in, in the dark, with her leg pressed up against a vacuum cleaner.

'That might be down to me,' Thea had to admit.

'Huh?' Rory's grip tightened.

'Delores offered me a deal. Apparently, I'm one of a really small percentage of people who can function on a small amount of sleep. Like two or three hours. For long periods of time. She

100

wants to pay me thousands of pounds to see if they can make me completely sleepless.'

Rory exhaled so sharply it sounded like he'd been punched in the stomach. 'Don't do it.'

'I was—'

'Just don't! Don't fuck about with REM sleep. That's your fucking *brain!* Are you crazy?'

He actually shook her a little, an angry parent telling off their child.

'*I wasn't going to!*' she hissed. 'I've told Delores that I'm leaving as soon as I can. With Rosie.'

'Good. That's good.' He nodded to himself.

Thea flailed about a little in the dark but managed to grasp his arm and took it in what she hoped was a reassuring manner. 'They're going to search the monastery. I'm going with them.'

For a moment there was just the dark and the sound of breathing. Thea felt Rory's warm hand cover hers and the heat went all the way to her face, but in the gloom there was no way Rory could have seen that.

'You do believe me, don't you?'

Rory's voice, when he spoke, was gruff. 'Yeah, I believe you. So be careful, okay?'

Chapter 22

There were monasteries that were flouncy, adorned debutantes, showing off on the ballroom floor with their spiderweb arches, delicate carvings and high curved windows. This monastery was one of the grim-faced old chaperones stuck in the corner, sucking its teeth at the frivolity before it.

The entrance was a simple gothic arch of stone with a thick oak double door.

'We'll do a sweep of the ground floor first.' The chief of the security team was called Len, a no-nonsense, stocky man in his fifties. He had been unfailingly polite, but Thea got the distinct impression that he thought this was as much a waste of time as Harriet did. 'Best to stay with me. The floors in these old places can be lethal.'

The sky had started to darken and bruise, turning a Hallowe'en green at the skyline as fresh snow built up.

'We'll have to make this quick,' Len had said. 'We don't want to be caught in that.'

Based on what Thea had told them, they had decided to skip the main nave and chapel and head towards the two-storeyed living quarters, where the windows looked out over the path the three of them had taken about a week ago.

'They could be long gone now,' Ethan muttered to her.

Thea was glad she'd pushed for him to accompany them. It had been a last-minute idea, one she had been surprised to find had been allowed.

'Really? He can come too?' she had said to Harriet.

'I pulled some strings,' Harriet had replied, pushing her glasses higher up her nose. 'And Rory, your sleep technician, he put in a good word. In my opinion, if it gets this foolishness sorted out quickly, you can take the whole Centre with you.'

Despite it being mid-morning, the inside of the monastery was a wet cold that, when breathed in, would grow like mould on the bones and stiffen the fingers.

'Mind your step, miss.' Len helped Thea over a pile of fallen rubble.

Her mind was still stuck in what she had seen yesterday in the hospital room: tortoise-Richard and his rage, that wild-eyed glare as he had struggled and then the realization at the end when he'd locked gazes with her. What had happened? What had the trial done to him?

They hurried through the echoing main nave and Thea only caught a glimpse of empty pews, broken glass and a ceiling so high it was lost in the gloom. Once, in this place, people had lit candles and prayed. There had been warmth and devotion; but also in this place there had been abuse and unhappiness: dark corners where darker things could be hidden.

They moved on.

The monks' living quarters resembled an abandoned council office. The monastery had been active until the late 1980s and so the living quarters hadn't been able to escape a safety door and carpet tile renovation. A corridor stretched out before them with doors on the one side leading to each monk's room. Next to Thea was an old noticeboard, the sort that was covered by sliding Perspex that locked with a key. There was a lone notice left, reminding everyone of the fire evacuation route and a cluster of pins huddled in one corner, ready and waiting to never be used again. A fluorescent strip light hung at a drunken angle just above their heads.

As the security team went first, opening doors and flashing torchlight around, Ethan and Thea followed.

'How's Rosie?' Ethan asked.

The carpet squelched under Thea's feet and, when she touched it, the plaster on the wall felt springy and alive.

'They say she's doing well. There doesn't seem to be any damage to her brain, at least, and her other injuries are healing.'

Still the machine beeped, still Rosie had not moved.

'So? What's Phase Two like?' Thea whispered to Ethan.

'Well, it's like … sleep.' He peered in through an open door. 'I slept for the whole night. No nightmares, nothing. There was some wave music stuff at the start, or whales, or something.'

Thea stared into one of the rooms. A plant grew in through the window, its narrow leaves like fingers reaching up. The bed was still there but the slats were broken and jagged and black mould darkened the walls. It was a bare, miserable box. Maybe the monk who had lived here had been jolly and well-liked, maybe he'd told jokes to the other monks and believed in a just and fair God. Maybe, though, he had been cruel and twisted out of shape, maddened by the silence, thinking a loving God would forgive him no matter what he did.

Thea couldn't get the tremor out of her voice: 'Ethan, I didn't sleep. Again. And I don't feel terrible for it; in fact, I feel fine.' She paused. 'I can't help thinking how Delores could just start testing on me whether I said I was leaving or not.'

Ethan remained silent but gently moved her hand away from her temple. She'd been scratching at the disc and the skin around it felt sore.

'Don't you just want to get these bloody things off sometimes?' she said.

Ethan tapped his torch against his hand thoughtfully. 'You

know, a week or so ago, I'd have said yes. If you'd left then, I'd have gone with you. But today? After the night I've had. *The sleep.* I feel … God, I can't explain it. I just don't want to go back to how it was.'

'Yeah. I know.' Thea sighed. Then, in a smaller voice: 'What if I'm wrong about this place? What if no one's here? It's just me, isn't it? I'm the only one who saw anything.'

He took a moment to stop and look at her, so intently it made Thea shift her feet uncomfortably. But, finally, he said, 'I believe you.'

That made two people at least. The problem was Thea wasn't sure if she believed herself anymore.

'There's no one here, miss,' Len said to her, while around her the rest of the security team assembled in the courtyard, blinking in the daylight. 'We've scoured the whole place and there are drones currently mapping the rest of the island.'

Thea was acutely aware of everyone looking at her, these men in their black combat gear, the expressions on their faces, all of them thinking that she'd wasted their time. The hysterical woman, can't even trust her own eyes, making a drama out of nothing, out of an accident. Stupid, hysterical woman.

'It was worth checking though, Thea.' Ethan was being supportive, which was worse in a way, because perhaps he didn't believe her now either; he just liked her enough to not want to make her feel bad.

Her cheeks grew hot.

'What about the lighthouse?' Thea asked.

Had they checked that? Someone could have run there quite easily.

Something like annoyance flickered across Len's stony face and he took a deep breath. His men shuffled their feet and muttered quietly to one another.

'Look, Miss Mackenzie, you've led us a merry dance all

morning. The drones will map the lighthouse. Right now though, that's not our main concern. See that vicious-looking patch of sky there? I've got orders to get us all back before that bitch hits. So, if you wouldn't mind?'

There were a few sniggers.

Thea had a choice then. After all, she was used to it. She had been the good little girl for her entire life so she could do it again: behave and do what the sensible man said.

Or …

They hadn't checked the lighthouse. She caught Ethan's eye and a muscle twitched in his jaw. He nodded ever so slightly.

Her cheeks continued to burn but she didn't have any dignity left to lose. 'Well, I'll go and check on my own.'

Len rubbed the bridge of his nose. He sighed. Thea held his gaze. She might not be crazy, not just yet, that face in the monastery window might still be real and the lighthouse might be all the proof she needed. She was going there.

'I'm afraid I have orders,' he said, reaching into the back of his waistband.

It had never happened to Thea before and it all happened so quickly her brain didn't have a chance to tell the rest of her body what to do. One minute Len was reaching behind him and Ethan was standing next to her, then suddenly Ethan had thrown himself at Len, knocking the older man to the ground, where the two of them grappled for control of what was now, very definitely, a gun.

'Run!' Ethan yelled as the other men closed in.

Fight or flight, it was called. Thea had hoped that, in such a situation, she would fight, that she wouldn't just stand there and gawp, feeling as if her body were a very long way away. She wouldn't freeze up, or roll over. She would instead, for example – *try and grab the gun.*

Fight or flight. The world moved very slowly. She may have hoped for fight but there, in the moment, she found out her first instinct. Ethan yelled at her again. 'Run!'

So she did. She scrambled back onto the path and then barrelled straight across it into woodland, moving without really thinking, knowing she couldn't outrun any of those men, if they came after her.

But she could hide.

Chapter 23

It was her mother Thea thought about as she hid in the wood.

What she thought about most was her living room.

The other women all called it "HQ". It was the hub of every-thing they did: their marches, protests, talks, meetings, charity plans. They ate there, sloppy bowls of pasta or noodles, whatever the choice of the person whose turn it was to cook. And tea, so much tea was made, endless cups of it, weird concoctions of bark and roots that made the room smell as earthy as a burrow.

One whole wall had been shelved out years ago and was filled with books and whatever else her mother didn't know what to do with: the odd pebble, a corn dolly, some photos of Thea in school uniform, a piece of stained glass shaped like a peacock feather, a kaleidoscope. There were books on shamanism, philos-ophy, talking to the dead and making a living from selling on eBay. Trashy horror novels in Seventies' binding with yellowing pages were jammed up next to a row of pristine Harry Potters, a *The Joy of Sex* and a copy of *The Tiger Who Came to Tea*. There was no arrangement in any of it, no alphabetizing, no grouping by genre, or topic. As a child, Thea used to close her eyes and jab her finger randomly at the shelves. Mostly her mother had let her read whatever she found that way. It had made for some interesting conversations with teachers at parents' evening.

The room was always dimly lit, usually by candles, but only as long as they were beeswax because the women worried about toxins. They worried about a lot: about the overuse of plastic, about the effects of social media on young girls, injustices in far-flung places, bees, abortion laws, the closing of libraries and opening of too many fast food restaurants. They turned that worry into plotting and planning, running web chatrooms and designing placards on newspaper on the floor.

The warmth wasn't just from the candles though. It was the women, mostly in their sixties and early seventies, who refused to fade quietly into old age like their mothers had done before them, who wore bright colours and dyed their hair odd shades and dressed how they pleased. They bickered and gossiped, teasing Thea, telling her off, lecturing her, making her one of them because she never really had friends of her own age. However, it didn't matter because she had that room with those women whenever she wanted, whenever she got a little tired of the quiet in her own house.

She wanted to see that room again.

And her mother.

Blinking back tears, Thea tried not to move. She'd seen enough horror films in her life to know that the heroine always got caught because she dropped something, or slipped, or knocked something, or sneezed. This felt very much like a film. It couldn't be real life, could it? Her life? Her life didn't involve running for cover, running so hard her legs felt shaky and her heart seemed huge in her chest.

She'd found a spot by a tree and some tangled, spiky undergrowth, so she'd crawled her way into it, as far as she could go, her hair caught in thorns, her hands squashing beetles, feeling them pop like bubble wrap as she pushed herself in, knowing she had to get out of sight and then she had to be very still.

So still.

A latticework of branches closed over her, like a confessional screen. *Forgive me, Father, for I have sinned.* Only bugs would be able to offer penance. Her breaths moved a strand of spiderweb that had got caught on her jacket collar and it floated elegantly in time with her breathing.

She tried not to think. Not of the gun that Len had been reaching for under his jacket, tucked into his belt, at the small of his back. Not of the lighthouse, which they really didn't want her to see, and what could be waiting there, hiding like her. And finally, she really, really tried not to think of the pale face at the monastery window, mouth stretched wide, a dark O of fury and the sound of bone crunching into stone.

And then Thea, in her leafy confessional, heard footsteps.

Quiet, carefully placed footsteps.

The footsteps of someone who didn't want to be heard, someone who knew how and where to step gingerly.

Someone who was searching and didn't want to startle its prey.

Someone trained.

Thea understood then why the heroines in those horror films screamed, throat-straining, long gulping screams. She understood because it was taking every ounce of self-control for her not to scream, to just let out some of the fear, give herself away and get it over with because this was a terrible hiding place and she was going to be found and she couldn't stand the waiting any longer …

Her mother's ridiculous safe phrase floated into her mind as a pair of boots appeared by her head and then she was suddenly being dragged out from her hiding place by her feet, arms flailing uselessly, her screams cut off when her feet were dropped and a hand clamped over her mouth.

I'm really missing the cat, Mum. I'm really missing the cat.

Chapter 24

It was a miserable morning in a forgotten seaside town.

Vivian had been right. The little red light on her answerphone had been a warning: she had not heard from Thea for over a week.

'I don't think anyone's going to show, Viv. You sure Tristan said eight?' Delia asked, dabbing at the crumbs of cake on her plate.

Vivian was sure. He had said his contact from Ing Enterprises would be there at 8 a.m. at what looked like the Apocalypse Café where the oilcloth was always sticky, the tomato sauce bottle forever empty and the glass on the chiller cabinets clouded with greasy cataracts.

'Well, maybe they slept late.' Delia peeled her sleeve away from the table, studying the damage to her coat, though the pattern was such that any stain would have been hard to see. She ran her hand through her hair and sighed, ruffling the underside of it, which was still a light green colour from a recent flirtation with the hair dye aisle. It was part of the deal when you were someone's oldest friend: occasionally you had to haul your old bones out of bed at ridiculously early hours to go with them to clandestine meetings.

Well, it was the deal if Vivian was your friend.

'Why would you eat cake at this hour?' Vivian picked at the chip in the handle of her mug.

'Why wouldn't you?' Delia retorted, relaxing back in her chair and folding her hands comfortably over her stomach.

Fair enough, thought Vivian. She gazed out of the window. It was definitely not the morning for a seaside walk, but she noticed someone was out there on the promenade: a man, muffled in a scarf and woollen hat, who had stopped just outside and leant against the railings. Nothing peculiar in that, Vivian told herself. People often paused for a moment to take in the view. Except, well, they needed to be actually facing the view, didn't they? He was staring the wrong way, not even looking at the sea. Staring at them.

Paranoia. Vivian mentally shook herself: she was not paranoid. Not completely, anyway.

On the wall there was a clock the shape of a dinner plate with cutlery for hands. It ticked.

They ordered more coffee.

Tick, tick, tick.

Where was the tock? Vivian wondered, resolutely not looking out of the window. That was how it was meant to go: there was meant to be a tock. Tick, tock. Everyone knew that. The clock was clearly defective.

Who were they waiting for? Vivian had been disappointed with herself when she'd heard their contact was called Alex and immediately thought of them as a man, well, a boy really, some computer nerd in a bad jumper. She had resolved to give her first thoughts a good talking-to. Alex could be a woman. Anyone.

The man behind the counter slapped a wet cloth along the top of the chiller cabinet.

Tick, tick.

'Come on, Viv, it's been an hour. They're not coming.'

Maybe the stupid, tockless clock was wrong. She looked at her watch and sighed. 'You see, I know it's only been a week and that's no time, is it? I know I shouldn't be worried and, if I am, I should go to the police, not sit in dingy little cafés failing to meet complete strangers.'

She tried to imagine explaining it to an overworked police-woman behind the reception desk: 'You see, my daughter is on a technology trial and she said she'd phone every day but she hasn't for over a week now and I'm worried about …'

About what? That's where it all fell apart. What was she worried about? Thea had sounded relieved on the phone the last time she'd spoken to her. She'd got better sleep; it was all working. There was nothing to worry about.

'But this is Thea,' she continued. 'The girl has always been clockwork. She said she would ring every day.'

And just like that, she was right back in those hormone-soaked days after Thea had been born when just looking at her sweet solemn little face caused a rush of every emotion she had ever experienced to swell so violently in her throat she thought she might have to scream just to breathe.

She got up and wrapped her scarf around her.

'Maybe she's just forgotten?' said Delia as they heaved on the door, the cold outside air blasting over them.

'When was the last time Thea forgot something?'

Delia smiled.

Thea made lists, then she crossed things off when she'd done them and, if the list got too messy, she rewrote it. She kept a calendar and remembered birthdays, put the bins out on time and then reminded Vivian when it was time to put hers out as well.

'Well, maybe Tristan's contact forgot then – you don't know.' Delia stuffed her hands under her armpits.

'That's the thing, Dels. You've hit it on the head,' Vivian said. '*I don't know*. I don't know anything about this company, about the trial, about any of it. I don't like not knowing.'

113

On the promenade across from them, the man was still facing the café. Maybe he had a café fetish? That was it. He had a café fetish, definitely – it certainly wasn't that he was an Ing Enterprises spy sent to watch them. No. Café fetish was much more realistic.

Vivian didn't look away this time. She wasn't able to see if the man was staring right at her from this distance, but she was certain, somewhere in her gut, that he was.

If he carried on like that, standing there and gazing in, leaning against the railings in that irritatingly relaxed way, then she was going to put her umbrella up, march out of the café porch and stomp right up to him …

'Viv?' Delia followed her gaze.

Vivian slumped. 'I'm going to have to go to the police, aren't I?'

In the dark. That was the phrase, wasn't it? She was in the dark and she hated it and, worse, her little girl was in there somewhere too.

But that was the thing about the dark.

All you had to do was strike a match, or flick a switch, and the shapes you'd thought were monsters turned out to be just boxes and bags and old junk piled high.

It was time to strike a match.

Chapter 25

The dragging stopped and, when Thea opened her eyes, she was looking at a face, a concerned face, which was nice, but, nicer still, it was a face she knew.

Ethan.

He put a finger to his lips and moved his hand away from her mouth. She gulped in air, still lying on her back where he'd dragged her out, one trainer loose and her jacket rucked up under her shoulder blades.

He nudged her to get up and pointed off to the right, still gesturing for quiet.

There was a distant sound of men's voices, but they weren't coming closer, and Ethan was already pulling her up and leading her away by the arm, gently but firmly. She got a proper look at him. He was bleeding from the corner of his lip, but apart from that he looked okay, very much not shot, which was a relief. Questions butted their way to the tip of her tongue, but she padded quietly next to him.

Soon they came out of the wood and found themselves back on the path again, below them the monastery and above them, the route to the lighthouse. Ethan began to run, pulling Thea with him, until the path curved around along seal bay and they were hidden from the view of anyone looking up from the monastery.

Only then did he stop.

Thea's lungs were about to explode. She was pretty certain she'd turned bright red in the face and she sank gratefully into the grass at the side of the path. She really should have worked harder in those cardio classes.

'You okay?' he asked, standing with his hands on his hips as he took deep breaths.

'Fab,' she wheezed. 'What happened back there?'

The sky was now an inky wave of trouble about to crash onto them. The seagulls swooped and screamed, possibly telling each other to get in out of the coming snow, unlike those two stupid humans down there on the cliff. Ethan stretched out his shoulders, then touched at his lip, wincing slightly.

'It was only Len who was armed, not the others.' He showed her the gun, spinning the magazine and checking the bullets. It looked like a film prop to Thea. 'But I think something's happened at the Centre. The only reason I got away was because a message came through on their radio. I couldn't hear it properly but it sounded like there's been a fire, or something. They were being called back.'

'A fire?' Thea got to her knees, feeling the cold slush from the previous snowfall seep into the fleecy gym leggings she'd been issued earlier.

A fire at the Centre was unlikely but not impossible. Thea thought of Rosie first, the rise and fall of her breathing and the beeping machine marking out her life and, in doing so, she remembered Richard being held down, a syringe pushed into his arm. What had Rory told her? *Don't fuck about with REM sleep.* The rage had come from Richard like heat. Like fire.

'But we've only got a short space of time before they come back out to find us,' Ethan said, interrupting her thoughts. He wiped at his lip again and grimaced. 'If you still want to go to the lighthouse, we do it now.'

It was the tone and the way he handled the gun.

'You were in the army, weren't you?'

He pulled her up and she realized that her hands were smeared with dead bugs squashed into her palms. She rubbed them on her jacket.

'Yep.'

'Which is why the nightmares.'

'Yep.'

'And that explains how you tracked me so easily!'

'Uh, no, not really. You stuck out like a sore thumb. I didn't need training for that.'

'Oh.'

He took pity on her. 'There's something at that lighthouse though – you're right. It was at the monastery before and that search was just a big charade to put us off. It's at the lighthouse now. I don't know what it is, but they really don't want us to find out.'

'Dreams,' she said, gazing out over the cliff edge.

'What?'

'Dreams – it was something Rory said. He grabbed me before we left, told me they're not really interested in fixing sleep at all … that—'

'Yeah, well, it's not some stupid dream I'm worried about,' he said. 'Dreams can't hurt you.'

The wind picked up, lashing the first stinging tails of sleet in their faces.

'You don't have to come with me though.' Thea raised her voice against the wind, trying to keep it steady. 'To the lighthouse. You could go back. I don't want to drag you into this.'

She didn't want to drag *herself* into this. What she wanted was to go back to the Centre, where it was warm and dry and she could check on Rosie and then get them both out of there as soon as she could. She didn't want to pick this scab of a secret, because she feared that underneath was only blood and infection.

'I'm used to trouble,' he said. 'And after what just happened? I'd rather be at the lighthouse than back in that bloody golf ball. Why do you need guns for a sleep trial – on a bloody island? No, let's go.'

Rosie in her bed with her beeping machine.

Beep.

Thea didn't want to go to the lighthouse. Who would? It was crazy. She should be sensible and go back to the Centre.

Beep.

But she'd been "a *good* girl", "a *diligent* employee", "a *dutiful* daughter" for a very long time. She thought of the pale blob of a face with its mouth stretched wide and the blood that had matted Rosie's hair.

Beep, beep, beep.

Thea made her choice. She started walking.

Chapter 26

'Is this going to work?' Thea hissed at Ethan, smiling manically.

'Shut up and keep smiling!' He hissed back. 'I just need to get closer to him.'

As they had climbed higher and the lighthouse came into view, they had seen that outside the lighthouse there was a guard. With a gun.

Ambushing the guard had quickly been discarded as an option. To ambush, you needed surprise, and you couldn't surprise someone who could clearly see you coming. They continued walking up to him, Thea waving exaggeratedly and offering some weak "hellos" as they got nearer, close enough to see that he'd put one hand on his holster.

'What are you doing up here?'

The wind rough-housed them, snatching their words away and hurling them off the cliff edge.

'FIRE!' Thea called back. 'You're needed back at the Centre. We've come to take over.'

At least they weren't dressed in their cult clothes anymore. Thea's dark leggings and jacket was the kind of thing the staff would wear if they had to trek to the lighthouse.

'WHAT?' The guard shouted, holding out an arm to stop them.

'FIRE!'

As it was, with the wind and the sleet, it didn't matter what they said because the guard couldn't hear them properly and they just had to keep walking closer, smiling, smiling all the while. One foot in front of the other. Closer, closer. Smile, smile.

They saw him reaching for his radio. Maybe he'd already been told that there would be two escapees trying to get into the lighthouse.

'Fuck it,' Ethan muttered and sprinted the last few feet.

Thea instinctively wanted to squeeze her eyes shut, but she didn't want to be the pathetic sidekick, so she ran too – fully intending to grab an arm or a foot and hopefully not get shot in the face. It was over too quickly for any of that; in seconds Ethan had knocked the man out and was searching his pockets.

'Help me drag him in!'

He fumbled with the keys he'd found, opened the door and grabbed the guard under his arms. Thea got his feet and they staggered into the lighthouse as a tangled threesome, Ethan slamming the door behind them as the wind picked up its temper.

A light flickered on automatically.

Thea wasn't sure what she'd been expecting from the inside of the lighthouse. What she got was … cosy. A curving stone staircase hugged the wall and led upwards to the glass-topped pinnacle that held the light. In what space was left, there was a tiny kitchen, the cabinets old but the appliances all very new and shiny, and a comfortable chair next to a tall, thin, curved window. It was warm and smelled of buttery toast.

Any minute, something could come barrelling down those steps, something ugly and crazed, with a mouth stretched wide in a howl, hands reaching out to claw, scratch or strangle.

A clock ticked.

There was a newspaper on the chair, the crossword half-completed.

'I don't think anyone else is here,' Ethan said, searching through the kitchen cupboards. 'Help me find something to tie him up, and then we'll look upstairs. Handcuffs'd be great, but I don't think we're going to find any …'

'Next to the kettle?' Thea picked up a pair.

They both stared at them.

'Okay then.' Ethan raised an eyebrow.

A noise by the door caused them to both whirl round, just in time to see the guard on his feet wrenching the door open and stumbling out into the sleet.

'Shit.' Ethan ran to the door.

'Let him go.' Thea shrugged, marvelling at how cool she could act. 'What's he going to do? They already know we're here. He'd just be one more thing to worry about.'

She started to rummage through the plastic box of medicine on the kitchen worktop.

'There's enough sedative here to last for months …'

She trailed off as they both looked at each other. Who, or what, would need sedating? Thea half expected cold fingers to wrap themselves around her shoulder. She shivered.

'We need to check upstairs.' Ethan took the packet from her and glanced at the instructions. 'You can stay down here if you want.'

'No!'

Ethan went first. Action Ken, that's what Rosie had called him. It had made Thea laugh at the time, the idea of him in a camouflage outfit, poseable arms holding a pair of binoculars, plastic attack dog included.

Thea's hands started to shake. They passed another little room wedged in around the stairs on the second floor, this time a sparse bedroom. Inside was a single bed, plain woollen coverlet and a few clothes strewn on a hard-backed chair. They carried on up towards the light. Thea couldn't stop the shaking spreading from her hands to the rest of her, in particular her jaw. She tried to clench it, but it juddered like she was the kind of cold that led to freezing to death.

They made it to the light-room, the intricate structure of glass panels and machinery in the middle, a narrow walkway around it.

That was when Thea started to gulp in air because it felt like she couldn't breathe properly anymore. Because of the gulping and the shaking, she found herself half-sliding to the floor in a panic, no clue as to why she was suddenly on her hands and knees on the metal walkway, the grids cutting into her palms, her chest heaving, trying to suck in air like she was giving birth.

'Shh, it's okay. You're having a panic attack. You'll be fine …'

Ethan pushed her into a sitting position and sat with her, making her breathe with him, long steady breaths, and there was a part of her that was cringing in embarrassment, but she couldn't worry about that part until she got control of her lungs.

'You're fine,' he soothed. 'You've done really well …'

'Don't … patronize … me,' Thea spluttered.

'See? And you can still be really rude. So you must be fine.'

They sat there for a while. It would have been a beautiful view if it hadn't been for the sleet blurring the windows and the way the wind growled and raged outside. Downstairs, tucked away behind the thick stone walls, there was protection from it but up here they were vulnerable. There was just glass between them and it, *old* glass at that. Up close she could make out some of the pictures in the stained glass: one saint in a long grey robe bending to pat a dog, or sheep, or possibly a small horse – it was hard to tell. In the sunshine it would have been kaleidoscope-pretty. Right now though, it seemed that at any moment, the whole thing would shatter, the cracks speeding across the panes and then there would be a rush of air and sleet as the glass imploded over them, wicked shards aiming straight for their eyes.

'Let's go.' She took another deep breath.

'Tea. Everyone feels better after tea. With sugar.'

Ethan set about boiling the kettle and Thea crumpled into the chair by the window, trying to concentrate on her breathing.

'I know!' Ethan knelt to look in the lower cupboards, his knees cracking softly as he did so. Action Ken knees, Thea thought.

'I knew that guard would have some!' He waved a bottle. 'Here. Even better!'

He shoved a glass into her hand, filled with an amber-coloured liquid.

'Whisky. Just the thing. One glass, then we carry on looking. Okay?'

He raised his glass.

'Okay,' said Thea, swilling the whisky round and round, making a small orange whirlpool.

'To … I don't know … to Moses Ing!'

Thea raised hers. 'To Moses Ing, without whom we wouldn't be in this fucking mess.'

They drank.

And from beyond the door they hadn't even noticed was there, half hidden behind a tapestry, a small wavery voice could just about be heard.

'Hello?'

They froze.

'Hello? Did you call me? Moses? Anybody there? Hello?'

Chapter 27

Moses Ing. The man behind it all, near-mythical, a tech Titan, a behemoth of the internet, the man who made Morpheus … a man they had very clearly seen waving from the walkway next to Delores dressed in his chinos and deck shoes.

'*He can't be in there!*' Thea whispered.

Ethan shrugged helplessly.

'*We saw him with Delores!*' she added.

He downed the rest of his whisky.

'Did we?'

'Yes! You were there. Delores introduced him and he waved at everyone and …' Her brain caught up. 'Oh.'

'Well, one of them isn't the real Moses Ing,' he said. 'Want to find out which one?'

Stunned, Thea watched him unlock the padlock with the keys he'd taken from the guard. He got the gun ready as he pulled back the bolt and opened the door with a shoulder shove, legs braced.

They made a dramatic entrance into what looked like a room from a run-down bed and breakfast from the Seventies. Chintzy wallpaper peeled away at the edges and there was a rough carpet, made brown with age rather than by design. A window let in some light, but the panes were misted up and condensation gathered in pools on the mould-speckled windowsill. Towards the back there was a door, its wood veneer scuffed off, which led to what must have been a bathroom.

However, it was the bed that drew their attention. It was a hospital bed, with bars on the side and white cotton linen, a drip standing guard on one side. It looked hugely out of place amongst the genteel decay.

But not as out of place as the man lying in it.

He was hooked up to the drip, the bed adjusted so he was half sitting, propped up on so many pillows he looked like a doll amongst them.

A frightening doll.

Skinny and blue-veined, the man had stubble greying his chin and bare feet that were hook-nailed and calloused. His head was completely bald and as smooth as porcelain and, just like fine porcelain, which is ever so slightly transparent, Thea and Ethan could see this man's brain.

It was a tattoo. An elaborate, skull-covering tattoo.

Just as doctors sometimes had china phrenology heads in their surgeries and on those heads the brain was mapped out in neat little grids with tiny labels, so it was with this man. The design stretched all the way around his left eye socket, over his sparse eyebrows, the fine black lines giving his head the look of a cracked egg.

His eyes were closed as though in a restless, fidgety sleep.

Then they were open. Bloodshot and a bit wild.

And looking right at Thea.

She noticed he was handcuffed to the bed.

'Where am I?' His voice was croaky from lack of use, as cracked as his head.

'Don't go any closer,' Ethan muttered to Thea.

'Moses?' Thea asked gently.

'Who are you? Are you real?' He writhed in the bed, the hand-cuffs scraping on the metal bars as he twisted his wrists.

'Are you Moses Ing?' Ethan said, louder.

'I wasn't here before! Where am I? Are you going to kill me?' He started to wrench at the handcuffs, yelling and kicking his shackled feet hard against the mattress as he strained, his neck stringy with the effort.

Then just as suddenly, he flopped, completely still and stared at something in the far corner of the room.

'What are you doing, Max?' he said, quite softly now, watchful.

He listened to a reply that only he could hear.

'It's my tech, Max. I've told you. I get to choose. We're going to do this my way.'

He rolled his eyes at whatever the response was to that.

'You trust them? Really? Well, go work for them, then. I won't stop you. It's my … tech …'

His eyelids drooped.

'My … tech … remember …'

He slumped, his breathing evening out, muttering a few last unintelligible words.

Thea and Ethan looked at each other.

'Fuck,' Ethan whispered, rubbing one hand over the bristle of his hair.

'Yeah.'

She tiptoed a little closer to the bed. The man was sleeping again now, or at least seemed to be. She wasn't going to test that out by going any nearer, especially after what he had done at the monastery. Asleep, however, he looked weak, his breath whistling slightly.

'This has to be him, doesn't it? From the monastery. He said he didn't know where he was. That's because he's been moved.' She turned to Ethan.

'Or he never knows where he is because he's crazy …'

'What about what he said? The tech? *My* tech, he said. He has to be Moses! Maybe … I don't know … that Max person he was talking to did something to him … I mean, why hide him unless he's important? Unless he's Moses?'

126

Around his left eye socket, Thea could see the words "form", "size", "weight" and "colour" each in its own little grid. There wasn't anything written around his right eye, but, as Thea looked, she noticed a circular patch of scarred skin, red and raw, with a deep dent in the middle. It was the size of the disc on her own temple.

'Look.' She pointed to it.

Ethan's hand instinctively went to his own disc.

'I didn't tell you this before,' she said, keeping her voice steady. 'But back at the Centre yesterday I visited Rosie and I saw Richard.' Ethan looked blank. 'From our sleep therapy group, remember? Sleep paralysis guy? He was taken into another room and he was … well, he was screaming and fighting – and the others were trying to control him but it was like, he was seeing something else, something I couldn't … see.'

Ethan paled, then he set his jaw and marched out of the room.

With a quick glance at the peaceful Moses, Thea followed. She found him in the kitchen opening drawers with aggression, rifling through the things inside.

'I am done with that shit on my head. I don't care about the sleep.' He pulled one drawer out and emptied it on the worktop, forks and teaspoons rattling, skimming his hands through them until he found what he was looking for.

A sharp knife.

He raced upstairs to the little bedroom on the second floor.

'Wait!' Thea ran after him.

She skidded into the room just in time to see Ethan in front of the mirror on the wall. With one hand holding the skin tight around the disc on his temple, he gripped the knife, just about to jab it in.

'Stop!' She yanked at his arm. 'Just stop a minute and think this through.'

She was out of breath.

'We don't know anything about this tech, what they've

programmed into it.' She gasped, still gripping his arm. 'You can't just dig something like that out with a kitchen knife. It could have some sort of self-defence mode; it could, I don't know, short out and fry your brain if you do it wrong. Please let's think it through a bit before you do anything.' She felt his arm relax a bit. '*Please.*'

He dropped his arm.

'Surely, we're out of range up here anyway?' she continued to hold on to him.

He shrugged her off. 'All right,' he said. 'One more night. But if they work tonight, if I have a restful bloody sleep, I am cutting the damn things out first thing in the morning, whether you want to or not.'

'Agreed.'

Ramming the knife point into the little wooden dresser next to him, Ethan stalked back down the stairs.

Chapter 28

Night. Ethan slept. Thea didn't.

They'd decided not to bother with the sedative for Moses as they didn't really know how to dose it and he was handcuffed anyway. There was also a chance that they could get more sense out of him if he was lucid.

They had cobbled together a basic meal from the tins in the cupboards and had eaten it while perched on the kitchen work-tops, watching the sleet fatten and slow into snowflakes until it got too dark to see anything. Ethan had insisted on Thea taking the bed and had settled down on some blankets on the floor next to her.

It was normal for her to struggle to nod off.

Normal, normal, normal.

Adrenaline was probably still doing a conga line through her body after the day she'd had. Anyone would struggle to sleep.

Normal.

Anyone.

She would drop off at some point, she told herself. The Sleep Centre was too far away for the tech to work. She would be fine, fine, fine. Fine. She would definitely not end up in a room being held down by too many hands, punctured by a syringe.

She rolled over for the fiftieth time, trying to get comfortable on the somewhat musty-smelling bed. Or maybe it wasn't the bed that was musty. Maybe it was her. She hadn't washed since this morning and it had been quite a day. There was a shower downstairs next to Moses's room and tomorrow, she resolved she would use it. Trying it now was out of the question: she'd seen too many horror films and knew that a woman in a shower late at night in a spooky lighthouse was never going to end well.

Yes, tomorrow.

With Ethan on guard outside the door.

She sighed and sat up. There weren't even any books to read. Stepping carefully over Ethan's sleeping body, she walked barefoot downstairs to the kitchen and got herself a glass of water.

'Hello?'

Moses's voice. They'd left the door open.

'Is someone there?'

She crept to the door and peered in. He sat up straighter at the sight of her, using his shoulder blades to push himself up. There was a floor lamp next to him, bathing his bed in a cosy glow, but the shadows it cast, and his bald head, made him into a skeleton, albeit one that was trying to have a polite conversation.

'I remember you. From earlier.' His voice sounded different this time, not manic and strained but low, thoughtful even. 'They've moved me. But you're not a guard.'

She shook her head.

'Who are you?'

'Thea. I'm one of the patients at the Sleep Centre. Well ... I was, anyway. You're Moses, aren't you?'

He bowed his head. 'Yes.' He looked at his hands and stretched his fingers. 'So it's started.' With a cry of frustration, he kicked his feet against the mattress again.

Thea retreated a few steps.

'No!' He took a deep breath to calm himself. 'Don't go! I won't hurt you. See? I can't move.'

'You hurt my friend. She's in the hospital because of you.'

A look of confusion crossed his face. 'I-I ... the guard? I thought I saw a ... guard ... had to get out ... but they gave me these pills ...' He trailed off, his jaw slack, a peculiar glaze to his eyes.

With a shake of his head, he snapped back to Thea.

'You! I don't have much time. Only myself to blame for that though.' He chuckled bitterly. 'I did it to myself.'

Then he muttered things to himself that Thea couldn't hear, his head lolling back on the pillows and she wasn't sure if he was talking to her or to people she couldn't see.

'It's in my watch ...' He tried to sit up again but didn't have the strength. 'Do I still have my watch? Max wouldn't bother to take it off me. The truth ... about it all ... in my watch ...'

And he slipped into sleep once more.

Thea stayed rooted in the doorway. There was indeed a watch on his left wrist, but she would have to move closer to him to get at it. Worse, because the left side of the bed was pushed up against the wall, she would have to lean right over him and fiddle with the buckle. While she was doing that he could ... she didn't know ... break loose, try to bite off her ear, or jam a knife she never knew he had right into her stomach so the last sight she'd have would be her own insides, hot and shiny, flopping out like fish onto the dusty floor.

How could the truth be in a watch?

Maybe it was a hi-tech one, with an inbuilt Wi-Fi connection that held a kill switch of some sort, something that would stop the whole process over at the Sleep Centre. It was possible. He was Moses Ing, Tech Emperor.

Why were they drugging him? What had he done?

She didn't give herself any more time to think about it but crossed the room in a few short strides and bent over him, her heart beating fast in her throat. She held her breath, thinking to herself that it certainly didn't look like a hi-tech watch as she struggled with the battered leather strap.

131

It came free and she staggered backwards, slumping over and clutching her knees to get air into her lungs and stop the black spots swimming before her eyes.

Just a watch.

A scuffed brown strap, a plain dial with clear black numbers, the kind of watch a grandad wore.

Just a watch.

With a little compartment in the back that opened if a nail was hooked under it.

And in that compartment …

A very small memory stick.

Chapter 29

The building was a blank of mirrors and ageing brickwork, nothing to catch the eye, nothing to stand out.

This was not the police station.

That visit had gone as expected, except with the added discomfort that they'd seen the policeman at the desk keeping order at one of their recent protests. 'Still painting those placards, Viv?' he'd said with a chuckle. She had left with some vague reassurances and a promise of a police phone call to Ing Enterprises. 'Thing is, you know where she is, you see? And she's an adult. The girl's probably just lost track of time, that's all,' the policeman had said, kindly enough. 'Youngsters these days.'

Inside the Ing Enterprises building, a sticky-sweet gloss covered every available surface. Vivian half expected to touch something and bring her fingers away trailing thin webs.

She turned to her friend, 'Ready, Dels?'

'As ever.'

They had been to the café that morning, the police station straight afterwards and it was now late afternoon. Trying to find a UK address for Ing Enterprises had proved difficult but Thea had told her where she had gone for her preliminary testing and it seemed as good a place to start as any.

They could have done the well-worn routine, though Vivian was a bit rusty at it now. She and Delia had done the old "name and shame" for years. One of them would be in front of the camera at whatever firm they needed to "out" that week and the other would film and whip up the protestors outside. Then it all went on the website and, latterly, Delia's grandson would post it to YouTube with links to relevant articles.

Vivian had taken a step back from being in front of the camera, but Delia was embracing modernity and had lately taken to doing the filming on her new smartphone. Consequently, they'd recently had rather a lot of films of Delia's thumb.

Vivian had known that wouldn't work here.

She had been right.

There was no receptionist. There was no reception. There was just gloss and shine and a few discreet screens set into the walls.

'Viv? What do we do?' Delia whispered as she pushed her bright purple glasses up onto her head.

The only man in the room blinked at them confusedly and then turned to one of the screens. In a few seconds it had scanned his face and a doorway slid open next to him.

'Are we even in the right place?' Delia looked around anxiously and nearly dropped her phone. 'Only, there's no sign and, well, we can't afford another lawsuit this tax year …'

'Ms Mackenzie.'

Vivian honestly could not have said from where the woman and her two guards had appeared. One minute there was a blank wall bouncing her own voice around, and the next there was this … creature. She was a creature. Perhaps she had even slithered out from the very wall itself, so glossy and shiny was she. Vivian understood make-up, she understood the pleasure of using a bit of colour and powder to enhance your looks, or, in her case, to stop one from looking as if they'd been recently dug up. But she did not understand this mask that many women these days chose to wear; a mask an inch thick that didn't enhance, but hid. Why did women these days feel the need to hide?

'How—?'

'Facial recognition on entry.' The woman smiled. 'But we knew you would be coming.'

'I won't be leaving until I speak to someone in charge of the Morpheus trial going on right now.' Vivian nudged Delia to start filming just for backup, startling her so much that she nearly dropped the phone again.

The woman moved smoothly towards them, her gait almost unnatural, too effortless. Like a robot, Vivian thought. Maybe she *was* a robot – it wouldn't be beyond a company like this. Perhaps if you stabbed her silk-clad arm she would bleed blue.

'We cannot discuss individual trials, Ms Mackenzie.'

'My daughter is on it!' Vivian spoke very clearly for the camera. 'It is taking place on St Dunstan's Island and I can no longer get in touch with her.'

The woman sighed. 'You will find your phone has been blocked. Any filming on these premises is rather difficult, I'm afraid.'

Vivian glanced at Delia who was jabbing her finger at the screen of her phone and swearing imaginatively.

'Ing Enterprises is a respectable and well-established technology company.' The woman smiled again, baring her neat little teeth. 'The company pays its taxes in full, has a happy and contented workforce and quietly helps this country, and many others, to smoothly operate a variety of technological systems. It has a charity foundation and a community outreach programme—'

Vivian opened her mouth, but the woman continued without pause.

'Your ire, Ms Mackenzie, is mistakenly directed and will be tolerated no longer. Please bear that in mind.'

Vivian and Delia were being backed towards the door.

'Are you threatening me?'

135

The woman sighed. But she managed to even make that seem benevolent.

'We do not threaten, Ms Mackenzie. We never have the need.'

She smiled a perfect smile with perfect little teeth. Vivian was about to say something, to take control of the situation, which was oozing out of her grasp like caramel but then they were at the door, which opened for them with an eager whoosh and she was about to open her damn mouth but the guards were in the way and all too quickly …

… they were outside again.

The two women stared at each other.

Delia jerked her head to get her glasses to fall back onto her nose, began to say something, changed her mind and sighed.

Vivian had always liked this bit. Women like her had done what they needed to do to shake society up a bit. They had paved the way for these younger people, and the paving had involved dust and muck and getting your hands dirty. The sheer chaos of it all, the shouting, the protests, running and struggling and the brilliant feeling of *doing*, of getting something done. Activity. She'd known what to do and where she fit in.

The two of them stood on the pavement, Delia waiting for Vivian to take charge as she normally did.

But it was cold out on the street and it had been a long day and for a moment, all Vivian wanted to do was sit down and get a coffee somewhere where they had huge squashy sofas. And she nearly would have done, but, luckily, the familiar fury came streaking in once more, clearing her mind to a blazing white.

'So?' Delia said.

Vivian turned her back on the building and flicked her scarf over her shoulder with a little more force than was necessary.

'So,' she said grimly. 'I think it's time we were a little more direct.'

Chapter 30

'So, y'know, curses be upon ye if ye haven't got my permission to watch this. Okay?'

The same tattooed head, the same voice. It was the man in the bed, but with his batteries in properly: a shine to his eyes, a vigour in his movements, an eagerness as he leant in to the screen, looking at least ten years younger, healthy, tanned.

Thea had immediately powered up an internet-free laptop, one that the guard had been using to watch DVDs, and shoved the memory stick in. She was reluctant to wake Ethan if he was actually getting some rest, but too impatient to wait until morning. Shoving earphones in, she clicked on the first file that came up: a video diary.

'Obviously filming this for posterity. Once I've perfected the tech and the world has been immeasurably improved just by sleeping, I'll be able to sell this at auction and become so rich I won't be able to decide which super-yacht to use.'

Someone sniggered in the background.

'A good scientist always keeps a record. Also, I'm really vain. You'd agree with that, yeah, Max?'

Again the muffled voice.

137

'Agreed. So. Tech is amazing, right? We love it. We're in the Age of the Tech Nerd. Founding member right here, obviously. But more and more, right, I've been thinking about the tech we have always had. Yep. That's right, the human body. And it's not just amazing this body of ours, it's *absolutely astounding*. Particularly, the brain. Final-frontier stuff, man, working out how the brain does what it does.'

He tapped out a little rhythm on his knees. Behind him, Thea could see a living room, a huge floor-to-ceiling window looking out at some city skyline, tasteful furniture in whites and beiges partially obscured by a glass-brick partition.

'Like the new look?' He angled his head down so the camera could get a better view of the tattoo. 'Max doesn't. Says I look like a freak-show act. Side note: really painful, guys, and illegal in this country, so, y'know, don't try this at home, kids!'

He leant back in his chair and steepled his fingers.

'Sorry. Off-topic. I do that – you'll have to get used to it. Where was I? The brain! Yes! Or more importantly, the dreaming our brain does while we are asleep. Good old REM sleep.' He smiled and sang softly, '*Dream a little dream of me*. Or don't. Dream a little dream and start to reprogramme your mind while you do it. Want to quit smoking? We could get you to dream it, embed it in the dream and magically, you can do it when awake. Nightmares? Reprogramme them into something else, or just get you to turn around in the stupid nightmare and stab the evil clown that's chasing you. Get smarter, in your dream. Learn a language, in your dream. Supercharge your REM sleep. It can be done.' He paused for effect. 'I can do it.'

He rested his chin on his hand. The desk in front of him was a mess of paper, sweet wrappers and cans of fizzy drink scattered wildly.

'Now I can't tell you exactly how. Patents, y'know. I'm not stupid. Got to create a multimillion-pound company from this, guys; can't give my secrets away! It's all down to elves and unicorns, right?' He smiled. 'But you can come with me as we test all of this out. It's complicated and you've got to be delicate, y'know? REM sleep is what stands between rationality and insanity. You don't want to fuck about with that, do you? Currently it's all wires and huge equipment and not very consumer friendly, not at all. Got to work on that, got to work on it, lots to do.'

A figure crossed behind him in the background, too quickly and too far away to see properly. Max?

'Sleep on it, that's what they say. Ha! Thing is – *they're so right*! Ever noticed, yeah, how sometimes you're thinking about something, trying to work it out, and you go to sleep and the next morning you've just got it; it all slots into place? But maybe we can boost that, so that while we "sleep on it" we upgrade each and every night, like *we're* the tech.'

Thea paused the video. Moses froze with his mouth open as if about to break into song. Dreams. Rory had been right. But Ing Enterprises had never tried to hide that, had they? It was Phase Three, the part that went beyond sleep and started on self-improvement. There was nothing so scary in that, was there?

She pressed play.

'Meet Ted.' A man sat down next to Moses, his skin so pale he looked as if he hadn't seen the outside world for years, but he was smiling like a little child, waving happily at the camera. 'Ted's going to be our new flatmate for a while. Our lab rat. You don't mind being a lab rat, do you, Ted?'

'Nope!' He had a reedy voice and a rash of spots across his chin.

'Ted here has, of his own free will – it is your own free will, isn't it, Ted?' Here Moses grabbed a fistful of Ted's shirt and raised his arm as if about to punch him. Ted mugged horror for the camera. Then they relaxed, laughing and patting each other on the back. 'Ted's going to be hooked up and we're going to upgrade his mind while he's asleep. He wants to learn some languages. So we thought we'd start with six. Yeah?'

He high-fived Ted.

'Now, Ted, for the purposes of truth and accountability I'd like you to say on camera how many languages you can currently speak.'

'Uh … one. This one. English.'

'Ted, please hold up your exam certificates for the good people watching.' He did so. 'You will note that there are no languages listed there. Now, your degree?'

'Physics.'

'Excellent. One more time, you have never spoken fluent French, or Spanish, or Italian, or German, or Russian, or Polish? Right?'

'Nope. *Nyet*. Ha! Joking!' Ted grinned happily at his wit.

'I'll cut it down for the purposes of this diary but, if you want to watch the whole thing, I'll attach another file with all of Ted's sleep vids and the data we've gathered. So Ted, are you ready to get your sleep on?'

Moses came closer so his whole face filled the frame, lowering his voice.

'Let's do this!'

Thea liked this Moses. And Ted. They were goofy, clever guys, the kind of guys that no matter their actual age, still dressed like students. She guessed that Moses was in his forties. He had a babyish look to his face but there were fine lines around his eyes. Ted was somewhat younger. The energy from Moses almost fizzed out of the screen and Thea found herself always watching him, even when Ted was saying something.

The picture cut out and a new set of entries played. In these, Moses, jumpy and excitable as a puppy, proudly showed off what Ted could do after three, four, five days of dream therapy. It started off small and they focused on one language at a time, Ted a little uncertain and faltering at the start, but becoming confident and fluent in at least three of the languages by week two.

Thea clicked onto Ted's sleep diary to get an idea of what happened each night. The oh-so-familiar wires and electrodes were attached and checked by Moses, then Ted was left alone to settle into sleep. Mood music played at first, explained by Moses in a voiceover.

'Whales and waves and all that shit. Not strictly part of the tech, but I've got a feeling the punters will warm to that a bit more than to just listening to the clicks and whistles of what's really going on. Secret: most of the important stuff *isn't even sound* …'

Thea fast-forwarded chunks of it, until Moses came into the room halfway through the night. The voiceover came again.

'So, this is the bit we need to refine, but right now I'm waking Ted up in strategic parts of his sleep and getting him to read the language textbooks. We'll have to tweak that for public rollout as, much as I'd love to sneak into everyone's bedroom every night like the frickin' BFG, it's an unworkable part of the tech right now.'

Thea clicked back on the main diary. Ted was still speaking Italian, and Moses was nodding and tapping a pen against his teeth as he swivelled in his chair.

'Gonna need to get you someone Italian to talk with so's I can fully check this is working cos honestly, bro, I have no clue what you're saying …'

A hand and arm came into shot, placing a mug on the detritus of his desk.

'Uh-uh, come here, Maxie …'

Moses grabbed the arm and pulled the woman briefly into shot, kissing her as if they were in the final scene of a rom-com. However, that wasn't what made Thea gasp and nearly let the laptop slide off her knees.

The woman on the screen kissing Moses, wearing a floaty long dress and a brass twist of metal around her upper arm, had very *long*, very *red*, very *familiar* hair.

Moses wrapped an arm around her shoulders and kept her in shot, despite her trying to wriggle out.

'Everyone, meet the very clever, very wise, incredibly sexy … Delores Maxwell!'

Chapter 31

Delores.

Delores Maxwell. Max, as he called her.

They had been a couple; he had created Morpheus while with her, living in an apartment together, laughing, kissing, making each other cups of tea.

The Delores back at the Sleep Centre, she knew this Moses, the sedated wreck of a man only a few feet from where Thea sat now. She'd hidden him in the monastery, left him to his madness. She'd stolen the tech from him and shoved him out of sight.

No wonder she hadn't wanted him to be found.

Back on the laptop screen, the next entry was different to the last, just an empty room, Moses's desk in the foreground. At first Thea thought the camera had been left on by mistake until she heard Delores's voice.

'We're not going to get another chance like this.' She moved into view.

Seeing this Delores was like having your favourite comic book character drawn by a different artist: you knew who they were, but there was something wrong with the line work and shading. She'd tied her hair up into a messy ponytail and was wearing a long skirt with a belt that had moons and stars hanging from it.

'Shouldn't this be about what's the right thing to do, ethically? Not about money?' Moses appeared and moved around Delores, so he was centred on the screen. He rubbed at his eyes; his clothes were rumpled and his face unshaven.

'Ethics? Really? *Now* you're worried about that?'

'I guess I've made enough deals with the devil to get a Christmas card from him each year. I know the sleep data we will one day collect: how long people sleep, what they dream of, what scares them, how they learn, all of it …'

He paused and rubbed at the stubble on his chin.

'I know we'll sell it. To a Big Data company that is currently trying to integrate robotics, gene therapy and the rest of it. Human 2.0. The ultimate upgrade. I don't care about that. I don't think people will care either because they'll desperately want to be a part of it, won't they? They won't want to be left behind. Reverse ageing, get smarter, run faster, heal quicker. They'll sell their data for it like *that*.'

He clicked his fingers.

'The ship for data privacy has sailed. We all waved it off years ago. But … there are other ships that we can still halt …'

Delores rolled her eyes and crossed her arms over her chest, 'Really? This is about … rumours and scare stories? You are planning to turn down the only offer we have that will get us out of debt because of some stupid conspiracy chatroom horror stories?'

She disappeared out of view for a few seconds and came back with a cloth rucksack that had happy faces on it. As Moses spoke she stuffed a jacket and a pair of shoes inside.

'They're not horror stories. What we're doing with Ted, it's real. What a company like Aspire could do with that is fucking scary and, yes, I get that a business has to make money—'

Delores flung the bag onto a chair and gave an exasperated

144

scream. 'Do you? Do you really? Because we haven't made any for years now and we have no money left. Where do you think all of this comes from? Do you think I just magic it up?' She threw her arm out to encompass the room and the desk, full as it was with wires and screens.

Moses took a step towards her, reaching for her arm, but she jerked it away.

'But, imagine it, Max,' he said softly. 'I give you this sleep tech. You get the opportunity to reboot your brain and dream your way to a cleverer, better you. Imagining it? Good. Now imagine that in those dreams, so subconsciously embedded you won't even realize, you are actually being influenced to buy a certain brand of trainers, or drink a certain type of water, or, fuck it, vote for a certain politician. Like product placement. But in your dreams.

'Actually no, *not* like product placement because right now, you notice it, don't you? In a film, when the handsome action hero gives you a flash of his designer watch? You know you're being sold to. Well, *hopefully*, you know. In your dream it won't be like that. You won't know it's happening and it will change the choices you make the next day, *every day*. Not little choices. It might start with the small stuff: what food to buy, what colour to dye your hair, what toy a child wants for Christmas, but slowly and surely, it will spread. It will fucking spread. Whoever has the money and the opportunity to use the tech, *will* use it and they will use it for a host of things we haven't even thought of yet.'

Thea paused the video again, her hand shaking. Phase Three wasn't self-improvement. Phase Three was … mind control? That couldn't be right. There was no way any company would be allowed to sneak into people's dreams like that and use them for their own gain. There were laws against that kind of thing. Or there would be.

In the freeze frame, Delores had been caught about to sit down and, paused mid-movement, it looked as if she'd been winded, as if Moses had given her a kick to the stomach, which had doubled her over. A silver moon glinted on her belt.

Thea pressed play.

Delores sagged onto the arm of a chair and didn't say anything for a while. She played with one of her bangles and then sighed. 'But, I mean, anything like that, it's so far in the future, it's … I don't know, sci-fi. We don't have to worry about that now.'

Moses stayed silent.

'Isn't it? That's what you said.' Delores looked up at him, her eyes sharp.

'That's what I thought at the time.'

'Jesus!' Delores started to pace, coming in and out of view. Moses sank into his desk chair. 'Building blocks, you said. Just building blocks that no one else would be able to work with …'

'But that's the thing about building blocks, Max – they can be built upon.'

Delores continued to pace. 'But there would be all sorts of checks and controls on any kind of tech like that—'

'We've all seen how honest and transparent big business is, right? And tech can't be mishandled at all? Right? *Right?*'

He sat forward in his chair and this time successfully grabbed Delores's hand as she walked past him. He swung her to face him, her belt jangling.

'If we own the tech, we own the choice of what to do with it. Or what *not* to do.'

For a moment Delores's face softened as if she might let him pull her into his lap where the two of them could sit entwined, while they figured it all out. Then she pulled her hand away.

'But we don't have a choice, do we? We've gone way past the point of having a choice. We're broke. We have no more money to do this on our own. And … I don't *want* to do this on my own anymore; it's too big for us. What you've created, we can't cope with that by ourselves. Not even the great Moses Ing could, even if that guy existed anymore. If you don't want it to get into anyone else's hands, well then – there's a solution, isn't there? Just stop.'

Moses slumped back into his chair. 'Stop?' Disbelief made his voice crack. 'But, I'm so close, I can't just stop …'

Her eyes burned into his. 'All you are is a name now, Moses. You've spent all your money, called in all your favours … There's nothing left. And, fool that I am, I've let you drag me down with you.'

Moses put his head into his hands, but Delores wasn't finished.

'I didn't come back here today to rehash this argument. You know how I feel. Sell it to Aspire. Nothing you've said today has changed my mind.'

She crossed her arms again but this time she held her elbows, like she was trying to get warm, or stop her body from splitting in half.

Thea glanced at the apartment behind him. It didn't look quite the same as it had done in the previous video. Before it had been neat and ordered; now there were clothes strewn over the chairs, one of the tastefully coloured rugs was half kicked up and there were pizza boxes and cans on the big glass coffee table. Had Delores left him because of this?

Delores picked up the bag, walked out of view, and in a few seconds, Thea heard a door slam.

Moses stayed sat in his chair for a while, head bowed, long enough for Thea to hover the cursor over the stop button. But then he turned suddenly and faced the camera, looking into it like it was a friend who understood, expectant almost, waiting for whoever was watching to give him the answer he so craved.

Today, he was wearing a Superman T-shirt.

'A good scientist always keeps a record, eh? Don't even know what I'm recording here, or why. Guess it's … Let the records show that Max wanted me to stop and that I wouldn't, that I can't, despite knowing how it could be used.'

He stared at the camera for a few moments longer. 'And let the records show that, if I'm ever not around, she'll sell the tech to Aspire as soon as she can.'

Eyes grim, jaw set, he reached towards the camera and flicked it off.

Chapter 32

There was no voiceover.

Ted's sleep diary cut into the footage, a few weeks later. Night vision mode showed him hooked up and sleeping and a little superimposed clock in the corner said the time was 2.38 a.m. At first, it was almost as if Thea was looking at a still photo – there was so little movement, only the digital clock counting off the minutes as they passed. Ten minutes in and Thea almost lost concentration, until, suddenly, just as she was beginning to wonder whether she should start fast-forwarding again, Ted sat up in bed.

Bolt upright.

There was sound on the diary and Thea could hear him breathing, short, panicky breaths as he scrambled back in the bed, thudding against the headboard, speaking so quickly that she couldn't catch what he said. He put his hands out as if warding something off, then kicked the covers off his feet, bundling the sheets up in a frantic movement. Before Thea could see what he'd caught in the sheets, Ted was up and out of bed, straight to a big window that opened outwards just enough for a person to squeeze through, if they were determined.

Ted was determined.

He climbed onto the sill, still muttering, and opened the window to its furthest point, then he threw the bundle of bedclothes out with such force that it made him wobble.

From another corner a second figure rushed into the room, yelling, 'Stop!' It was Moses but though he tried, he couldn't get across the room fast enough to save Ted as he teetered at the window, his feet twisting and trying to grip the windowsill. He turned to Moses, one arm stretched towards him, his eyes pleading for help but there was nothing Moses could do.

Thea watched in horror.

The diary cut out and Moses's face filled the screen again, his voice serious.

'Ted hallucinated during his sleep periods, specifically in the REM part that we'd been using to help him learn the languages. That night you just saw, he said he could see spiders, the big furry ones that can jump, and they were all over the bed covers. So he bundled them up and threw them out of the window. Then threw himself out too.'

Moses paused.

'There is a wide ledge underneath that window, part of the roof for our downstairs neighbour's balcony. Ted fell onto that, then rolled into our neighbour's balcony canopy, which broke his fall.'

Thea unclenched her hands. Moses reached up and adjusted the camera, widening the view until Thea could see the person sat next to him.

She clenched them again.

It was Ted. Except this wasn't the Ted she had seen previously, with his shy smile and goofiness, the one who had joked about knowing Russian.

This Ted could no longer joke.

Propped up next to Moses was a blank waxwork of the man Ted had once been.

But even waxworks have the illusion of life about them, a

twinkle painted onto the eyes, a smile carved into their faces. This Ted was empty and unfinished, eyes vacant, head lolling to one side with drool gathered at the side of his mouth.

Moses didn't look at him but rubbed a hand over his forehead as if trying to massage away a headache.

'He's been like this for … three days now. His body functions, so he'll swallow if he's fed something … like a … like a baby … but—'

A jagged half-cry, half-gulp made him stop talking and he bent forward over the desk suddenly, his shoulders heaving. Ted remained upright due to the strap around his chest, his eyes glassy.

Moses pushed himself up again and angrily swiped at the mess on his desk. 'Max was right – I can't do this on my own. Look what I've done!' His voice broke again. 'I thought I'd factored it in. I know that if a body's REM sleep is tampered with then hallucination is a possibility. The brain goes into stress mode and compensates where it can. I knew that. I thought I'd dealt with it. And anyway, when the person gets normal sleep again, the body would reset itself. The person shouldn't become …' he turned for the first time and looked at Ted '… *this*.'

For a few minutes it seemed as if Moses was transfixed by Ted. He gazed at him. The only sign he'd not become catatonic as well was the slight tapping of his fingers on the desk.

'I won't believe this can't be fixed. I just need to be able to think better. I'll edit all of this together, my record. Put it on a memory stick, keep it safe – just in case.' Moses turned to the camera once more, a manic edge to his voice. 'I did this. So I will undo it. On my own. No one else gets hurt.

'I think I know what to do.'

Thea let out a breath. The video stopped.

Upstairs, something smashed.

Chapter 33

The knife had been left embedded into the dresser earlier that day.

Now it was in Ethan's hand.

She had left him peacefully sleeping less than an hour ago but now, as she skidded into the bedroom, he was neither peaceful, nor asleep.

The crash had come from the dresser, which was on its side, its drawers spilling out, and Ethan stood next to it, awake, motionless, holding the knife.

Thea didn't move. Maybe if she stayed still, he'd stay still too. He looked awake, but Thea knew he wasn't. Not really. This wasn't one of his normal nightmares. She knew exactly what was happening because she'd just seen it happen to Ted in the video diary. Poor Ted in his pyjamas, trying to throw imaginary spiders out of a window.

But Ted hadn't had a knife.

Thea realized that this wasn't Moses's tech anymore. Delores had taken it from him and who knew what they'd done to it, or how quickly it worked.

Or how quickly you got to the dead-eyed, dribbling stage …

Did the bedroom door lock? Maybe Thea could just lock him

in. But then he'd be locked in with a knife and Thea didn't want to imagine what he might do to himself. She couldn't leave him to that, after what they'd been through.

She had to try and get the knife from him.

'Ethan?' she said softly.

Almost as if he had become voice-activated, he sprang to life, marching over to her. She willed herself not to cower against the wall.

'Ma'am. I'm going to have to ask you to stay here. We have a situation.'

Thea couldn't take her eyes away from the knife, how sharp it looked with its evil, serrated edge.

'Ethan—'

'I'm sorry, but this is no place for—' His eyes flicked upwards and he suddenly gripped her with one hand. 'MA'AM! DOWN! INCOMING!'

He threw her to the ground with such force, a searing pain shot through her shoulder. His weight pinned her down, protecting her from an imaginary blast and she gasped, the air crushed out of her lungs, spots forming in front of her eyes.

Don't faint, don't faint, don't faint, she chanted to herself.

She screwed up her eyes and blinked furiously as, above her, he shouted out instructions to the wallpaper. Mercifully, after a few minutes, he moved and she rolled into a half-seated position, gingerly prodding her shoulder as he crouched in front of her, the knife gripped firmly in his hand.

'Ma'am.' He spoke to her over his shoulder, warily watching the door. 'Stay here. Stay down.'

At least he didn't think *she* was the enemy.

Yet.

Quietly, he ran to the bedroom door and then he was gone, off down the stairs, his body pressed to the wall, waving the knife in front of him. Thea shakily got to her knees. As much as she would have liked to have stayed where she was, to curl up into a ball and try to block out everything she'd just seen, she had to follow him. There was no one else to do it. Her shoulder was beginning to throb, a dull drum beat punctuated by the occasional top note of needling pain and she felt tears forming, hot and stinging.

She would not cry. She would get up, she told herself, like a nanny to a recalcitrant child. She would stand. See? There she was – she was standing. Now she would walk to the door. It was not so far away, not so much of an effort. There was nothing wrong with her apart from the shoulder; her legs and feet were fine. See? She was at the door. How easily that had happened. Now she would walk down the stairs even though her knees were a bit wobbly and her shoulder a bubble of pain. Hopefully, by the time she got to the bottom, Ethan would not have killed himself and she could get the damn knife away from him.

And throw it far out into the snow.

She staggered into the kitchen, bracing herself for she didn't know what, with nothing to defend herself, shaking and alone, to find …

… Ethan asleep on the floor, curled up around the knife as if it was a cuddly toy. Peaceful again.

She bent down and quickly slipped it out of his grasp before she allowed herself to crumple to the floor next to him.

Chapter 34

There was so much blood.

It wasn't so much the amount of it that was making Thea feel sick, but rather the doughy, fleshy flap of skin Ethan was gouging out of his head.

She hadn't been able to stop him this time. It was the morning of the next day. Before she could finish describing his hallucination, he had been halfway to the knife in the cutlery drawer. They were currently sitting on the floor in the bedroom.

Head wounds bled. A lot. She'd read that somewhere. Something about the fact that there are numerous blood vessels and so even a minor cut could cause major bleeding. What Ethan was doing was not a minor cut though: he was digging into the skin around the disc on his temple, blood running down his cheek, his jaw trembling, his hand trembling, Thea trembling for him.

She watched helplessly. The knife continued to twist and jab and the obscenely squishy flap of skin was deluged by another welling of blood. At least she'd managed to pour boiling water over the knife and sterilize it first, but at this rate, it wouldn't matter because he was bound to go into shock at any minute.

With a pent-up scream of frustration, he hurled the knife away from him, where it clattered against a skirting board, smudging red on the paint.

'It won't budge.' He put his head in his hands despondently while his shoulders heaved. 'How does it do it?'

Thea pressed a dishcloth to his temple. She had come prepared. The dishcloth had been folded neatly in a cupboard, so she guessed it was clean and she'd cut another one into strips to wrap around his head once the bleeding stopped. She'd also brought up the whisky, to dab at the edges of the wound primarily, but there was too much blood for that. So she wiped the blood away from his cheek and neck with a towel and he took a swig from the whisky bottle instead.

She edged the dishcloth away from his skin, had a look, stopped herself from heaving, and pressed it firmly back.

'It doesn't look as if it's attached itself into the temple,' she said. 'It hasn't drilled down with a prong or anything. I don't get why you can't just lever it off.'

Thea got off her knees and sat next to him, their backs against the wall. He offered her the whisky, but she shook her head.

'What can they do with these discs? Can they work at long range? Could they ...' He stopped and his shoulders drooped. He spoke softly. 'Could they even kill us with them? Zap us with some kind of electrical charge?'

Ted's empty stare flashed back into Thea's mind.

She dunked the towel in a bowl of hot water she'd brought up. Ethan's blood swirled into it, spirals and curlicues of red drifting lazily out across the surface. He closed his eyes and rested his head back against the wall, still holding on to the dishcloth.

'How were we so stupid?' He sighed. 'To get involved in this?'

'Because we were desperate, that's why.'

They sat there for a few moments. A fresh trickle of blood ran down Ethan's cheek. Thea shifted uncomfortably, her shoulder throbbing.

'Ethan, there's something you should watch.'

'Is that …?' Ethan glanced up from the laptop.

'Yep. Our Delores.'

'Wow.'

He went back to watching intently.

'Wait, wait, wait.' He paused the video. 'So people were trying to buy Moses's tech, and they were going to use it to put adverts in people's dreams. Correct?'

'Well, kind of. I think it would help people learn quicker and be smarter, but it could also influence people without them even knowing they were being influenced.'

'Or it could programme people to say, or believe, or *do* anything?'

Thea looked at the image paused on the screen: Delores was caught mid-gesture in a blur, which made it look as if Moses was reaching out to a ghost.

'Yeah, I guess so.'

Ethan pushed the laptop away from him a little and rubbed at the cloth taped around his head.

'Well, this just gets better and better,' he said sarcastically. 'Not only am I acting out my hallucinations, but if I'm lucky and the tech works properly, I get my mind reprogrammed to eat a certain brand of crisps, and – gee – I don't know … maybe go kill the prime minister.'

'Keep watching.'

He did. Thea didn't want to see it again, Ted's face, so she watched the snow come down. At first, she'd thought it wouldn't settle. The ground had been so wet from the sleet, but it had and now big, fat, feathery flakes floated lazily in the dark, giving the fields a duvet day that Thea would see the next morning. She was beginning to lose track of time. They'd been at the lighthouse for only one day and the trial itself was in its fourth week. The snow fell and the window was a square of static interference on a television screen. They couldn't have got back to the Sleep Centre even if they'd wanted to; they were wearing warm layers, a fleecy top and thermal jacket, but only trainers on their feet, the monastery search party intending to be back well before the snow.

No, that was wrong, Thea thought; they could still get back to the Centre. It would be cold and miserable and they'd probably twist an ankle because they couldn't see the path anymore, but they could do it. They just didn't know whether that was the best idea yet. And the snow was a good excuse.

One day gone already. Why hadn't anyone come to get them? The Centre knew where they were and, yes, there was snow, but that wouldn't stop them. Ethan had heard of a fire at the Centre from the radio of one of the search party guards. Was that keeping them busy? How much longer would that last?

Ethan was silent when the video diary ended.

'I think it's when you go into Phase Three, remember – the bit where we get to improve ourselves?' Thea spoke quickly. 'I think that's where it all starts to go wrong. Ted was learning all those languages—'

'Jesus! Did you see him?'

'So Moses tested it on himself, scrambled his brain and Delores needed money so she sold it to Aspire.' Though, Thea realized, Delores had continued to look after Moses, had made sure he was hidden, yes, but safe and cared for. Kind of. 'They've probably fixed any problems,' Thea said eagerly, wanting to believe it.

Ethan stayed silent.

In the afternoon a little FM radio picked up a local channel playing old songs and if Thea squinted with her brain she could almost believe that she and Ethan were a happy couple enjoying a weekend break in a cottage picked from PlacesInTheMiddleOfNowhere.com.

158

They found tins of custard in the cupboard and heated them up, dunking biscuits in them to really make sure they made up for any sugar restriction they'd had back at the Centre. The pain in her shoulder had dulled and she tried to keep it fairly still, hoping it would get better on its own. Luckily, there were painkillers in the medicine box that had been left on the counter.

She couldn't help wishing Rory was with her. He'd probably have had a chocolate bar in his pocket and his laugh would have instantly made her feel like things could be worked out. Though, she had to admit, he would have been rubbish at getting a gun from an armed guard.

'My mother is probably haranguing the Centre right now, if they've allowed her call to go through,' Thea said. 'She thought it was a cult.'

Thea pictured her mother at the helm of a small motorboat, nosing it through the waves, the other women stood behind, heading to the island to rescue her. The post-menopausal army.

Ethan had been quiet up until that point. 'So is it just you and your mother?'

'Yep. We don't live together, or anything.' She wasn't quite sure why she added that so quickly. 'I've got my own place, but yeah … just me. What about you?'

'I was married. Once. Didn't work out.' He paused and Thea didn't think he would say any more. But he cleared his throat. 'We met before I joined up. It was good then but being in the army meant I was away a lot, too much really. And even when I was home, I was always kind of still away, half the time – y'know?'

What Thea knew about marriage she'd got from books, but she nodded sympathetically.

'I don't blame her,' he quietly said. 'Between the nightmares and the sleeplessness, the memories … there wasn't any space for anything else. For her.' He looked down. 'I wasn't the same person she met.' He sighed. 'So, I'm on my own now.'

They were silent for a while until Thea looked up and caught him gazing at her so intently, she began to squirm.

'Don't you think that's odd?' he said.

'Well, lots of people get divorced—'

'No, Thea – think! A few of the others I spoke to,' he said, frowning, 'they were all single, not much in the way of family – loner types ...'

Thea was beginning to guess where this was going.

'And, apart from you and your mother, no one at home waiting for them to call.' He paused for emphasis. '*No one to care what happens to them.*'

Thea thought back to that first meeting with Delores in her office: '*You are the one who is important. You are ... different to the others.*' Delores had meant different as in white-crowned sparrow, but had she been different in another way too? Was she the only one out of those fifty clients who had someone waiting for their call? So why take the risk – unless the chance to trial out sleeplessness on her had been too hard to resist?

'What should we do?' Thea asked. 'This fire back at the Centre, the one the guards at the monastery ran off to help with – they'll sort it out soon enough and we'll be next on their to-do list. Should we try to get off the island? Go back to the Centre?'

Thea's tongue felt furry and coated with sugar. She couldn't think of anything. No matter how many times she moved the pieces around, the game always ended with her and Ethan dead. *Not dead – they can't do that,* one part of her brain murmured. The other part sniffed and rolled its eyes.

'There must be working Wi-Fi at the Centre somewhere, probably in the Staff Bubble. We just need to sneak in and email that memory stick to someone, anyone. My mother, a newspaper ... At least we'll have tried to do something.'

'Or we could just carry on sitting here, in the warm, eating custard and listening to the radio until they come for us.' Ethan sounded serious. 'We might not even have to wait; they could just programme me to kill you and then kill myself, any moment now. Problem solved.'

Thea got goosebumps on her arms. It was the tone in which he'd said it, so bleak, so emotionless.

'You're going to have to handcuff me tonight, you know.' Ethan screwed up the empty biscuit packet and fixed her with a look.

'I'm not sure I know you well enough for that just yet!' Her joke was met with stoniness. She blushed.

That was when Moses started to wail.

Chapter 35

Thea hadn't expected to see the sky. There it was though, peeping through a hole in the roof of Moses's room. No wonder he had been wailing. Snow steadily drifted in, enough to have already covered his blankets, melting where it touched his skin, piling up in the furrows of the bed sheets. Luckily for him, the fallen bits of soggy wood, plaster and a few cracked tiles had missed the bed.

'The weight of the snow must have caved that bit of the roof in,' Ethan said, squinting upwards. 'Pretty weak roof to start off with. Guess they didn't have time for roof repair before shoving him in here.'

'What are we going to do?'

They stared at Moses. He pulled the squelching bed sheets up under his nose and stared back at them, his wide eyes moving from one to the other. *God knows what his brain thinks we are right now*, Thea thought.

'We can't leave him in here,' Ethan decided. 'It's cold, for one thing.'

'I don't know …'

'I get it – he's dangerous. I'm not stupid. But I can handle it. We've just got to move him to the kitchen, put him in the chair, handcuff one arm to the radiator. I've had to take him to the toilet enough times. He knows the drill.'

Thea eyed Moses warily. Moses was definitely awake more often and, though quiet, Thea often saw him watching them. She remembered the Moses in the video diary, the happy-go-lucky, joking one from the start … the clever one. Clever enough to make the technology. Clever enough to outsmart her and Ethan.

Thea sighed.

Around the lighthouse that night, a new, cushioned, white world formed in the quiet dark hours that saw Thea awake, Moses shackled to the radiator and Ethan cuffed to his bed.

It was the morning of their third day in the lighthouse. They sat on the floor, drinking tea and eating crackers.

'We can't stay here much longer,' Ethan said, while dipping a cracker into mayo. They were running out of food now too. All that was left was a pot of jam, the crackers and mayo, some tins of beans and the dregs from a box of cereal.

'I know.'

Thea rolled her shoulder experimentally. It hurt.

'I had a date not so long ago.' Ethan snapped a cracker. 'Before we started the trial. Met her on the web, hooked up for a drink. Thought it would be awful, because dates generally are. It wasn't.'

He tapped the lid of the jam and paused.

'Didn't think I might not see her again.'

Thea's cracker snapped in half, one end mired in mayo. A lot of sensitive, compassionate comments could have been made at this point.

'It's probably best you only got one date.' She smiled. 'No time for you to screw it up.'

Ethan puffed out a breath of air like he'd been punched. 'Harsh!'

But it had worked: he smiled and rubbed his hand over his bristly hair.

163

She munched a dry cracker, which coated the roof of her mouth.

'What about you?' He leant forward, his arms over his knees. Thea noticed his forearms. They were tanned and strong-looking, then she blushed for paying attention to something like that when they were stuck here. In the lighthouse at the end of the world.

'Yeah I screw it up too. Sometimes on purpose. Sometimes not.'

Rhodri popped into her mind. She'd met him at the train station. Their train had been delayed and they had both gone to sit on the same spot on a bench. They'd laughed, he'd offered the place to her and got them coffees for the wait and, when the train finally appeared, they'd chatted and flirted on the train ride. Numbers had been exchanged.

And she'd ignored every one of his calls.

'What did you see?' Thea changed the subject. 'When you hallucinated?'

Ethan sighed and rolled the jam lid on its edge with one finger. 'Mistakes I made.'

'When you were in the army?'

'I don't talk about it much because, well, I don't need to – I relive it most nights in my nightmares.' He rubbed at a spot on the carpet tile. 'There was a hostage situation on one of my postings and … well, decisions had to be made quickly. Not the right decisions, it turned out. Not the right decisions at all. It's when it's kids – that's what hits you hardest, that's what you can't forget …'

At night. On your own. Sleepless.

'It was pretty much this, the trial, or prison. I mean, not straight away, but I just wasn't thinking straight half the time and that's where I'd have ended up, eventually. Short fuse.' He laughed bitterly. 'No fuse, more like. In hindsight, prison would probably have been the smarter choice, wouldn't it?'

If she had been someone who was used to hugging other

164

people, Thea might have tried giving Ethan a hug then. He looked like he needed it. Rosie would have done it, she thought, in that easy way she had, and then she'd have made them all laugh by producing chocolate from her shoe, or something. Ethan hung his head.

'Max?' Moses woke up, his free hand smoothing the spot on his temple where Thea knew a disc had once been, the skin dented and scarred.

Ethan and Thea generally ignored him. His brain was poorly set jelly in a trifle and it was impossible to keep track of what he was talking about.

'Where am I?' There was something different to his voice this time, something sharper. Thea glanced at him. He leant forward in the chair, peering at them both intently. He smelled: a sour, musty funk and Thea could see, where he was gripping the arms of his chair, that his fingernails were edged in black.

'St Dunstan's Island. The Sleep Centre,' Thea replied, unable to take her eyes from his. They were so focused on her.

'She sold it then.' He sighed. 'I guess I didn't leave her much choice. Where's Max?'

Ethan shook his head at Thea, but she answered anyway.

'At the Centre. We're at the lighthouse. Max hid you away because you …' She suddenly felt embarrassed at calling him crazy. Even though he was. 'You tried the tech on yourself and it kinda messed with your brain.'

'But she's trialling it anyway?'

'Yep. They think they've worked out the problems.'

'They haven't,' Ethan interrupted. 'What you've created could probably destroy lots of people, like it destroyed Ted. How does that feel?'

'Ethan!' Thea shoved him.

'What? In two minutes he's probably going to go back to thinking we're goldfish or something. What does it matter?'

Moses hung his head so Thea couldn't see his expression.

'How long have I been gone?' he whispered. 'How long have they kept me drugged?'

The video diary had been date-stamped and the final entry had been the previous summer. She kept quiet.

'I should never have tested it on myself, but I'm not mad ... not anymore, at least. They didn't need to keep me locked away. You can help me, set me free. I could talk to her, help stop all of this!'

His eyes shifted warily from Thea to Ethan.

'Is there some way we can destroy it?' Thea tried, despite Ethan rolling his eyes.

Moses laughed, a harsh, raspy sound.

'Destroy my tech? It's beautiful.' Moses slammed his palm against the side of his head a few times. 'I wanted to make us gods. We could have been better than AI, the human machine, super-charged ...'

'Yeah well, now you're cuffed to a radiator and I've got the key.' Ethan came towards him and Moses flicked a wary glance his way. 'Life sucks.'

Moses started to scrunch up his blanket in his fist. 'Wait! If you take me there,' he said, stretching out his sinewy neck, 'to the Centre. I'd help. Everyone ... needs ... to ... hear ... the ... truth.'

He blinked and shook his head, his last few words slurred, his eyelids drooping.

'See?' Ethan said. 'Useless. He'll be asleep soon anyway. Leave him.'

Useless. Thea wasn't so sure. As she watched his chest rise and fall peacefully, she also wasn't so sure that he was really asleep, there was something tense about his shoulders and jaw. Could they believe what he said? Not mad or dangerous – but drugged by Delores so she could steal his technology? She kept thinking of the Moses in the video diary, the one at the start. He would have helped them. Somewhere inside his shattered brain that Moses must still be there.

Ethan didn't look convinced.

Thea went for a shower in the bathroom at the end of Moses's room, even though she had to pick her way through snow and the fallen roof to get there. The soap was old and cracked, and she didn't look too long or too hard at the plughole.

She felt better when she stepped out, fumbling for the towel. She wasn't tired, despite the fact she'd had no sleep again last night. Those old exhausted days that had felt like a bruise seemed so long ago, though she would have gone back to them now in a heartbeat. The gritty eyes, pounding head, furred tongue and dizziness would have been better than … this. The feeling that her brain was being continuously doused in water so freezing it made her eyes sting.

Too awake.

What kind of society would it be if everyone always got a perfect night's sleep? Thea wondered. All those bright-eyed people skipping about, being polite to each other, being considerate and patient and making calm, measured decisions. Freaky.

She quickly dressed and it was when she sat on Moses's bed to put on her socks and shoes, lost in a utopia of well-slept citizens, that she noticed the little lumps in Moses's pillow.

Little round, tablet-shaped lumps.

They tumbled into her hand when she shook them out. His old sedatives. Whoever had been giving them to him before they arrived had clearly not checked that he had been swallowing them because here they all were. Thea realized that for the whole time he had been with them in the lighthouse Moses had been steadily getting more and more alert.

Something fluttered in her stomach.

She ran back into the kitchen to tell Ethan … only to find him unlocking Moses.

Chapter 36

'Ethan?' Panic gave an edge to her voice.

He didn't respond, but kept crouching at Moses's feet, fiddling with the shackles. Moses looked at her though, his gaze clear and attentive. He smiled bemusedly and raised his eyebrows as if this was a joke they were all in on.

'Ethan?'

Cold water dripped down her neck from her shower-wet hair. Ethan casually glanced over his shoulder at her, his eyes glassy.

'One mission objective located and secured.' He wasn't talking to her; it was like he was talking into an imaginary headset. 'Other hostages still not found.'

He pulled the shackles away and Moses sighed with relief, rolling his ankles round and round and flexing his toes.

With mounting horror, Thea watched Ethan reach for the wrist cuffed to the radiator.

'No!' she yelled, her body acting on instinct.

She ran the few steps to him and was about to try and yank the keys from his hand, but Moses was quicker – and nearer. With a grunt of effort, he kicked his feet up hard, right into Ethan's face, connecting with such power it snapped Ethan's head back. As he toppled backwards, clutching at his nose, Moses delicately plucked the keys from Ethan's hand.

But it wasn't only the keys he'd taken from Ethan.

Moses pointed a gun at her.

It was the gun Ethan had taken from the security chief, Len. There was another one somewhere, the one from the guard who had been standing outside the lighthouse when they first arrived, but Thea had no idea where Ethan had put that.

'Sorry,' Moses said, still pointing the gun at her. 'I don't even know if this thing is loaded. I like you. I think. Both of you. But this is my chance. I need to speak to Delores.'

It had to be loaded, Thea thought with dismay. Why would Ethan have bothered having the gun on him if it hadn't been loaded?

'You'll have to uncuff me,' Moses said. 'Can't do it while holding a gun.'

Thea was suddenly hyper-aware of everything. Ethan, on his hands and knees, retching and trying to get to his feet, the scrabble of his boots against the wooden floor as he attempted to stand up. A sound outside, like the crunch of snow on tyres, but it couldn't have been that. The tiny jangle of the keys in Moses's hand.

'Now!'

She moved around Ethan and gingerly took the keys from Moses, that sour smell of rank, unbrushed teeth engulfing her as he breathed on her. But his face, when he pushed it closer to hers, softened surprisingly for a moment.

'I don't want to hurt you. I just have to get to the Centre.'

Thea opened up her hand and showed the tablets to Moses.

'Ah. You found them. Not the cleverest of hiding places but I didn't have a choice.'

'How long have you been off the sedatives?'

'Long enough for them to wear off. Mostly. I've done enough sleeping. I'm not dangerous—'

'You hurt Rosie.'

169

Moses's face crumpled. 'I thought she was a guard, I thought – I don't know – I was confused, and I just wanted to get free. But I'm not confused anymore. If I can talk to Max, she'll listen to me. They shouldn't tamper with the tech – you know what it can do, don't you?

Thea nodded. Dreams. Control. Then out of control: hallucinations and finally an empty shell of a person. Unless Moses had fixed that? Thea looked into his eyes. They were bloodshot and puffy, but clear. She felt she could see a person in them, not just a scramble of neurons and some medication. He definitely wasn't an empty shell.

'See?' he said, reading her thoughts. 'I can talk to Max. I know her … or, at least, I knew her. I loved her. She loved me. I can help. I could try to stop all of this—'

'Destroy it?'

He almost flinched and there was a definite pause before he answered, 'Maybe.'

Was "maybe" good enough? Thea looked at the handcuff key in her hand. She thought of dreams and madness, of dribbling wrecks and sleepless soldiers. Ethan groaned nearby.

Thea thought of the Moses she had seen in the video diary – the one with the messy desk and kind eyes, who joked with Ted and pulled Delores in for a kiss. That Moses would have helped.

But was that Moses in front of her?

She could only spin the roulette wheel and hope for the best.

The handcuff clicked apart almost on its own.

Moses pulled his hand free, immediately heading for the door, the gun forgotten in his hand. Thea watched him go. He probably wouldn't get far. None of them would. What did it matter?

Ethan had other ideas, however, and swayed to his feet. Whether he was still in the grips of a hallucination, or whether he just wanted to pummel Moses for getting free, he staggered, but then launched himself at the older man, fury personified.

They both hit the floor with a slam that reverberated through the soles of Thea's feet. Moses wailed and wriggled, a blur of flailing limbs, the two of them wrestling on the floor, Thea just standing there. She knew she should be doing something, but she didn't know what and she couldn't get her body to move. There was a skittering sound and the gun spun across the floor towards her.

It came to rest only a few inches away from her foot.

Just as she bent to pick it up, Moses finally managed to writhe free, making a desperate run for the door as Ethan howled in anger and scrambled after him.

Moses yanked open the door, a rush of cold air hitting them all, the world outside mostly white. For the briefest second he stood triumphantly on the threshold, the bright light bathing his face, the wind making his pyjama trouser legs ripple. With a guttural yell of glee he barrelled out through the doorway.

Straight into the person standing on the other side.

Chapter 37

It was the beard she recognized. The rest of the face was muffled by a fur-lined hood so big that the face was lost in shadow. But the beard … that was familiar.

'Rory?' Thea realized she was pointing a gun at him – but she wasn't going to lower it either, not until she'd worked out what was going on.

He shoved the hood back off his face with one hand, his cheeks ruddy with the cold, and with the other he held Moses's arm. Ethan stood, a little shakily, and took a few steps to stand by Thea's side. With relief, she noted that he no longer had that glassy-eyed hallucinatory stare.

'Rory, how are you here?' Thea steadied the arm holding the gun, because she was trembling. From the cold, obviously. The gun was heavy, but it was a heaviness that felt good; it was the heaviness of power, of being able to defend yourself. For once.

Rory came in a little from the doorway, his free hand raised in a gesture of surrender.

'Look, I've got a lot to explain. A lot has happened back at the Centre, but I'm here to help you, okay? You're safe.' Another figure came out of the cold beside him. Thea tensed. 'It's okay, this is Kyle. He's with me; he's helping me.'

Kyle had a bright red scarf wrapped tightly around his neck and very bleached-blond hair, as if he was auditioning for a part in an Eighties tribute band. He pulled down the scarf and gave a smile that hooked up the corners of his mouth in an almost convincing way. Thea moved the gun so it pointed at him.

Everyone stood there for a few moments, waiting for someone else to say or do something first.

'So, we've got a lot to fill you in on.' Snow fell in chunks from Rory's boots. 'Could we maybe come in? And could you maybe put the gun down now?'

Thea looked at Ethan. 'Are you okay?' she said quietly.

Ethan nodded, his eyes darkly shadowed and red-rimmed.

Her heart beating so fast it made her feel sick, she took a long look around the room and an even longer look at Rory who had one hand stretched out to her, dark hollows under eyes that she recognized – kind eyes. Rory, she reminded herself, the man she'd been having lunch with for weeks, who staged battles between the action figures on his computer and gave her contraband chocolate.

She finally lowered the gun, keeping hold of its comforting weightiness.

'Okay then.' Rory dropped his hand, warily eyeing Ethan. 'Shall we close the door? Get started? Also …' He glanced at Moses who he had gripped by the arm throughout this exchange. 'Who is this?'

'Basically. The shit hit the fan.'

Rory began to recount his tale after he had got over the shock of meeting the real Moses Ing. This mostly involved him becoming extremely wide-eyed and stuttering how much of an honour it was while Moses fell into a stupor once more. Moses reached out and twirled a bit of Rory's beard, saying 'shiny' in a slurred voice, before sleep got him. Rory had looked as proud as if Moses had let him in on the code for Morpheus.

Thea watched Moses's eyelids flutter. He was playing possum. If he'd stopped taking them when he was brought to the lighthouse, then the sedatives were pretty much out of his system now. He wasn't asleep. She could have told Rory that, but Rory was with Kyle.

She studied Kyle. He let Rory talk but his eyes missed nothing, and she saw them range around the room, like an eagle searching for prey. She was glad she'd pocketed the sedatives and that they weren't scattered on the floor as clues for his keen gaze to follow.

The kitchen had never been designed to have five people squeezed into it, especially one who was now once more cuffed to the radiator. Despite the snow outside, the air inside was a tepid dishcloth. Thea touched her hair that had now dried to a rough, frizzy mess. *I've got Rosie's hair*, she thought. It was oddly reassuring.

Rory's tale was not.

'All hell was let loose the night you guys left. I mean, have you been experiencing the hallucinations?'

At this Ethan nodded curtly.

'Well, they must have been milder for you guys because you were further away from the Centre, but for us? It was brutal. We weren't prepared for it at all. The things I saw people do …'

Here Rory trailed off, staring into the middle distance. He looked as if he hadn't slept much himself over the last two nights, slumped and floppy like a finger puppet without the finger. Kyle cleared his throat and Rory jolted back to life.

'The lucky ones were the ones who hallucinated something nice … but there weren't many of them.' He paused and swallowed. 'We tried to get them into their rooms. I saw … I saw someone sat in the corner of a corridor and I thought to myself, here's someone I can help at least. He had his back to me and when I got closer he smiled at me and reached out for my hand. Which was great, right? I could help him.'

Rory didn't meet their gaze as he carried on.

'But his hands were all bloody and his smile was filled with blood because he'd got the blunt end of a knife and had smashed out every single one of his teeth. They were scattered on the floor around him.'

Thea couldn't stop herself from imagining it. She put herself in the corridor she'd walked so many times to get to her room, so white, so glossy, now smeared with blood. The toothless man smiled up at her, blood running down his chin, holding up his hand to her and in his hand were teeth, rattling together in his palm like dice. She could feel them crunch under her feet.

'I tried to help. I really did. But there was only a handful of sleep techs. We tried to call for backup, but no one came. We learnt later that Delores ordered the first two floors to be put on lockdown until the morning. Cut off, you understand? People got hurt that night.'

Thea, Rory and Kyle sat on the floor of the kitchen, Ethan still perched on the counter, his face turned to the window, but Thea knew he was listening. The metal barrel of the gun was cold in her hand.

'Rosie?' Thea whispered. In her imagination, the toothless man's face changed to Rosie's – it was her bloody smile, her frizzy hair with streaks of red in it.

'Everyone is fine,' Kyle butted in before Rory could speak. Thea couldn't be sure, but she thought she saw Rory redden. 'But the trial has been stopped, to be on the safe side. Ms Maxwell has stepped down and Aspire, the company that actually owns Ing Enterprises, have sent a team to take over.'

Moses stirred in his pretend-sleep, muttered something and shifted in his seat.

'Safety is of the utmost importance,' Kyle continued smoothly, in a voice used to getting attention. 'There has been a small fire, probably caused by one of the clients in their hallucinatory state, so we are evacuating the island. Clients first, of course.' He smiled that hook smile.

'And Moses?' Ethan said.

Kyle flicked a glance to him. 'Well, he is a bit of a surprise to us all, but that is a private matter for Ms Maxwell and the company to deal with between themselves.'

Thea didn't believe him. Aspire must have known that Delores was parading a fake Moses, surely? She closed her eyes, squeezed her lids shut for a minute, trying to think it all through.

'Thing is, we don't have much time.' Kyle stood up and opened the rucksack he'd brought with him. Inside was a box. 'We need to get the discs off you. Boat's waiting. We have warm clothes and boots in the truck. You're getting off the island.'

'Wait.' Thea blinked a few times, as if that would help her think. 'That's it? Delores is being held somewhere and everything is okay now? What about the tech? What it does, what it *can* do?'

Rory frowned, puzzled. 'What do you mean – what it can do?'

'What it can do is now no one's business except the owner of the tech. Which is Aspire,' Kyle said. 'Ing Enterprises have been negligent and foolhardy with it. Aspire is a safe pair of hands, rest assured, Miss Mackenzie.'

Thea thought of the memory stick in the tiny slit pocket of her leggings. It was a good moment to tell Rory about it. She might not get another moment like it. But there was Kyle by his side, with his sharp eyes and sharper smile.

She stayed quiet.

Kyle opened the box. Inside were what looked like an expensive set of the kind of headphones a pretentious DJ would wear.

'What's that?' Ethan asked.

'It's how we get the discs off. I see you have already worked out how impossible it is to remove them without help,' Kyle said as Ethan put a hand to the bandage around his head.

Rory had fallen silent, Thea noticed.

'It's really easy.' Kyle offered the fancy disc-removing headphones to Thea to have a look. 'Doesn't hurt.'

She took them, dazed. This morning they had had little hope

of getting off the island. Now, they were very nearly on the boat. It was happening too quickly. But, she reminded herself again: *this was Rory.* The man who had put himself at risk trying to warn her about all of this in the first place.

This was Rory.

But there was also Kyle.

'It should be Ethan first,' Thea said, passing the headphones back to Kyle. 'I'm not hallucinating yet.'

She thought she saw a fleeting look of annoyance cross Kyle's face.

'No,' came Ethan's voice. 'If we're rushed for time, it should be Thea first. I might have damaged mine by trying to get them off.'

'Quite so.' Kyle snapped the empty box shut and the noise made Thea jump. 'So, Thea?'

He was right. It took seconds. He put the headphone disc-removing whatsit on her head, left it for under a minute and, when they slid off, the discs came with them. He showed them to her. She touched the spots where they had been on her temples, not sure what she was expecting to feel. There was just smooth skin.

Ethan jumped down off the counter. Kyle stared at the head-phones in his hand, smoothing the metal with one finger and then looked up at Ethan, with an expression Thea couldn't read. She touched her temples again, marvelling at the soft skin under her fingers.

'Me next?' Ethan asked.

Kyle opened out the headphones.

'It's been a long couple of days, right, buddy?' he said to Ethan, in a clear and confident voice. 'A strain on everyone. Let's get this sorted.'

Rory glanced at Thea with a frown and fidgeted. 'Kyle? I—'

'Not now, Rory.'

Ethan came and sat cross-legged by Kyle, his Action Ken knees clicking again.

'Okay?' Kyle adjusted the headband.

'Okay.'

Thea took Ethan's hand. 'Wait!' She turned to Kyle. 'You've checked it, right? Because he might have damaged the discs when he tried to remove them on his own.'

'Yeah, Kyle … I think—' Rory began to shuffle closer to Kyle, reaching out for the headphones.

'The discs are fine. He's done more damage to himself, by the looks of it.'

Ethan laughed a little and Thea realized his laugh was lovely and she hadn't had enough time to hear it.

'Thea!' Rory's eyes widened and he lunged for the headphones, but he was too slow.

Kyle placed them onto Ethan's head.

Chapter 38

Too late.

Too late Thea reached for the headphones on Ethan's head, some sixth sense moving her hand.

Too late because Ethan's smile disappeared and then it all happened so fast she wasn't able to move quickly enough. The veins in his temple and neck bulged, even his eyes bulged, the capillaries in them bursting as froth started to form on his lips.

Only then did Thea manage to knock the headphones off.

Too late.

A single trickle of blood crept down from the corner of one eye. His body stilled.

She couldn't find the strength to move and someone was pulling at her arm and shouting at her, but she couldn't focus on them because she still couldn't take her gaze away from Ethan.

The trickle of blood changed course slightly, made its way determinedly towards his cheek.

There was a ringing in her ears as if a bomb had exploded and she knew people were talking but the sounds were fuzzy and she couldn't stop looking at that trickle of blood, now

179

slowly making its way across his cheek and down towards his ear.

Everything. Needed. To. Stop.

Noise smacked at her.

'We've got to go!'

Then Ethan's body was moving away from her. Which was odd. How was it doing that? But she realized that her feet weren't on the floor either and that someone had picked her up, put her over their shoulder and she was being carried out.

An air pressure bubble popped inside of her. She kicked and she screamed. They couldn't leave Ethan there, on that dusty floor, his head lolling to one side, blood coming from his eye. It was open, staring at her as if he was still alive, accusing her. *Why did you let this happen to me?*

She screamed and choked and gasped and was thrown into the back of a car, knowing the thunking sound she heard were the locks clicking into place.

Time disappeared for a bit. Rage filled Thea; she'd never felt anything like it before, didn't even know she could feel something like this: this heat of anger. She kicked out against the Plexiglas that separated the front passengers from the back, kicked hard, her feet thudding in a satisfying way again and again against the plastic, smearing it with the soles of her trainers. She slapped her hands against the windows and cursed, streams of words she'd never used before, screaming until she was hoarse, kicking and punching and yelling until, at last, the rage left her limp and sweating in the back seat.

She could see Rory and Kyle at the front, Kyle driving. Not once did Rory turn to her. The car was some sort of four-by-four – big, with monster wheels that ate up the snow without any effort. Moses pretended to sleep in the seat next to her.

The silvery edges of her vision pulsed in time to her heartbeat. Her chest heaved and she tried to get her breathing under control.

Now the anger had dissipated, she tried to think. Not of Ethan. Not yet. The only way she was going to get through the next few hours was by resolutely not thinking about him and the lifeless stare that was now imprinted in her memory.

This didn't feel like rescue anymore.

Rory. Had he known what was going to happen to Ethan? He hadn't turned to look at her once since he'd thrown her in the car. She remembered the way he'd glanced at her just before it had happened, how he had reached for the headphones, but not fast enough.

She remembered how Kyle had taken over.

Kyle. His little wave, his Eighties hair and smooth, cultured voice. The one driving the car this very minute. Could she believe anything that Rory had told her? Could they have killed Ethan through the discs, a remote-controlled death switch – just as he'd feared? But why not kill her too?

The car braked suddenly, with such force that Thea jolted forward on her seat, nearly going head-first into the Plexiglas. Moses slithered down next to her, crumpling into the footwell. It seemed that Kyle and Rory were having an argument of some kind; she couldn't hear it because she'd just realized the Plexiglas was something else entirely, something soundproof. Kyle thumped his hand against the steering wheel.

She wished she could lip-read.

They seemed to have reached some sort of impasse, glaring at each other. Then Rory's shoulders hunched and he crouched forward, his head in his hands. Was he crying? Thea couldn't tell. From where she was sitting, she could only see the back of his head. Without warning, he reared back up and struck the dash-board with his fist. Kyle shrugged and calmly took the handbrake off, getting the car moving once more.

Thea needed Rory to look at her. But he wasn't going to.

In a way that told her more.

So, when they neared the Centre but didn't go straight to

the front, instead skirting around it, towards a back entrance Thea hadn't even known about; when she saw who was stood waiting for them, her flaming red hair a warning flag: she knew.

She knew she'd been betrayed.

Chapter 39

Vivian liked train stations.

She liked cities. Specifically, she liked being right in the middle of them. In a city you could walk out of your house or flat at almost any time of the day or night and within five minutes you could pick up a snack, or a paper, a drink or a person. She liked noise and bustle, neon signs, twenty-four-hour convenience stores and light-soaked streets.

'Your train's in ten.' Delia plonked herself next to her on the bench, making an "oof" sound as she did so. Old people did that. Vivian did yoga and cardio, ate a ridiculous amount of vegetables, walked briskly past cake shops without a glance and poured away at least half the wine Delia served her. There was no time for old.

It was a few days after their trip to the Ing Enterprises building.

Delia handed her a coffee, knowing that, without it, Vivian would not be able to even consider the rest of the morning. Not for the first time, Vivian thanked the (obviously female) gods for Delia: their friendship was her longest standing relationship. Men came and went but Dels remained.

'You know, Dels, I'm finding myself feeling … like a bit of a dinosaur with all of this. It's not the technology so much. I just can't shake the idea that I'm going about this all wrong, that I'm not understanding something. Am I being rose-tinted, or did it all seem … well, just easier in the old days?'

'Nostalgia, Viv? Didn't think that was your thing.'

'It's not.' Vivian smiled wryly. 'The old days were god-awful half the time; that's why we wanted to change so much.'

Delia sipped her coffee. It took her a while to answer and, when she did, she chose her words carefully.

'Everything's so much more … knotty these days. But we still need to scream about things, if that's what you mean. It's the only way to get heard. Problem is, everyone's doing so much screaming, it's hard to listen to it all.'

Vivian nodded. She was just one more scream.

'I looked at a few of those sleep apps, like the one Thea's trialling.' Delia produced a pack of biscuits from her pocket and offered one to Vivian. She hesitated because it was still early but then she sighed, thinking that sometimes in life you had to just take the biscuit.

'And?'

'It's nothing so new. Mood music and whale song, mostly. Some of them track how well you sleep but it's not that accurate. Why would Ing Enterprises be so secretive about that?'

Vivian gazed up at the glass roof of the train station. It was a jaunty Victorian-built affair, constructed at a time when public buildings had been special occasion cakes that needed as many flourishes as possible. Pigeons waddled around like serious, but very small, commuters.

'I tried to learn Italian once,' Vivian said thoughtfully. 'I got one of those CDs and put it on at night, fell asleep to it because I'd read somewhere that your brain would pick it up while it slept.'

'I didn't know you'd learnt Italian.'

'I didn't. It didn't work.' Vivian turned to Delia excitedly. 'But

184

think if it had! Think if someone had actually figured out how to make something like that work …'

She trailed off. Delia frowned and paused in the middle of sipping her coffee. They both let that last sentence sink in.

Vivian stretched her legs out and heard her knees click. 'Maybe I'm over-reacting. Maybe Thea's just forgotten to phone. For over a week. Maybe I've become one of those terrible grasping mothers who can't let their daughter out of their sight for a second. The police already think I'm a mad old conspiracy theorist. Maybe I am.'

Delia smiled.

Vivian finished the coffee, but really wanted something stronger. She could almost imagine what Thea would have said if she'd caught them both drinking before they'd even digested breakfast. She'd get that expression on her face, the one she'd practised since she was a little girl, the frown of disapproval at whatever her mad mother was doing at that moment.

She had been a bit of a mad mother, she had to admit. The itinerant lifestyle, the shared houses, sudden moves to random places where the next protest was; the unending succession of well-intentioned, mostly stoned strangers who had wandered in and out of their lives. So yes, she may have been mad, but she had also been constant. Constantly there. Constantly around when needed, when called upon. She had been good at that at least.

The announcement screen switched to 'Train Due'. People started to shuffle closer to the platform edge, bags were picked up, tickets found.

'I don't know what I expect to do when I get there,' she said to Delia, suddenly wanting to stay there on the platform, safe amongst all these people, the pigeons, the litter.

'You'll think of something. You generally do,' Delia squeezed her hand and Vivian squeezed back hard before quickly boarding the train.

She watched the station and Delia slip past her, then the city, then the suburbs, then the green belt until the landscape opened up and swallowed the little train that was taking her away.

To the island.

Chapter 40

The wind twisted Delores's hair, a tongue of fire stretching out to see what else it could burn and destroy.

The Sleep Centre was damaged and crying. Smoke poured out from the punctured side of the Client Bubble, and streaks of black ran down from it: thick, smudgy mascara trails. Thea pressed her face up to the window of the car. She had heard of the chaos that had happened here, but actually seeing it smouldering in the snow in front of her made her gape.

Kyle opened the car door for her. For a moment, she thought she might refuse to get out, but then she realized they'd probably just drag her and she preferred to meet Delores again with some kind of dignity still intact. Her trainers sank into the snow and she could feel the cold start to numb her toes, her breath misting out in front of her.

Rory took her arm. Under the pretext of pushing her forward, he whispered, 'Rosie's safe. I've hidden her.' It took a few moments for the words to line themselves up in the correct order in her mind, but when they did she snapped her head to him, only to see the side of his face as he turned away.

Harriet stood to one side, bundled up against the freezing air. Normally she was composed and carefully made-up, but Thea could see a deep wrinkle in the middle of her brows and her lips were pale and bloodless.

Delores stepped forward. Thea put her hand to the small of her back, to the little slit pocket in her leggings originally designed to put a house key when running, but now holding a tiny, tiny memory stick. She could feel its sharp edges. It was the only thing she had to bargain with.

Delores opened her arms.

'Thea,' she said, her voice warm. 'I was worried about you.'

Then she stepped forward and folded Thea into a hug, her sharp chin pressing into Thea's shoulder, the one that she'd hurt earlier. Thea stayed rigid, her arms trapped at her sides, her gaze flicking from side to side, waiting for the person who was going to taser her, knock her out, or shoot her.

'If you want to stay alive, do as I say,' Delores hissed into her ear and then leant back quickly, raising her voice. 'So good to have you safely back.' She smiled and the effect was jarring. It didn't fit right on her face, the corners of her mouth twitching with the effort. Thea thought of animals who bared their teeth in warning.

While Delores had been talking to Thea, Rory and Kyle had been helping Moses out of the other side of the car, Rory holding him under the armpits, Kyle carrying his feet. Thea was very close to Delores at the exact second she clocked who they'd brought back to the Centre.

'Ms Maxwell,' Kyle said as he neared her. 'We found him at the lighthouse. Some sort of ... *vagrant*, yes?' He emphasized the word. 'Thought it best to bring him back.'

Delores was a master of this kind of thing and apart from a slight pressing together of her lips, she managed to keep her face perfectly expressionless. Something passed unspoken between her and Kyle.

It took Thea a minute to realize what was going on. They knew! Ing Enterprises and its parent, Aspire. It hadn't been only

Delores hiding him away, it had been all of them. And where better to keep him hidden than on the island?

Delores moved away from Thea and bent to look at the floppy body of Moses, just a brief glance, her hair swinging down to shield her face – and anything she may have felt.

With a swift motion, Delores flicked her hair over one shoulder, her long wool coat flapping in the breeze, and straightened up, holding out a manicured hand to Thea.

'Harriet will take you inside,' she said.

Kyle stopped and put Moses's feet down. 'No.'

'I'm sorry?' Delores said politely but in such a tone to suggest she wasn't sorry at all.

'Thea is to be taken straight to the boat. I've got orders to personally make sure she gets there. As soon as possible. I'm afraid you are no longer in charge, Ms Maxwell.'

Again that something unspoken between them, a weird emphasis on the word boat, which made Thea's skin prickle. She was fairly certain that that was not where Kyle had orders to take her.

Delores grabbed Thea's hand and almost shoved her into Harriet. 'I may not be in charge any longer, as you say, but I really wouldn't try disobeying me. It generally doesn't end well.'

Suddenly she was in a game of piggy-in-the-middle, except, as the piggy, she wasn't even sure which side she wanted to be on. Kyle, or Delores? Thea scanned around for an escape route but there was nowhere to run, and no hope she could outrun Kyle.

Thea wasn't sure how it would have ended had not Moses chosen that exact moment to start thrashing in Rory's weak grip, moaning loudly. Kyle shifted his feet uncertainly, looking at Thea and Delores and then over to where Rory was struggling to hold Moses. Moses flailed out one arm and caught Rory on the nose, who gave a muffled yelp.

Kyle sighed.

Marching back over to the two of them, he grabbed Moses's arms and, between them, they hauled him inside, his feet dragging uselessly on the ground.

'Go.' Delores pushed her, talking to Harriet. 'Make sure she's not seen. I have one more thing to check here.'

Before he was whisked inside, Thea was almost sure she saw Moses briefly open one eye and look straight at her.

Chapter 41

Harriet put her finger to her lips.

Thea had been in the Staff Bubble before on her first meeting with Delores. It was a weird mirror of the one that had been used for the clients and the design was identical: same huge central area with the cafeteria and strategically placed seating, a gleaming lift shaft in the middle and wheel-spoke walkways with light coming from the curved glass roof.

Empty. Echoing.

Thea grabbed both of Harriet's forearms and held on tight. 'Harriet, you've got to help, you—'

But then all the words stuck in Thea's throat and she clamped her hand over her mouth to try and stop any ragged gulps of air.

It wasn't even really crying at first; it was some kind of chest-heaving, head-thumping pressure in her body that needed to be released. She felt Harriet's arm across her shoulder, supporting her as her knees buckled and finally the hot tears came.

They were for herself, alone in a game being played by people a lot more powerful than her, with rules she hadn't been allowed to learn.

But they were also for Ethan.

'Thea?' Harriet's voice seemed very far away. 'Thea?'

She felt Harriet half-pushing, half-leading her into another room and forcing her to sit down.

'Breathe.'

So she did. And that was all she did for a while. It was all she could concentrate on, because, when she stopped, other thoughts came rushing back at her and clogged her throat.

Harriet busied herself to one side. Thea realized she was sitting on a bed, in a room similar to her own back in the other sphere, but messier, as if the person in it had rushed to leave.

'Here.' Harriet pushed a warm mug into her hands, holding her own over them to warm Thea up. 'Everything has happened so quickly. I'm not surprised you're in shock. The … problems … the fire. The new people taking over. At least you're okay.'

'Ethan is dead.'

Harriet fumbled the teaspoon and it clattered noisily. Saying those words nearly set Thea off again, but she took a deep breath, squared her shoulders and sat up straight like her mother would have done, her eyes gritty and sore.

'Kyle did it; he killed him. I was there.'

'But how—'

'We found Moses at the lighthouse. The real Moses, not the one we saw here. He tested the sleep tech on himself and it made him hallucinate. It made him mad – for a while. It killed Ted, kind of, pretty much anyway—'

'Who's Ted?'

'The tech, Harriet!' Thea gripped one of Harriet's wrists. 'The tech is dangerous!'

'We know it caused some issues,' Harriet soothed, gently wriggling her wrist out of Thea's grasp. She nudged the tea to her lips, making her take a drink. 'But that was only briefly. And then of course, the fire. We think one of the clients started it, in their … incapacitated state. But we've been told that all of the clients have now been safely evacuated from the island.'

192

Thea tried to read Harriet's expression: wide-eyed but steady. Would she be able to tell if she was lying?

'No! It's not just the hallucinations! It's what happened after. It just kind of mushes your brain, leaves you a blank. I've seen it! And do you know why they're so keen to get this sleep technology working?'

'Really, I—'

'Dreams! They want to get into our dreams – the REM sleep, remember? – and they want to … to … use them, to influence us—'

Harriet shot a quick glance towards the door. 'Thea! Slow down – you're not making any sense and anyway, I've got to get you to Delores before Kyle comes back. She wants to see you before Aspire get their hands on you. We don't have time for this.'

Thea took a deep breath, staring into her mug. Then she pierced Harriet with a fierce glare. 'You saw all the clients board a boat, yes? You actually saw it yourself?'

Harriet didn't answer. She took a step back and clasped her hands together, kneading her fingers.

'When was the last time you saw any of them? Moira? Richard? *Rosie?*'

No answer.

Harriet suddenly sagged and sat down heavily next to her. She rubbed her face, smearing the mascara into the dark circles under her eyes, her lips flaking as if she'd bitten them a lot lately.

It was quiet for a minute or so. Occasionally Harriet looked as if she was about to say something, but then she seemed to change her mind. Thea realized that Harriet was clutching her hand and she held on, thankful for the warmth.

'I'm so, so sorry,' Harriet whispered at last. 'I don't know what's going on and then this new company taking over, except they aren't taking over because they owned us anyway? I don't understand.'

The two women stared at each other, then Harriet bent closer to Thea, so close Thea could see the flecks of old mascara under her eyes. She whispered, 'I … don't think I like this …'

Thea didn't know what to say so she squeezed the hand holding hers. Harriet darted a glance towards the door.

'I have to go and see if Delores is ready for you. Please don't leave this room, Thea. I think it's – I think you'll be safer here.'

She hesitated briefly in the doorway and looked back at Thea, biting her lip and frowning before she left the room. Thea was alone.

She ran her hand over the duvet. Her head was so heavy, Thea thought blurrily, and it had to be down to her eyes. They felt like rocks. Her neck, in comparison, was a broken flower stem. The room was so warm and the bed was so comfortable that it made sense to just lie that heavy head down for a few moments …

Chapter 42

She was exactly where she wanted to be. This room was fire-lit and as warm as a burrow. There were scones on a cute little table in the middle and a bowl of thick cream and jam with big pieces of fruit in it. She had a blanket over her knees and her chair was big enough for her to curl up.

'See? I said it would be amazing.' Rosie leant over. Her hair covered one eye, but she was smiling and scraping cream from her knife.

It was amazing. She didn't have to do anything or be anywhere, and it was so cosy here, like living in a children's programme. There were pictures on the walls in delicate gold-rimmed frames: holiday shots of a bird in a shawl wearing glasses perched on her beak, sometimes standing with other similarly dressed birds in front of the pyramids, or the Eiffel Tower.

'Where is she?' Thea asked.

Rosie crammed a scone into her mouth leaving a purple smear on her lips. She swallowed a few times before answering. 'The cuckoo? She jumped,' she said casually, eyeing up another scone.

'But who's going to call the time?' Panic rose in Thea's chest.

'Oh, we can't do that. Don't worry. They'll kill us if we go outside.'

The fire crackled and a log split with a hiss. Thea was suddenly

195

angry with the cuckoo for jumping. She had a job to do; this was her responsibility. You couldn't trust anyone these days. An empty wing-backed chair stood by the fire with a single feather on the seat.

'One of us has to call the time,' she said.

Rosie broke open another scone and tapped the knife on her teeth; there was the sound of metal scraping on enamel. 'No, we don't,' Rosie said.

It was too warm in the room. She pushed the woolly blanket from her and let it slide to the floor. She didn't want to go out there. Rosie should go. It wasn't her problem. Rosie should volunteer because the time had to be called and it wasn't her job to do it.

'You should do it,' she said to Rosie.

'Do it yourself,' Rosie snapped back, impatiently flicking her hair back from the eye it had covered. Except there was no eye, just a red, gaping wound where her eye should have been, as if someone had taken an ice-cream scoop to her face. On her temple there was a heart drawn around the metal disc. 'I don't know why you have to spoil it. There's nothing else to do. Just have a scone, relax.' Rosie dug into the jam again and smiled as she spread it onto the scone, but the smile wasn't like before, perhaps it was the eye that gave it menace.

There was a diving board contraption in front of the double doors, on which the cuckoo stood before it shoved her out of the clock to call the time.

Thea didn't want to.

She got up. She didn't stand on it but edged around it, leaning over to push one of the doors open a little, just to see what was going on.

Down below her there was fire. The golf ball building was crumpling in on itself and the fire ate it up, swishing its tongue around and around, lapping up every last bit. Then her body jolted and suddenly she was too far out. She couldn't scrabble for purchase. Someone had hold of her neck and they were pushing her over the edge, even though she was trying to hold on, her body fizzing with

196

*adrenaline. Tensing, she tried to grab something, anything to stop
her from dipping, from moving, from lurching off the edge. She was
going to fall. Every muscle in her body tensed for impact as she …*

… woke up.

Standing on the edge of the bed, someone's hand on her hip.
'Thea?'

She looked down at Harriet's worried face as she wobbled on
the springy mattress.

'What was I—?' Thea stuttered.

Not a hallucination, not a hallucination, not a hallucination.
She was not turning into Richard and Ted and Moses. She was
not. Thea thought back to the lectures she'd had, which seemed
years ago now – micro sleep, that was it. The body snatching
some rest. That was all.

'Just a bad dream, I'm sure.' Harriet helped her to sit down
and then squeezed her arm, her eyes sad. 'Delores is ready to see
you now.'

Chapter 43

'We don't have much time. You will have to trust me.'

Delores's desk was covered in paper, some of which she was hurriedly stuffing into a satchel. She didn't even look up as Thea came in. Her coat had been thrown over the back of the chair, its arms trailing limply, and she'd pushed up her sleeves, crumpling the silk of her blouse.

Thea laughed.

She hadn't meant to – it had just come gurgling out of her throat in a spasm, like vomit.

'Trust you? Really?'

Delores stopped and considered her. She flung her hair over her shoulder in annoyance and then sighed, opened a desk drawer and got out a hair clip. She twisted her hair up and away from her face in one smooth, practised move. Suddenly the Delores from Moses's video diary was staring back at her.

'I'm trying to save your life Thea. When I say we don't have much time, I really rather mean it.'

'How can I trust someone who had Ethan killed, who drugged and hid Moses away, who … who—'

She paused. On Delores's desk was that heavy-looking ornament, a sinuous twist of stone on a plinth, veined with greens and purples, coloured like a bruise.

'I may as well tell you now that we had cameras placed in the lighthouse. I've seen what happened. What Moses gave you.'

Thea almost laughed at her own stupidity. Of course they had the lighthouse rigged! Who had she thought she was dealing with?

'You can keep the memory stick if you so wish. It doesn't matter to me now.'

Thea shifted her weight uncomfortably though she refused to sit in the chair behind her. Her trainers were soggy from the snow and one foot had gone numb. She had the feeling that she should be doing something: something action-heroine style, not just meekly listening to Delores.

'You have become a particularly sticky problem, do you know that? I believe you told Ms Stowe that your mother was retired from her activist days? Not quite true, hmm? She's being a bit … vocal.'

The mention of her mother was a punch to Thea's stomach that made her eyes water. If she had been by her side, Thea would have felt instantly smarter, stronger, braver but at the same time she wanted her mother as far away as possible from all of this. No megaphone, no placards, no petitions.

'What have you done to her?' Thea heard the crack in her voice.

'Done?' Delores frowned a little. 'We have done nothing to her. What kind of business do you think we are? No, your mother may be vocal, but nobody really listens to her anymore.' She attempted a smile that wasn't successful. 'You are lucky that you are special. Rare. It's the only reason you are stood here and not …'

Delores came around from behind her desk and brought a cup with her, a dainty, fragile porcelain bowl filled with a fragrant, hot liquid. Thea took it but sniffed at it suspiciously, remembering from somewhere that cyanide smelled like almonds. Suddenly everyone wanted her to have a drink.

'Drink the damn tea, Thea. If I'd wanted you dead, you would never have made it out of the lighthouse.'

'Like Ethan?'

Steam curled up from her waiting cup. She drank the damn tea.

'Really? We're not in the business of murdering people, Thea. I saw how Ethan died and it was due to some glitch in those badly damaged discs. Deeply, deeply regrettable.'

Delores was quite close to her, but her face was marble and the expression carefully carved. It was like trying to work out if a statue was telling the truth. Thea put down her cup, then did her best impersonation of Delores's icy cool.

'I don't think I believe that,' she said. 'And, you know what? I'm sick of being talked at. I'm done with listening quietly while you spin whatever story you're believing today. Let's start with Moses. The truth.'

Delores returned to her chair and sat down, unzipping her tall, spike-heeled boots before dropping them to the floor and massaging her feet.

'As you wish.' She took a sip from her own cup. 'Are you going to sit?'

Thea's legs made the decision for her – she crumpled into the chair, a bright shaft of sunlight instantly slicing into her eyes. She squirmed out of its glare.

Delores sighed. 'Moses.' Her eyes softened. 'I did love him, you know. You saw him in the video; you saw the man he was. Who couldn't love that man? And he loved me … but he loved his precious technology more.'

Voice hardening, she swung her legs up onto the arm of her chair, a jarringly nonchalant move at odds with her steely cool. It reminded Thea of the woman in the video, the one with silver moons on her belt and jangling bracelets.

'I couldn't see exactly what you were watching but I know he used to love making those stupid video diaries. Logs, he always called them, like he was Captain sodding Kirk. I thought I'd got rid of them all. So you've heard his side. But there are always two, aren't there? It wasn't just him, you know. He couldn't have done it without me. The great genius Moses Ing. But who spent hours reading all the data, hmm? Me. Spreadsheets, funding, even finding Ted – all me. Not the glamorous stuff, I'll admit. Eternal fucking female problem – we do all the legwork and get none of the glory.'

Her eyes blazed.

'So yes, when he did what he did – his choice, mind you – and tested it on himself, what could I do? He had to be cared for. Debts had to be paid. Aspire were interested in it, even though it was nowhere near ready, so I made the best choice I could … at the time. I've been able to keep him safe.'

'You were drugging him.'

'He is a liability to himself.'

'But it's easier to steal something from someone too drugged to know what's going on, right?' Thea lowered her voice, her heart thumping in her throat. If she was a white-crowned sparrow, she was a sparrow having a conversation with a leopard. 'I know the real reason for Morpheus. You want to get inside our heads.'

'Do we? You must know more than me. I'm not in charge of all of this, remember? In fact, soon I will be very much sacked. What the company wants to do with it is their concern.'

'Mind control?'

'Hah! Really? That is the stuff of silly sci-fi films. We can't even get the tech to work properly yet. I thought we'd ironed out all the glitches but, well, we're finding that REM sleep is a much bigger problem, one we haven't solved, no matter how hard we try. You've seen the result.'

Unclipping her hair with one hand, Delores twisted it absent-mindedly into a rope as she gazed out of the window, a demented Rapunzel. Thea stood, overcome with a wild urge to try running away while her back was turned, try to make it to a boat on her

201

own, just run and keep on running until the snow disappeared into the wood, then the wood changed to shingle and the shingle turned to sea … and freedom.

She would probably only make it to the ground floor if she was lucky.

'What really happened here?' Thea asked.

'The Sleep Centre …' Delores paused, and then tried again. 'REM sleep in some of our clients was disrupted, which led to hallucinations. The Sleep Centre became compromised and we dealt with it as best we could but, well, you saw the damage, yes? Someone managed to start a fire. We had to shut off that whole wing.'

'But everyone was safely evacuated?'

The mask didn't drop as Delores faced Thea, but behind her were the smoking remains of the Client Bubble, cutting a white curve out of the view.

'The company made the decision,' she said quietly.

Delores's next words dropped into Thea's brain like cold jelly, slithering into her very soul. 'Like they'll make a decision about you.'

Thea's cup trembled in her hand.

'But I can help you.'

202

Chapter 44

'Our little white-crowned sparrow.'

Delores stood behind her desk in a classic power pose, her palms placed flat on the desk-top, facing an imaginary boardroom. Thea sat down suddenly, as if someone had kicked her in the back of the knees.

They'll make a decision about you.

Her little sleep therapy group: Moira with her owl glasses and tortoise-Richard – where were they? What had happened to them? She hoped it involved a boat, all of them clambering aboard, making awkward jokes and choosing where to sit. She hoped that they were now on the mainland, maybe back at Sanity's End where the owner would be grumpily dishing out tuna and dandruff sandwiches for all.

That's where they were. That's where they *had* to be.

'*Rosie's safe. I've hidden her.*' Rory had told her – but could Rory be trusted anymore?

She was only vaguely aware that Delores was still speaking.

'I'm finished here, after what's happened. Of course, they know about Moses – the charade with our little fake Moses was just a bit of PR for the clients. His name has a certain power, after all. They didn't want to lose that.'

She picked up a piece of paper, scanned it and then crumpled it in her hand.

'I've been a fool. This is their chance to get rid of me. I'll be the perfect scapegoat. All those years! All the work, everything I've done – and I'll be sent off with a handshake and enough money to keep me quiet. If I'm *lucky*.'

Delores could join the rest of the dead for all Thea cared. The ghosts floating about this place could eat her soul, tear it apart like string cheese and suck it down slowly.

'I don't feel very much like keeping quiet, however,' Delores said bitterly. 'I don't see why they should get to keep it all and just push me aside as if I'm nothing! Me! I'm the reason this is all here. So this is where I need you. I think you'll like it, Thea Mackenzie – my offer. You've been trying to play the heroine since day one so now I'm going to give you the chance.'

Thea's heart beat a little faster. She'd been here before, in Delores's office, being offered a proposal. It felt so long ago, that day: a different Thea. The same Delores.

'You see, they think they know everything. They know about you, my little white-crowned sparrow and they know about your potential. That's why our friend Kyle was so reluctant to leave you earlier.'

Delores scanned another piece of paper and then tossed it aside.

'But they don't know *me*. They think I'm finished, that I'm licking my wounds in a corner somewhere while they clear up. But I have my own plans, as long as I can keep the Aspire watchdogs out of them. You and I, Thea Mackenzie, we're going to get off this island together. I have a private boat moored at another hidden cove further on from the beach where you landed, have had it there since we set up on the island. No one knows anything about it. I've always been a big believer in having a Plan B.'

Voices floated to them from outside the office. Delores

tensed briefly, but they drifted away and she snapped her satchel shut.

'You keep the memory stick and when you get to the mainland, you expose it. Blow the whole thing open. The real reason for using the tech, the side effects … everything. Blow it apart so there's nothing left for them. Raze it to the sodding ground. I don't care.'

Whenever Thea wasn't sure what to say, she said nothing. It made people believe she was thinking something over carefully. Most times though, her brain was actually leaping around like a frightened frog too far from the pond.

'I know what you're thinking,' said Delores. Thea doubted it: *she* didn't even know what she was thinking. 'You'd blow the whole thing apart … and blow me apart at the same time. Why send myself down with the ship? Like I said, I don't care anymore. If my ship goes down – well – so will theirs. I'll have the payoff and I'll be able to afford a good lawyer and a bolt-hole until it all blows over. Aspire will take the brunt of it … After all, as they keep insisting, they own the tech. I'll get Moses the care he needs. And, meanwhile … I'd have *you*.'

She tapped her fingernails on the desk.

'Later, when the dust settles – there's a lot we could do with you.'

The little white-crowned sparrow. Ranks of sleepless soldiers trooped across Thea's mind in orderly lines, shiny-eyed and eternally awake.

'So, let me sum up the choice. Get to play the heroine and bring down the company, or, well … the island is quite a dangerous place at the moment, no? Aspire plan to get rid of any evidence of what's gone on here. *Anything* could happen to you, and I'd be quite helpless to prevent it. It would be … regrettable.'

Thea's frog brain continued to writhe.

'Oh, and you wouldn't be able to wriggle out of the latter stage of our agreement either, in case that's what you were thinking.

Getting to work with you in a few years, that's non-negotiable. Let me be clear as well, your mother will have to be muzzled. And there would be … consequences … for reneging on the deal.'

Every other scenario her brain had whirred through over the last few minutes all ended in the same way: her death. At least with this offer she got the real reason behind the tech out there for everyone to see, and she got herself a few years while Delores stayed low. Anything could happen in those years. But she would get off this island. Right at that moment, that was all she wanted.

'Under normal circumstances, I would give you some time to mull it over. Unfortunately, these are not normal circumstances.'

Delores had her back to the office door.

So she didn't see Moses slip in.

Chapter 45

Shuffle, shuffle.

Moses was a horrifying puppet come jerkily to life. With his bald head and the spidery writing all over it, the grids marking off his skull, his gaunt limbs and hook-nailed feet, he shuffled closer and closer. He was something from a nightmare, the kind of thing he might have wanted to fix in someone else, years ago, before he knotted up his own brain so tightly there was no way to pick it apart.

Shuffle, shuffle.

He looked at Thea and put a blood-stained finger to his lips. *Where had the blood come from?*

A little game for him and Thea. Creep up on the girlfriend who had drugged him, stolen his technology and then locked him away for all that time – surprise! The shock she'd get, how she'd clutch melodramatically at her chest, but then she'd smile when she saw who it was. They'd laugh together, oh how they'd laugh …

Shuffle, shuffle.

There was a spray of blood on his T-shirt and deeper-coloured blotches on his pyjama bottoms. A biology lesson from a long time ago resurfaced in Thea's mind: darker coloured blood comes from veins, not from arteries. He smiled and there was blood on his chin.

How had he got free?

In his hand he held a wooden chair leg, weighting it on his shoulder as if it was a baseball bat. The tip of it was matted with something Thea did not want to think about.

Shuffle, shuffle.

Something about Thea's frozen expression must have alerted Delores who whirled around, one hand indeed going to her chest, just as Thea had imagined.

Surprise!

As if this was a mime exercise at school, they all held their positions. Thea could see Delores's hand moving carefully over the smooth surface of her desk, searching for something. Did she have a panic button? Even if she did, was there anyone left in the Centre to panic?

Moses followed the direction of Thea's gaze and darted forward so quickly it took Delores by surprise, not giving her enough time to move her hand and avoid the chair leg Moses smashed into her fingers. Delores's legs gave way as the pain flooded through her, her mouth an open O of shock and agony, her crushed hand still trembling on the desk as she crouched down on the floor, her forehead resting on the edge of her desk.

Thea nearly screamed with her, springing out of her chair and backing away, hands outstretched as if that could protect her.

'Max, I don't want to hurt you, I really don't, but it's been pretty difficult finding you.' Moses wiped his forehead and shot sudden glances about the room as if someone might jump out on him. 'We need to talk.'

He took a slim tablet out of his pocket and swiped at it with his thumb, scrolling through options, his other hand still gripping the chair leg.

'You don't have many people left here, Max. There was a lot

of stuff left unattended. Like this. Nifty little thing. Now let me see …'

He scrolled through a couple more times and then stopped.

'Ah, yes. There we go.'

The office door closed smoothly.

'No interruptions. Do you know?' he said conversationally. 'I feel better than I've felt for … ooh … ages. Less fuzz up here.'

He tapped the side of his head with a grisly finger.

'Not being sedated helps, I guess, doesn't it?'

Delores clenched her teeth and got to her knees, steadying her good hand on the desk as she hauled herself back up into a drunken standing position.

'Look, I know that I don't want to hurt you, Max.' He started opening the drawers in her desk. 'But what I don't know is if you feel the same way … ah, there it is.' He held up a slim little handgun and then tucked it into the pocket of his pyjama bottoms.

'We've got a lot to catch up on, yes? Sit.' He tossed the device he'd been holding into the corner of the room and pressed down hard on Delores's shoulders, forcing her into her chair as she tried to take deep breaths and cradled her hand. Moses loomed over her, one hand on the armrest.

'I said sit!' Moses whipped his head round to Thea.

She clumsily fumbled her way back into the chair.

He started to slowly rock Delores from side to side in her swivel chair.

'Maxie, Maxie, Maxie, what did you do, Maxie? With *my* tech?' He spat out the word "my". '*Dream a little dream of me.* Of you. And I did. All the time, Maxie, I was drugged up to my eyeballs, I dreamt of you. You were always in my fucking head and I couldn't get you out of it.'

He started to spin the chair in lazy circles, keeping it moving the whole time he spoke, Delores clutching on with her good hand. He looked alert, aware, manic almost, but not crazed.

209

'You did it to yourself!' Delores managed, paling at every jolt.

Moses slammed his palm against the chair back and it jerked to a halt. He bent over her again, little veins standing out on his head, mistakes on the phrenology tattoo markings.

'Yes, I did. I did. But then what did you do, Maxie? *What did you do?* You see, I thought you loved me. You'd left me and we disagreed on the tech but I always knew you loved me—'

'I did! I do!'

'You locked me up and took my life's work. Not a loving gesture, that, is it?'

'To look after you! I needed money to keep you safe.' She held her crushed fingers in her good hand, letting her hair swing down and hide half her face. 'What else could I have done, Moses? Come on, tell me! You left me. You chose. You chose that bloody tech over me!'

Moses bent to sweep her hair back, an oddly affectionate move for someone holding a chair leg as a weapon. Delores moved her face a little so her cheek rested in the palm of his hand, her eyes not gazing into his but flicking down. It was a move Thea was familiar with and, despite the pain she must have been feeling, Delores did it with speed and ferocity. Moses had his legs planted apart in front of her and so she kicked, kicked hard upwards; it would have had more effect if she'd still been wearing her boots but, even using her bare feet, Moses gasped and crumpled at the hips. She clambered out of the chair and went to the door, pressing against it, then thumping it when she found it locked. Meanwhile, Moses was half slumped over her desk, still clutching the chair leg and yes, Thea was quite sure, he was chuckling softly to himself.

'*There's* the woman I loved,' he said and then took a few quick deep breaths. 'Never one to miss an opportunity to knee me in the balls.'

Delores paced at a safe distance away from him, Moses blocking her from the corner where he'd thrown the tablet. Thea was rooted to the chair, once again the audience for someone else's drama.

But then Moses's laughing turned to crying, huge racking sobs that he almost choked out, one hand over his face, sprawling over the desk.

'My God, Max – what have you done? Do you even understand?'

Delores slowed her pacing and exchanged a glance with Thea. Moses's hand kept its grip on the chair leg. Thea looked from one to another, like a child caught between dysfunctional parents. With which monster should she side?

'What have I done with it?' Delores kept her voice even and calm, moving nearer to him. 'If you had really been so worried about that, you would have taken my advice from the start and just stopped. Destroyed the thing.'

Moses's shoulders slumped and he sat in the chair, leaning over the desk with a hand to his forehead.

'But it was good tech – wasn't it?'

He moved the chair leg like a rolling pin on the desk, back and forth, back and forth, hypnotizing himself with it.

'Yes, Moses, it was good tech,' Delores said, never taking her eyes off the chair leg.

'I could have worked it out! I still could! I could fix all of this!'

Back and forth went the chair leg, each roll sending it a little further out of his reach.

'You could.' Delores moved nearer still.

'I could.' He gripped the chair leg again, not looking up.

But Delores had got hold of something else, the heavy-looking, bruise-coloured sculpture on the desk. She didn't hesitate but swung it quickly, just as Moses moved to shove the chair leg away from him. It went rolling off the other side of the desk.

The ornament had been aiming for his head. It smashed into his shoulder instead.

211

With a cry of surprise, Moses threw his arms out, pushing Delores away with such force that she, already imbalanced and still clutching the ornament, teetered, tilted and fell. Hard.

Her head hit the corner of her stone desk with a sickening crack.

Chapter 46

Moses gathered Delores to him, keening as if he were the one in pain.

'No, no, no, no,' he cried.

Her body began to slip away from him.

Delores didn't make a sound. Her mouth moved and her tongue slapped wetly but there were no words. The woman who had been so eloquent over the past few weeks, snagging Thea in clever, sneaking speeches and plans and threats, was all gone in one sudden short burst of violence.

Thea could hear her own ragged breathing, her eyes almost hurting from being so wide and her heart a nauseous thud in her throat. She'd been halfway to picking up the chair leg that had rolled towards her when Delores fell and now she was frozen in a crouch on the floor. She could only think to stay still, make herself as small and unnoticeable as possible, so maybe they'd forget all about her.

Delores's legs sagged and Moses couldn't hold her up. They sank to the floor together, Moses smoothing Delores's hair away from her face and the blood running into her eye. Her head lolled to the side and Thea nearly gagged. She'd seen her share of violent films in her time but the blood and … wrongness …

of it had always been safely contained in her television set, comfortably squared off. It wasn't twitching slightly right in front of her.

Moses struggled to keep her upright, both of them on their knees. He tried to prop her up by gripping her shoulders but then gave up, letting her body sink awkwardly against him. His face was a mess, tears trying to sluice their way past the blood and dirt as he continued to smooth her hair and wail.

'No, no, no, no ...'

Thea crawled a bit closer, bringing the chair leg with her. Delores's legs were splayed at painful angles, her neck twisted as Moses pushed her head against his chest. She had pretty feet, Thea caught herself thinking, her brain trying to focus on something that wasn't gore and shreds of flesh. Cute little toes and neat nails.

'Moses?' Thea said softly.

He tried to shift Delores's body a little higher but she slid down even further, one arm dangling, her fingertips brushing the floor. Her hand spasmed.

'Moses?' she tried again. 'Moses? I think maybe she'd be more comfortable if you laid her on the floor.'

He sniffed and took a gulp, his eyes skating over Thea, as if he could hear her voice but didn't know where it was coming from. Thea gently held Delores's shoulder, never taking her gaze from Moses, expecting him to lash out at any minute, and together they eased her onto the floor.

Kneeling next to her, Moses sniffed and wiped his forearm across his nose, a peculiarly child-like thing to do. Delores kept trying to say something, opening and closing her mouth, her lips moving though she couldn't force out any sound. Thea had been taught CPR once on a training course years ago; she'd spent a morning bandaging up her colleagues and blowing ferociously into legless plastic torsos, grimy with over-use. She couldn't remember any of it now.

'Moses? We need to get her to a hospital. Get her on the boat? I need to open the door.'

Again, he seemed to hear her but didn't look at her. Thea glanced over to the device Moses had so casually tossed away into the corner earlier. What she really wanted was that. It could give her a way out.

Thea felt something nudge her wrist and she looked down to see Delores's hand shakily trying to grasp on to hers. Her hand was cold and bloodied hair covered one eye but the other was fixed on Thea as she convulsed a few more times. It was instinct to allow those trembling fingers to clutch hers, but she couldn't help thinking of Ethan. He hadn't been given the same comfort. He'd died so suddenly, nobody had stroked his hair, or cried over him – or held his hand. His body was still at the lighthouse, dust settling on his open eyes.

She thought about gently sliding her hand out from under Delores's chill grasp but, in the end, she couldn't do it. Her hand was so cold, Thea couldn't take away the warmth of hers, just when the woman needed it most.

She watched as Delores took a breath and then stilled, a stillness Thea was becoming all too familiar with, the body relaxing into death. Whatever had been Delores dimmed and disappeared from her gaze. Moses howled, still on his knees, bending to bury his face in the dead woman's stomach.

Pushing herself away from them, away from death, Thea closed her eyes momentarily, leaning her head back against the desk. Almost immediately the black sucked her up and, even though she knew she should be making a grab for that device Moses had thrown aside, even though she had no idea what Moses would do next and Kyle was probably on his way, she allowed the darkness in because it was soft and soothing and she only needed a moment of it, sailing gently on it like it was …

Chapter 47

... the sea. She was in a little boat on the sea. The waves were choppy, spitting at her as they slapped at the boat's sides but then her mother was going too fast, wasn't she?

There she was, her mother, at the back of the boat, a firm grip on the tiller, her vagina-printed scarf fluttering out behind her, her grey hair slicked back against her skull by the force of the wind. Thea should tell her that she was going too fast. They couldn't bounce and jar over these waves at this speed – they'd capsize and then what would happen to the owls?

There were owls in the bottom of the boat.

Baby owls, owlets, full of fluff with tiny sharp beaks pointing through. Their heart-shaped faces and worried-looking eyes made them seem like wizened, fluffy, old men. They hopped and jostled amongst each other and Thea tried not to step on them though they squeaked when, accidentally, she did. It was unnerving. All the owls had to make it to the other side. It was important. Some kept trying to hop over the side of the boat and Thea had to gently knock them back down. They nipped her fingers.

'Do you think they're in a cult?' her mother yelled to her from behind.

Were the owls in a cult? She wasn't sure.

'Because I want to try golf and they keep stealing the golf balls,' her mother shouted.

The owlet closest to her foot had a golf ball on its head, balancing it there like it was playing keepy-uppy.

Thea decided to go and tell her mother to slow down. She tried to get up, but her feet were stuck amid the owlets.

'You should kick them out of the way,' Ethan said. He was sitting on the opposite bench to her, his arms folded. There was an owlet on each shoulder, their faces turned into the wind, fluff ruffling. He frowned.

Once again, Thea tried to raise her foot but the owlets were too heavy. They screeched and pecked her ankles, nodding and bobbing to each other as if they were complaining amongst themselves.

'Or kill 'em. Throw them overboard.' Another two owlets hopped onto his knees, flaring stubby wings as they tried to find their balance.

She couldn't kill them!

They all had to make it to the other side.

'Mother!' she yelled, her voice trembling.

Her mother wasn't listening. She had her hand on the tiller, but she was leaning over the engine talking to Rosie. They were laughing, slapping their knees and squeezing their eyes shut in merriment. Because of the salt and moisture in the air, Rosie's hair was twice its normal size.

Her mother should be concentrating. She was going too fast.

Golf balls rolled around the bottom of the boat, which was becoming an owlet play-pit. They waddled through them, nudging them with their beaks, rolling over them by mistake and toppling, a heap of scraggly fuzz and feathers. When they toppled they looked at Thea like it was her fault, blinking at her, stunned and serious.

'Would you like a mushroom?' Ethan asked, holding out a punnet of them, raw, white little cushions. He had an owlet on his wrist. It cocked its head at her and pecked thoughtfully at his watch.

'Mushrooms are full of sleep. They help you to date.' He shook the box at her.

She was too busy to have a mushroom. She wanted to move her feet but she couldn't even see them properly beneath the owlets. Lifting a knee, she heaved. And again. Nothing. The golf balls rolled, the owlets fidgeted and shuffled and twittered, and she felt fear ball itself in her throat.

They were going too fast. Her mother wasn't paying attention. There were too many golf balls and she was stuck.

The boat juddered over a set of waves, sending owls and golf balls sliding to the side. An owlet used the opportunity of finding itself on top of one of its siblings and hopped its way up Thea's trouser leg to her knee.

It put its head on one side and stared at her with little round wet eyes. She could feel its sharp claws digging into her jeans. Then it started to retch, a horrible choking sound that shook its entire body, its throat working manically, its stubby wings flapping to no avail. Was the owl going to die? None of the owls could die! She'd tried so hard!

The owlet shook its head and made one final retching sound, spitting something up onto her knee. There were little bones and a kind of bracken-like material all balled up together around a tiny metal memory stick.

Oh, so that's where it was, Thea thought to herself as a massive wave crashed over the front of the boat and she was slammed down face first into owlet fluff and …

Chapter 48

… her elbow.

She reared up with a gasp.

She'd been asleep. She'd actually fallen asleep in the middle of the horror show.

Not a hallucination, not a hallucination, not a hallucination.

Morpheus had been tasked with doing something different to her sleep than the other clients, but it seemed the outcome was the same: the brain craving some REM relief. One minute, she'd been watching Moses cry over the dead body of Delores, the next she'd been in an owl-filled boat with her mother, Ethan and Rosie, a retching owlet on her knee coughing up …

The memory stick!

Thea got to her knees, black shapes floating in her vision, twisting and squirming like bacteria under a microscope. For the first time, she registered how quiet the room was. No wailing. Where was Moses?

How long had she been asleep?

Delores's body was still on the floor, a waxwork of the woman she had once been, the red of her hair mingling with the obscenely glossy blood oozing from her head.

Nearby, someone started speaking in a dead, monotonous tone.

'Morpheus' – it was Moses – 'was the master of dreams. He ordered the dreams of heroes and kings. He influenced the dreams of the gods themselves …'

On her hands and knees, Thea crawled around the edge of the desk and found Moses, huddled against the wall in a tight ball, his eyes a blank stare.

Above Moses's head, on Delores's desk, was her laptop. A laptop that would definitely have internet connection. Thea instinctively checked that the memory stick was tucked safely in the waistband of her leggings.

Moses sniffed. He'd smeared blood around his eyes trying to wipe them and now, with the markings on his head and the streaks on his face, he looked like one of those frightening tribal masks.

'Moses?'

'Thea, wasn't it?' he asked vaguely, never taking his eyes from Delores.

'Yes.'

'Look what she did. This place.'

'You could help stop it.' Thea hauled herself up, her arms wobbling.

'Me? It's done. There's no coming back from this.'

She looked at him, in his blood-spattered T-shirt and dirty pyjama bottoms, hunched and crying. Outside the office door, Thea didn't know what was waiting for her, but it wasn't a red carpet to freedom. She needed Moses, as help, leverage, or bait. She wasn't yet sure which one.

'Delores had a private boat waiting for her, in a cove,' Thea told him. 'No one knew about it. If we get off the island, if you open the door, you could tell people the truth. What they're planning to do, how dangerous it is …'

'She should never have sold the tech. How could she?' His voice took on a child-like whine. 'She took it away from me.'

He stared at Delores's body and then clutched at his face, rubbing his temples hard.

'I've killed her,' he moaned. 'But it wasn't my fault. You know that, don't you? It wasn't my fault.'

He flicked his eyes up to her guiltily, then back over to the body.

Thea steadied herself against the desk. It had all happened so quickly, but no, she didn't think Moses had meant to kill Delores. She'd lunged for him and he'd swung out his arm in defence. But it was no matter. They had been two children in the playground, stamping their feet, crying 'Give it here! It's mine!', while the school burned down around them.

'Open the door, Moses.'

Thea tapped at the laptop and then thumped it angrily when a password box instantly appeared. Her only chance to get the video diary out lay behind a locked screen.

'Pangolin,' Moses muttered.

'What?' Thea tried a few of the drawers, looking for convenient Post-it Notes with secret passwords on them.

'Pangolin.' Moses looked at her from where he was sat on the floor. 'It used to be her password. Little snouty creatures. They're endangered. She liked them.'

He covered his face with one hand and then started thumping at his forehead with the other.

Thea gaped. But she typed it in and, when the welcome screen appeared, she took a deep breath. An internet connection may not have been provided for the clients, but Thea knew that the staff would have needed it and she was in the Staff Bubble.

The internet connection icon showed three bars.

She glanced towards the locked door, her hands shaking, expecting any second for Kyle to start pounding on it. Delores's email account was already open and Thea shoved the memory stick into the laptop.

From outside, there came shouting.

Moses staggered to his feet, briefly looked at the screen and the title of the email she was frantically typing: 'MUM, READ

THIS. IT'S FROM THEA!!' He stilled and she almost expected him to swipe the laptop away from her, perhaps get that ornament that now lay chipped on the floor and begin using it to break her own skull …

He blinked and rubbed at his chin, smearing blood onto it from his hands.

Then he nodded, just the once, his face serious, his eyes clear and focused. He turned to the door.

On the screen the email was marked "pending" and the circle spun.

'Moses!' Kyle's voice roared from outside.

Thea nearly whimpered. The circle continued to spin. There was no way that Thea was going to leave the memory stick in the laptop – it was coming with her.

Moses lay a hand on her arm. 'It's okay. I can't undo any of this,' he said quietly, picking up the tablet he had dropped earlier and getting Delores's gun from his pocket. 'But there is one thing I can still do.'

He tapped on the screen.

'I can give you a bit more time.'

The office door opened and, before Thea could say anything, he left the room.

Chapter 49

The circle spun.

Thea could feel the sweat making her thermal jumper stick to the skin under her arms. She looked away, hoping that when she looked back, the email would have sent.

The circle spun.

There was more shouting: Kyle again, then Moses and then … quiet.

The circle spun.

She couldn't wait any longer. Yanking the memory stick out, she gave a quick prayer to any god listening in, hoping that the email would eventually send. Running to the door, she knew that if she let Kyle corner her in the office, there was a good chance she would never leave.

Out on one of the suspended walkways leading to the shiny central lift, she saw Moses: he hadn't run far. In fact, he wasn't planning on running much at all by the look of him. He was balanced precariously on one of the flat-topped handrails, his feet purple with the cold, a demented eagle surveying his hunting ground.

'Moses!'

Thea wasn't alone.

Kyle was at the opposite end of the walkway. The lift was in the middle between them, but there was a narrow walkway around it to get from one side of the building to the other.

'Moses!' Thea came closer to where Moses was balanced.

Kyle noticed Thea. She hadn't seen him since he'd carried Moses into the building earlier that day, however many minutes, hours or millennia ago that had been. Thea had lost track. He looked as if he'd had a pretty rough time. There was blood on his face and his T-shirt was ripped. The Eighties tribute band wouldn't be so keen to have him now, Thea thought. It had clearly been harder looking after Moses than he'd bargained for.

For a second or so, Thea was back at the lighthouse. Kyle had done it so smoothly. He had taken charge of the headphones, said something light and reassuring in his refined, Eton-Old-Boys'-Club voice. He had placed them on Ethan's head, knowing they would kill him.

Delores might have ordered it.

Kyle had done it.

Thea realized why he was keeping his distance as she took a few steps to Moses's side. Moses was holding the gun, and it was pointed at Kyle.

Moses turned his head to throw her a beseeching look. 'What am I meant to do now, Thea?'

'You don't have to do anything,' she soothed. 'Not anymore, Moses. It's over. Please come down.'

Her muscles trembled and even her bones ached; all she wanted to do was sink to the ground, close her eyes and let herself fall into the black.

'I always knew what to do,' Moses muttered. 'I could always fix the problem.'

Holding one arm out in front of him, Kyle tried to walk closer to Moses who wobbled dangerously as he turned his head to look at him, waving the gun.

'Fuck off!' Moses snarled.

Kyle faltered and stopped.

Thea held out her hand to Moses.

She had spent so much time thinking and talking about this man in front of her, with his weird skull tattoo. Ever since she'd landed on the island, she had been dogged by his name and the rumours around it: inventor, genius, recluse, madman.

The Great Moses Ing.

'You don't have to fix this problem, Moses,' she said. 'It's over.'

He swayed on his handrail perch, a living phrenology head. She didn't know if they could get past Kyle, even if she got the gun from Moses and coaxed him down from the handrail, and she didn't know if they'd find Delores's boat. But she knew she couldn't watch another person die.

'Moses?' She held his gaze as he turned his head back to her. 'You don't need to do this. Come down – you can help me. You're Moses Ing, after all – you can tell people what happened here. They'd believe you. We can get out together.'

He gazed at her sadly. 'We're not getting out.'

Kyle smiled that smile, the one that hooked up the corners of his mouth. 'He's right, you know – you're not getting out. Not that I care what happens to him – we can buy in another Moses if we need one. And you? Aspire have got plans for you but if you prove too difficult, well, they can find another you as well. Either way, this is the end. Jump, old man, or use the gun. I'm waiting.'

'No! Stop!' Thea turned to Kyle. 'You need him! He could probably fix Morpheus – if you gave him a chance.'

She wasn't quite sure what she was saying. Her only thought was to keep the two men safely where they were: Moses on the walkway and Kyle at a distance.

'They're not my orders.' Kyle shrugged and took another step nearer, Moses between them. 'Aspire has world-class laboratories which I'm sure can do any fixing for themselves.'

'The world-class labs don't matter.' Moses smiled grimly and tapped his head. 'You need a world-class mind. I used to have that. Not anymore. I wouldn't help them anyway. Look at it all,' he said, his voice breaking and tears forming again. 'Look at what I've lost: Morpheus, Max … all of it. Look at what you did with my beautiful ideas. I gave you the tools to make gods of us. Do you understand that? I gave you the chance to be more than human, to be *better*, and look what you did instead … instead you created monsters.'

Thea didn't have time to worry about being a god; she was too busy trying to stay alive. She tried to reach for his hand, but he refused to take it. Instead, he sniffed and wiped the tears away, smudging them into the blood and dirt on his face before squaring his shoulders, taking one last look at the ruins of the Centre from his vantage point.

'What use am I without Morpheus? Without Max?'

'No! Moses!'

And she lunged for him, but it all happened too quickly. Moses shot at Kyle, squeezing his eyes shut as he did so and Thea could already see that the bullet went wide, but Kyle staggered back anyway. Moses had twisted to fire the gun so when his body began to tip, his arms out as if he was going to float lazily down to the ground, he stared right into Thea's eyes.

She would never forget his expression at that moment. It snagged onto her so she couldn't look away, and it seemed as if it took forever for him to fall, so long that she saw it all: the pain and sadness, the confusion and then … as he dropped further away, one hand stretched towards her: the fear.

Thea felt the bar of the handrail press into her stomach as she rushed into it, leaning over, still trying to grab a hand that was plummeting to the ground below, out of reach.

When his body smashed onto the tiles, she closed her eyes, almost feeling the floor below wanting to suck her into it as well. The backs of her legs tingled as if the muscles were preparing to jump and, gently, she tilted from her waist, just a touch too far forward. If she fell asleep, right now, she'd tip and then tumble after him …

It would be easy to tilt a little more, and she was so very tired …

She heard Kyle's footsteps coming for her.

Her body jerked at the same time her hand slipped and, with a sudden rush of adrenaline, she felt herself lurch forward in one sick, dizzy movement, until she planted her feet firmly and hauled herself back from the brink.

Kyle moved fast, but Thea was closer to the lift. Head spinning, she wrenched herself away from the handrail and ran to it. The doors shut her in, and the polite female voice came too soon: 'Ground floor'. When the doors opened once more, she nearly raced straight to the huge glass entrance doors.

Stupid.

Kyle was still up there on the walkway, mercifully without a gun as Moses had fallen still holding it. If she got out of the lift, however, he would simply call it up and follow her. She needed a head start. She needed to be *smarter*.

Keeping her foot between the doors to keep them open, she cast her gaze around for something to jam the lift. Of course, there would be stairs and Kyle would use them but that would take longer. She needed that time.

There was an upturned cafeteria chair within reach, one of many strewn about messily. Perhaps the staff fleeing the island had pushed them over in their haste to get out.

Moses was nearby, though she didn't look in that direction.

She couldn't think about that.

Blessing the days recently spent in yoga, Thea stretched flat out on the floor, her arm out while still keeping the lift door jammed with her foot. Her shoulder didn't throb quite so much now, but it wasn't up to helping out in any way. High on the walkway above her, she saw a bleached-blond-framed face bob into view. Kyle was trying to work out what she was doing. She didn't want him heading for the stairs yet. Maybe he thought she'd become prostrate with grief or shock. Or she'd fainted. Or started hallucinating again. She stretched some more. It felt like she might tear a muscle somewhere any second, but she managed to claw her fingers around the chair and shove it into the lift entrance.

The doors banged open and shut on it uselessly, a giant mouth masticating a piece of gristle.

Then she ran.

The glass doors were there. They were so close she could see the smudges on them, handprints of people either gone from the island, or dead. She didn't look back because there was nothing to look back for; she needed no final picture of the hell this place had become.

She skidded to a halt.

Nothing to look back for.

Thea was close enough to touch the glass.

She was wrong. She'd forgotten.

Rosie.

How could she have forgotten Rosie? She was still in the building, if Rory had been telling the truth. Hidden somewhere and unconscious, making it too difficult for Thea to move on her own. She couldn't drag her through the corridors, down to the beach and into a boat all by herself with Kyle chasing her.

Wouldn't it be more sensible to escape and then send back help, especially as Kyle was, at this moment, leaping down the stairs towards her?

She *should* leave – Rosie was probably dead.

She *couldn't* leave – Rosie might be alive.

She had to go back for her.

She had to because ... well, it was her fault she was lying in that hospital bed, wasn't it? Rosie had followed her and her point-less little quest to find a face in the monastery window. If she hadn't, she might still have been happily sticking pencils in her hair and flirting with Ethan, not lying motionless in a hospital bed.

Thea could watch Ethan die, she could walk over Delores's dead body, she could look away as Moses hit the ground ... but she *could not* run out of this building without knowing she'd at least tried to help Rosie. If she did that, she would know that the island had changed her forever – and she wouldn't be able to live with the person she'd become.

The glass of the front doors was cold. It felt good on her forehead as she rested her head against it. She gave herself a moment. Carefully and deliberately she pressed her palms against the glass as well. The imprint of her hands joined all the others, a smudgy marker, a sign that she too had been here. She had been alive in this place. Once.

She took a deep breath and faced the nearest corridor.

Chapter 50

'Why are you 'ere?' The man eyed Vivian suspiciously.

'I would have thought that was fairly obvious. The sign said rooms available. I want a room.'

The pub's name, "Sanity's End", was probably going to be more accurate than Vivian had at first thought.

The train journey had done terrible things to her bones, but worse things to her soul. So much emptiness had stretched out around her, fields and fields with just a horizon line where they met sky, no friendly rooftop or chimney buttressing the void. The light had begun to dim as the mountains set in. Vivian thought they might provide some relief from the unwavering flat lands but they proved to be worse, great hulking things bending down to work out whether the little train chugging through them was worth crushing.

The station had been deserted but there had been a dog-eared noticeboard, the plastic covering warped and brown in places as if someone had tried to set it alight. She'd phoned the only taxi firm available.

Despite the fading light, she could see the island through the pub's streaked windows.

'Why are you 'ere? No rooms available.'

The man had appeared like a terrible magic act from behind a stained velvet curtain, which was still half open and gave a peek into a cluttered living space beyond. A muted television flickered light over a defeated chair, a scuffed side table and carpet that rightfully belonged to the Sixties.

'Clearly not for a pleasant holiday,' she muttered to herself and then decided to lose any attempt at subtlety. 'What's going on over on that island?'

She was sure he paled a little; it was hard to tell because his face looked as if it had been left out too long in bad weather.

'What island?' He narrowed his eyes.

Vivian fought down the urge to laugh, but instead pointed through the window. 'That island, right there. The one we can both clearly see.'

He sniffed. 'Oh, *that* island. Ain't nothing there. Used to be. Monastery and the like. People used to come to take their stupid pictures. All gone now.'

'But there is something there, isn't there? Ing Enterprises owns it. My daughter came here not so long ago and then went over to that island to take part in their trial. She told me.'

The man sniffed. 'No.'

'No?'

'No. Looks like the trial's over. They're moving out.'

Vivian snapped a glance at the island, but it was a late winter's afternoon and she wasn't able to make out anything more than a blocky, misshapen lump. 'Why?'

'Why would I know? They'd not tell me.' He opened a ledger with a thump, the spine breaking immediately to the right page. 'You can't 'ave a room.'

The trial was over; Ing Enterprises was moving out. Vivian fumbled in her handbag and retrieved her phone once more – no messages, no missed calls. But if this man was right and Thea was at this moment sailing over to the mainland then this was exactly where she wanted to be.

She plonked her bag on the reception counter. 'Why bother opening if you don't want anyone to stay?'

There was silence. The man sniffed again and crossed his arms over his chest. 'I'm a man of 'abit.'

Behind him were two large keys hanging from hooks on the wall. There was a conspicuous streaking in the dust around the key on the third hook, as if someone had carelessly swiped it from the wall recently. Vivian put her hands palm down on the reception desk and, feeling the stickiness under her fingers, instantly wished she hadn't.

'My daughter's name is Thea.' Vivian's voice softened. 'She's twenty-seven and I am very proud of her: she's funny and smart and worth much more than she thinks she is. Do you have children, Mr—?'

She thought he might not reply, but he did. 'Alastair. Name's Alastair.'

Then he shuffled his feet and loosened his crossed arms. Only a little. 'Gotta boy. Don't see 'im much,' he said.

'You see, Alastair; my funny, smart, precious girl came here because she doesn't sleep very well and that made her desperate. Desperate people do silly things. And the silly thing she did was to put her trust in those people on that island. They promised to fix her, even though she doesn't need fixing in my opinion. And then I stopped hearing from her.'

Vivian held Alastair's gaze.

'It's been a long day,' she carried on. 'I don't admit this to many people, but I'm getting old and long days make me tired so I need a room for the night. I'll most likely be out of your hair in the morning and you can say you've never heard of me.'

She saved her best until last: 'I'll pay extra.'

Alastair let his arms drop to his sides. He scratched at his head and then examined the result under his fingernails. Frowning, he got out a handkerchief so grubby it could keep a microbiologist busy for weeks and blew his nose.

'Money fully paid upfront,' he said. 'No loud music, no animals, no extra guests permitted in your room. There's a TV but we don't get much of a reception up here. No meals provided. Ain't got no chocolates or petals and ain't gonna get 'em neither.'

Vivian got out her purse and Alastair fetched a key, which, when he pushed it over the desk towards her, she saw was the kind of heavy black metal that wouldn't be out of place in a Victorian prison.

He kept his hand on it and cleared his throat.

'It sounds to me,' Alastair said thoughtfully, 'like this girl of yours would be the kind of girl to leave a nice comment on one of them feedback card thingies what have to be sent off ...'

Vivian suspected this was, perhaps, a breakthrough moment. That, or the man was having some kind of episode.

'My name's Vivian.' She held out her hand. 'Vivian Mackenzie.'

He took her hand and crushed it in his, holding on to it for his next words.

'If they have finished out on that island' – he gave her a long, considered, knowing look – 'I'll need to start makin' a living with my own customers.'

He let go of her hand and she massaged some life back into it.

The perfect idea popped into her head like snapped cartilage.

'Excellent!' She smiled brightly. 'Now, I wonder if you know anyone who could lend me their boat?'

Chapter 51

Thea really was a lab rat in a maze with another rat literally on her tail.

Something smashed somewhere. Thea ducked instinctively and whimpered to herself.

The black spots in front of her eyes sinuously twisted into shapes to distract her – rabbit ears, bow, teardrop – until she had to stop, place a hand on the wall and take some deep breaths, too afraid to close her eyes in case she disappeared into sleep or hallucination. Now her discs were off, sleep was claiming her, inch by inch.

What if she fell asleep just as Kyle rounded the corner? He could slit her throat while she talked to imaginary owls.

The corridor was as bright and white and glossy as it had always been, like the shine on panna cotta. No, she couldn't think about food. The last thing she'd eaten had been those crackers back in the lighthouse: thin, diet things made mostly of air.

A floor plan would have been great. She couldn't really remember how she'd got to the clinic when she'd visited Rosie here in this Staff Bubble. There had just been corridor after corridor, swirls of cream that all looked the same. Not that there was any guarantee that Rosie would be there anyway.

Were there footsteps behind her?

Skidding to a halt, she listened. Even her swallowing sounded loud and she realized how thirsty she was, recalling how little of that tea she had got to drink back in Delores's office. Blood pounded in her ears.

There.

Footsteps. Running.

Thea moved, doors flashing past her, some open, some closed, hardly looking as she turned a corner and nearly hurtled straight into a man sitting on the floor.

It was Richard.

The last time she had seen him, he had been in the hospital room next to Rosie with a group of people trying to restrain him. He was dressed in just a pair of pyjama bottoms, his feet dirty and bare, eyes blank. She had seen that vacant stare before, on a laptop screen – Ted sitting next to Moses, silent and empty. It had made her heart jump faster then, but this was real and right in front of her.

Richard did not move.

Slack jaw, slack arms, neck wilting under the effort of supporting his head, he slumped on the ground, eyes dulled and lifeless.

But he was alive. Thea could see the gentle rise and fall of his chest.

There was no time to stop and wonder how he had got there, nor to think how, if her hallucinations continued, that might be her soon, alone and empty on a cold, tiled floor.

Now she was on an incline, the corridor curving around and up slightly suggesting that this was maybe an outside wall. Everything was so white, so clinical, it felt like a nightmare – running and running and searching through these white corridors and never getting anywhere. At any moment she expected to come to a dead end and get an electrical shock for taking the wrong turn, a zap for her rat-mind.

The footsteps followed her.

These were all just rooms and offices and labs, no sign of a medical wing. Signs! Signs would have been useful! Thea ran past room after room, shoving doors open, glancing in, moving on. So quiet, so deserted. Everyone fled by now. *The company made the decision.* Delores had told her that, back in her office. Thea didn't want to find out the decision they'd made.

Another corridor, big double doors at the end.

But this corridor wasn't white.

Tramlines of red cut a path on the floor. They led from each room and then joined into one track heading straight for the double doors. It took a while to sink in, her brain soggy and flopping about.

Tramlines = dragging.

Dragging = something heavy.

Red = blood.

People had been dragged – no, not people – *bodies* had been dragged to that room at the end. There were no handprints on the walls, no signs of struggle, only the odd red footprint where the someone doing the dragging had stepped in blood.

The company made the decision.

The picture popped into Thea's head; she couldn't help it. Moira from therapy, with her thick, round glasses – the woman who used to get up at night and eat while asleep. Maybe she had been lost in a hallucination, a nice one perhaps where she was surrounded by fluffy roast potatoes and buttery parsnips all dancing for her. Maybe she'd smiled at the person coming towards her, thinking them a part of her vision, or maybe she couldn't smile anymore, locked in her own body, unmoving. Like the slaughtered cows Thea had seen once on television, the bolt pistol pressed to their heads, the jolt, their legs scrabbling for purchase as they went down.

No one at home waiting for them to call. No one to care what happens to them.

There had been no boat for the clients. No evacuation. Had she ever really believed there had been?

Those double doors at the end of the corridor waited for her. There was a fly crawling on them.

If she really was the lab rat scurrying through the maze, she had found the end in that room, the rotten, decaying heart at the centre of it all. She knew what was in there and she couldn't bring herself to look. There was no getting out. All paths led to that. She was just one more body for a company that wanted to erase what happened here, forget it, smooth it over like a plasterer smoothing over a wall, hoping the blood wouldn't seep through.

She cowered in the corner of the corridor and was too numb even to cry.

Rosie was probably in there, not that Thea would be able to bring herself to go in and check.

She was the only one left.

No.

There was Richard.

Somehow, he had been overlooked, had wandered out of reach or been forgotten in some way: however it had happened, he was still alive. She may have failed Ethan and Rosie, but maybe she could help him, maybe she could at least try to salvage someone from this charnel pit.

She was not going to cringe in this corner. Instead, she was going to try; get up and keep on trying until they caught and killed her.

Running was not an option anymore for her battered legs, so she staggered back.

Richard was still there, she saw with relief, as she rounded the corner into the corridor. Taking a few steps towards him, she realized how long his legs were and worried about how she would get him up and moving.

That's when Kyle appeared at the other end of the corridor.

He was closer to Richard than she was, and he broke into a

shockingly fast run, arms pumping. Hardly breaking his stride, he jammed the knife hard into Richard's throat in one smooth practised move.

It was done with such force, Thea almost felt the punch of the blade in her own throat. She saw everything so clearly for one shocked moment. Wide eyes … arms twitching … the knife handle smooth and black and obscene …

Then Kyle wrenched it out.

He stepped over Richard like he was litter, the knife dripping in his hand and carried on running.

Straight for Thea.

Chapter 52

She had always been the last girl to be picked for school teams, but Thea ran like she'd never run before. She wasn't hoping that she could beat the man behind her with that steely, emotionless glaze to his eyes, but she was hoping she could hide.

She was better at that.

Those double doors loomed once more, and she really didn't want to, but she had no choice because that was the end of the corridor.

The double doors it had to be.

Dead end.

As she slammed into the room, a hand shot out and covered her mouth. A warm, living hand, gently but firmly guiding her back from the door, into a shadowed corner. The hand didn't move but a face edged into her vision.

She blinked.

Rory.

He was holding a fire axe.

What he was still doing here, Thea no longer wanted to know. As he gestured to her to keep quiet and nodded to the door, hefting the axe, she knew what he was planning to do: hit Kyle as he came through. She knew lots of things in that moment. She knew she didn't trust Rory. But she also knew that Kyle was going to appear any second and she hated him even more.

She grabbed the axe from Rory whose mouth dropped into an almost comical O.

There was no time to explain because Kyle opened the door and she swung the axe as hard as she could. It felt good in her hands, having something with which to fight back and she put all of her fear and hate and anger behind the swing, yelling gutturally. The blunt end of it missed its mark a bit but enough of it smashed into Kyle's face and he stumbled.

She'd been expecting him to crumple and fall, immediately felled like the bad guys in a PG-rated film.

He did not.

He staggered, touching his face where the cheekbone had shattered, disbelief in his eyes. Then he lunged, swinging wildly because there was blood in one eye but barrelling towards her with surprising strength too. It was instinct, to close her eyes and drive the axe down once more, into something that snagged the axe blade and then nearly pulled her down with it.

She opened her eyes.

Kyle lay motionless on the floor.

Thea breathed hard, gulped in air, her face wet with what she first thought was blood, but what surprisingly turned out to be tears. Her knees seemed to dissolve and her legs gave out, sending her sprawling onto the floor, still clutching the handle of the axe. Vomit burned in her throat and she put out a hand to support herself.

It slipped in some sort of thick fluid.

Rory crawled towards her and reached out, big-eyed and pale. Rory.

Her breath hitched.

She turned to him, tightened her grip on the axe handle and tugged at it, her face turned away, until it slid free. Rory, reading her expression, started to scurry backwards, but not quick enough …

She swung the blunt handle of the axe right into his soft, fleshy middle.

He bent double, making a weak "oof" sound.

She hauled herself up, feeling every joint scream at her as she did so, then she turned back to the doors, her chin high, the axe clutched in both hands, not thinking because thinking would lead to feeling and she couldn't feel anything right now. If she did, she would just crumple—

'Wait!' Rory gasped.

She shoved one of the doors open.

'Please … wait!'

Her footsteps were muffled by the cushioned hi-tech floor material, but she knew her steps were confident and determined as she left the room. She wasn't going to speak to him. She didn't know how much of a part he'd played in all of this and she was tired of being lied to, tired of having to try and work out the real motive behind what everyone was saying and doing.

Just tired.

'Wait!' he called again. 'Don't you want to know about Rosie?'

She slowed, just a little, the name tangling her steps.

'Rosie's safe!' he continued. 'I managed to keep her safe! She's still alive!'

Chapter 53

'Do you have any idea? Any fucking idea, Rory Thirwood?' Thea marched back along the corridor to him, eyes blazing, raising the axe in front of her, gesticulating with it. 'I saw you sit back and watch Kyle kill Ethan. I watched him die! And Delores. And Moses. I've seen those bodies in there. And do you know what? I am sick of it. Of watching. I'm not watching anymore. This is it. I don't trust you. I think I might even want to use this axe on you and if you are lying right now about Rosie, if this is yet another elaborate trap you're setting for me, I swear to God I will take this axe and I will ram it right between your eyes.'

She marched up close to him, her chest heaving.

'I know,' Rory said meekly. 'I know what you saw. I've seen a lot too.'

She didn't drop the axe.

'I didn't know what would happen to Ethan.' Rory stretched out his hands to her, supplicating. 'You have to believe me! I would never …'

Belief. She'd asked that of him, days ago when the two of them had whispered together in a cleaning cupboard. '*You do believe me, don't you?*' And he had.

Rory dropped his gaze. 'I thought we were rescuing you …'

This was Rory.

He rubbed his eyes wearily. 'Please. Delores told me I had to go and get you, keep you safe from Aspire. I had no idea what would happen to Ethan, or what they'd done to the clients. I …'

Thea swayed on her feet, her eyelids getting heavier with every blink.

'I swear to you I am not lying about Rosie,' he continued. 'She's hidden. I hid her in the Client Bubble, the damaged one, as soon as the chaos started, to keep her safe. I guessed no one would go back there. Thought I'd get her out with me, but before I could do that Delores ordered me up to the lighthouse to fetch you. But Rosie's there. She's awake.'

'Awake?' Thea snapped back into the room.

'Yeah. A bit groggy. Can't move much. But awake. I was getting supplies from the canteen here' – he showed her the rucksack over his shoulder; it was full of nut bars and fruit – 'when I came into that room and saw what they'd done … to the clients. I didn't know before, I swear I didn't. And then I heard someone running and … there you were.'

Thea glanced at the door at the end of the corridor. 'In there, they're all …'

'I know,' he said softly and then paused. 'We were told that the clients had been evacuated – you have to believe me on that. We would never …'

There it was again. Belief. *'You do believe me, don't you?'*

Did she?

He trailed off. In the short time since she'd seen him last, it was as if his face had sunken in on itself.

Thea lowered the axe.

Thea had never been much of a hugger, but when she saw Rosie propped up in bed in a client room, her face still a mess of bruising, blood and bandages, but smiling, a wicked glint in her working eye – she was in the hug before she realized. And then she was crying, and Rosie was crying too until they couldn't even understand each other because all they could make were incoherent sounds, hitching gulps and sobs.

For Thea, every cry was the loosening of something hard and knotted up inside her. It was something that had been twisting itself tight ever since she had seen Ethan die, so tight it had kept the rest of her together like an overstretched ball of rubber bands, liable to snap at any time.

Eventually they quietened and Thea sat back on the bed, holding Rosie's hand.

'But – important question' – Rosie sniffed and smiled weakly – 'how's my hair?'

Thea considered the tangle of fluff, wild at the front and flat at the back where Rosie had been lying on it.

'Best ever.' Thea returned the smile, but it faded quickly. 'You know, that day at the monastery, I thought you were … that I wouldn't …'

Rosie squeezed Thea's hand, her own so much bonier than it had been. 'I know.'

She shifted herself on the bed and Rory came over, adjusting the pillows behind her so she could sit up more.

'It's all gone to hell, Thea.' Rosie's voice slurred a little. 'Rory's filled me in a bit.'

Thea tried to keep her own voice steady. 'Everyone who took part in the trial is dead. Ing Enterprises isn't in charge anymore; possibly it never was. A company called Aspire owns it all and the trial went wrong – the hallucinations – but not just that. After the hallucinations there is just this … this blankness. The person becomes a living, breathing shell. So, they've covered their tracks. Killed them all.'

Rosie took a breath, as if she'd just dipped her feet into cold water.

'You know they were all pretty much alone?' This Thea aimed at Rory. 'No family, no friends nearby, no one to make a fuss?'

He dipped his gaze away again.

Thea clasped Rosie's hand in both of hers. 'Has Rory told you about Ethan?'

Rory interrupted, 'She maybe doesn't need to—'

'Ethan's dead.' She flicked her gaze to Rory before saying the next part. 'They killed him too.'

There was no better way of saying it. However you arranged the words or however soft the tone – they still sliced. Rosie looked bloodless.

'No,' she whispered.

Thea held her hand tight, hoping that would hold her together.

'But they can't all be … And Ethan was so …' Rosie looked at Thea and what she saw in her eyes made her own harden. 'Then … we're the only ones left?'

Thea considered them: a man, one injured woman and another one with an axe. It sounded like the start of a bad joke.

'There might still be a way out. Delores had a boat hidden for herself, and for me. We could still use it. We've just got to get to the beach.'

'Delores is going to help us?' Rosie said hopefully.

'No, she's dead too. There's no one to help us. We're going to have to help ourselves.'

Rory cleared his throat. 'Why would Delores tell you about this boat?'

The suspicion in his voice made her chest burn. She'd put the axe down beside Rosie's bed, but suddenly her fingers itched for it.

'White-crowned sparrow, remember? Use Morpheus to completely get rid of the need for sleep. I was to be her star guinea pig. Couldn't let the guinea pig die here, could she? Like the *others* …'

She may as well have had the axe then, because she saw him flinch. *Ethan.*

'Well, we've got to get to this boat, then.' Rosie tried to push herself up even more.

245

Rory clasped and unclasped his hands. 'I don't know, you've only just woken up from a serious head injury—'

'She'll be fine – we'll help her,' Thea snapped at him. They were on either side of Rosie's bed and Thea put a hand on Rosie's shoulder.

Rory gave an exasperated sigh.

Rosie looked from one to the other, stuck in her bed in the middle of them both.

'So you want to stay here like sitting ducks and just wait for Kyle to find you—' Thea began.

'Kyle won't be finding anyone. You took care of that!'

It was her turn to flinch. Thea opened her mouth to reply but found there were no words. There were images though, and sounds too, ones she would never be able to forget.

She abruptly sat down.

Kyle was dead. She had killed him. He would have killed her, and he had actually killed Richard and there were all the reasons and excuses in the world but, strip all of that away and she was left with that small, bleak sentence. She had killed him. Was she the same as them now, the ones who had dragged bodies into that room at the end of the corridor?

Rosie interrupted her thoughts in a small voice: 'Thea? Please don't leave me behind.'

And there it was. The need. Somehow, on this island, in these days, she had become the person people needed – to agree, to act, to help, to forgive. Such a lot that they expected her to do, little weights pulling on her eyelids.

She turned to Rory. 'I'm sorry. Look, I don't know what to do, okay? But we're still alive. We've just got to keep making the next decision that keeps us alive a little bit longer, and then the next, and the next until we get off this island.'

Rory nodded. She'd got this far – somehow – but now it wasn't about just her anymore. It was about the three of them. Three people to keep safe. It seemed like such a huge number.

'Get Rosie up and out of bed. Find something warm for us all to wear. Boots if possible – there's snow.'

But, even to her ears, her voice sounded drunken, and suddenly she smelled the patchouli joss-sticks her mother always had burning in her house. In fact, there was her mother, sitting on the end of Rosie's bed, with her glasses perched on the edge of her nose reading a newspaper as a teapot poured tea all by itself—

'Thea?'

She woke with a start, Rory's hand on her shoulder.

'Don't let me do that again!' She sprang up and paced to the cupboards, searching through an abandoned cosmetic bag left on the bedside table. 'It's been so long since I slept. But I can't sleep – I might hallucinate!'

Unspoken between them was the thought, *and after the hallucinating, what would happen to her next?*

'What will you do?' Rosie asked, her eyes much bigger than her voice.

Thea smiled grimly as she picked up a pair of nail scissors. When she'd hugged Rosie, those knots deep within her had loosened, but now they tugged and tightened once more.

'Stay awake,' she said, testing the points against her palm, ready to stab the ends into herself the very next moment she felt herself drift.

That was when the first explosion came.

Chapter 54

Running, again.

Heart-thumping, throat-closing, hand-shaking – again, again, again.

To Thea it seemed she was always running in this nightmare place and never getting anywhere; even when she made it out as far as the lighthouse with Ethan she was flicked back to the Centre again: a counter in a hellish game of tiddlywinks.

There was a deep booming that reverberated in her chest, and the feeling of something pressing down on them, squeezing the floor and making it tremble.

'What is that?' Thea shouted to Rory.

Between them, they supported Rosie.

'Clean-up's started!' he yelled back.

Scorched-earth policy had never been so true, Thea thought grimly as she tightened her grip across Rosie's shoulders.

They hadn't even had time to get boots. After the first explosion they had got Rosie out of bed and run from the room, heading back to the damaged cafeteria that Rory had led her through only about half an hour ago on the way to where he'd hidden Rosie.

It was the dark twin of the other sphere. The original fire had started somewhere near here and there were black smudges on the stainless steel and white walls. Surfaces had warped, and the sticky gloss that had so unnerved Thea was charred to an acrid toffee. However, now there was new damage from the recent explosions. The chairs and tables, which had been neatly arranged, were upended and had a fine layer of dirt on them, whilst the floor was littered with chunks of stone and a few bits of metal. Thea warily eyed the walkways above them.

This Client Bubble was where it had all started to go wrong. Thea remembered Rory telling her about the man who'd hallucinated that his teeth were falling out, and she imagined once again his bloody smile, the rattle of enamel in the palm of his hand.

Another boom made the floor undulate again and it was a sound that Thea felt in her body, deep in her rib cage. All three of them cringed, trying to keep moving when all they really wanted to do was hide.

Above them, the suspended walkways groaned.

Thea and Rory glanced at each other.

Then there was the terrible sound of tearing metal: the kind of thick, solid metal that should never tear. A walkway juddered as if a giant was jumping on it, shuddering violently until one of its welded joints split into ragged teeth, one end swinging down and spraying brittle chaos onto the floor below.

'Run!'

Thea didn't look up again. She looked ahead, her path to the door suddenly a computer game obstacle course of chair legs and falling danger.

She felt Rosie stumble and though she tried to keep a grip on her she couldn't stop her from pitching forward, all three of them tumbling into a heap on the floor.

Despite the heat coming from somewhere, Rosie was pale and her lips mauve. A spreading blot of dark red was already beginning to bloom on the bandage covering her eye.

A crisscrossed square the size of a coffee table thudded into the floor about a metre away from Thea where it stuck, point deep. She whimpered and tugged at Rosie who planted her hands flat on the floor and tried to push herself up.

'Rosie!' Rory shouted, grabbing her under both armpits and hauling her up.

It was only a computer game, Thea told herself. One where, if a massive chunk of scorching walkway fell on her she would simply blip out on the screen and reappear safe and well back at the start. Dodge that chair leg, keep that grip on Rosie, jump that sizzling lump.

Then there was white. Snow.

Cold air hit her.

They were out and on their way to the green where they'd spent hours doing yoga and eating their lunches. Behind them, the Sleep Centre burned against a dimming, late afternoon sky. Had it really been only that morning that Thea had been dragged away from Ethan's body? The previously undamaged Staff Bubble was now ablaze, the top curve of the golf ball completely caved in and the rest of it starting to warp and twist like melting marzipan. Thea, Rory and Rosie picked their way through smouldering debris and headed for the copse of trees on the way to the shore.

The three of them swerved a ruined bedstead that hissed in the snow, the heat searing Thea's back.

'Please,' Rosie gasped, her legs crumpling.

'No! We have to keep going.' Rory yanked her up, her feet now dragging between them, leaving trails in the snow.

Tramlines, Thea thought. Like in that corridor.

She wished she could stop and look back at the building, just take a moment to watch it crumble and fall, fully take in each pop as the windows shattered, each bit of cladding a piece of skin peeling away.

Rosie drooped between them, a toy with her stuffing pulled out.

250

'What are they – up there? Do you see them?' Thea twisted to gaze into the sky, pointing up at the shapes she could see.

They looked like birds from a distance, dark, thin shapes hovering in the sky. But they weren't, Thea realized with mounting terror. Birds didn't hover over a burning building, they got the hell out of there before their wings singed and they plummeted to their death.

'They're not birds, are they?' She turned to Rory who had paled, despite the effort of dragging Rosie around.

'No,' he said, 'they're not. They're drones.'

'Wait … they blew up the Centre by drone? Bombs are heavy, aren't they?' Thea frowned. 'How can a little drone like that carry a bomb?'

'I don't think they can.' Rory hurried her along, panting. 'I think they're just recording the demolition …'

Thea kept an eye on the sky. 'Do you think they can see us?' she said nervously.

'Well, they will if we keep chatting out in the open like we're having a bloody picnic. Move it!'

The old gift shop was nearest and, without needing to decide it amongst themselves, they ran for it. Thea half expected they would have to shoulder the door open, but the handle gave way without a fight and they skidded into the musty black, just as Thea was sure she saw one dark, bird-like shape angle itself away from the others and come straight for them.

Chapter 55

They found themselves in the rotting corpse of a gift shop.

Ing Enterprises hadn't bothered to clear the old place out. As Thea's eyes grew accustomed to the gloom, she made out display cabinets and shelves still full of the souvenirs that sightseers would have snapped up to gift to unsuspecting relatives who would, in turn, donate them to charity as soon as they could. A row of cuddly monks grinned at her, dust cataracts dimming their eyes.

Rory slammed the door shut and Rosie sank to the ground.

The windows were grimy, but Thea tried to peer through, scanning what she could see of the sky.

'Do you think it'll be able to see anything through those windows?' Thea cast around for somewhere to hide.

'It won't need to if it's got thermal vision,' Rory said.

'Huh?'

'Heat detector spots the heat from our bodies – but it might not be able to do that through these walls.'

They quickly checked the windows didn't open, piled anything heavy in front of the door and then they pressed themselves against the walls on either side of a window, Rosie slumped under the sill.

Drones. To Thea, drones were wobbly, whirring things that

children flew in the park, an upgrade on the old toy helicopter. Or they would one day deliver parcels, though no one was very clear when that day would come. The ones she'd read about and seen, they would not help blow up a building; they would not hunt and track and use horrible little sensors on their horrible whirring bodies to hunt down three people who only wanted to get off an island.

Thea was breathing too hard.

She tried to think of something else. And there she was. Back on the green but it was daylight, a bright winter day with just enough sun to keep the chill at bay if you wrapped up warm. There was the smell of the grass and Rosie's chatter, and they had their lunch spread out before them, sorted into piles of "healthy", "too healthy" and "too healthy to actually eat". Then there was Rory with his chocolate, his stolen contraband, and in that freeze-frame of sun and with the sugary sweetness starting to melt on her tongue, in that moment, though she hadn't realized it at the time, she'd been happy. She'd fit in.

'We're going to die, aren't we?' Rosie's face was pale and big-eyed, her swelling and bruising still vivid blues and greens, the dingy bandage hiding the worst of it.

Thea couldn't get her mouth to open to offer any comforting words; the signal between it and her brain had fritzed.

'I saw a programme about field mice during a harvest,' Rosie continued, dreamily. 'The harvester comes, churning up all the wheat, cutting it down, rolling over it and the field mice they run, and they run but they can only get so far. In the end they have nowhere left to run. The harvester gets them. Chopped-up little field mice.'

Rosie's voice took on a faraway quality, as if she wasn't really talking to anyone, only herself. When she'd been little, Thea had read a book about a field mouse family who had escaped the spinning blades of the harvester, despite one of the little baby mice being ill and unable to move. She couldn't remember now how they'd done it. But she wanted to tell Rosie about it, about how the mice could escape, after all.

'That's us, isn't it?' Rosie continued. 'We're chopped-up little field mice. We just haven't quite got to the end of the field.'

She rested her head against the wall and closed her eyes.

'Rosie, keep your eyes open,' Rory whispered, bending to nudge her shoulder.

'Why? I'm tired.'

Thea wanted to sink down with her. Her eyes had begun to throb, holding the beat of a miserable tune that only they could sense. The floating black shapes in front of them melted into the general gloom, which was worse because now the whole place pulsed and squirmed as if she'd got herself stuck in a very dark lava lamp. She blinked a few times, her eyelids almost sticking together each time she did so.

One of the blinks went on longer than she'd meant it to. With a jolt, she bobbed her head up again.

Blink.

Blink.

Bli—

Pain shot through her hand. She'd stabbed herself in the palm with the scissors she'd been carrying in her pocket. Keeping the point embedded she wiggled it slightly, feeling the pain needle, a white-hot focus for her mind.

Just as she was thinking perhaps they had been wrong, perhaps the drone hadn't spotted them after all, that it had just turned in their direction on its own special, drone business – just as she was allowing herself to think of getting to Delores's boat ... something scratched the wall directly behind her.

Thea and Rory tensed.

A bumping, skittery scratch, like a drunken bumblebee careening away from its flower of choice. A questing, snouty little scratch.

Bump, scrape. Bump, scratch.

It came again.

Bump, rasp.

Then, lazily, it made its way along the wall until it knocked and buzzed against the window in the middle of them.

A light flashed in.

Chapter 56

She tried to steady herself using the meditation techniques she'd derided so often in her first few weeks on the island.

One long breath in … and hold it … one long breath out …

The light came from the window between them. It was methodical, the way in which it tracked across the room, starting at the corner furthest from them and meticulously making its way along the floor, no patch escaping its beam.

Eventually it would track its slow careful way right over to them.

Thea nearly forgot to take the in-breath.

Rosie's one good eye was huge in the gloom as she turned her face a little towards Thea. Her hands were pressed up against the wall behind her as if she was holding it back from collapsing and she made a strangled gasping noise. Thea tried to look reassuring, but she wasn't sure that translated well in the dim light.

The snouty, questing scratch had turned into a snouty, questing light.

One long breath in … and hold it … one long breath out … and hold it …

Rosie's mouth stretched wide in fear.

The torchlight beam focused on the far corner, a tea towel

with a print of a saint patting a cow suddenly bright in the spotlight, the cow's face looking almost shocked by the illumination. Then the light slowly crept over display shelves, badges, rows of crucifixes and the line of cuddly toy monks with their stitched smiles.

It paused.

Thea couldn't see what had caught its attention. In her imagination she saw dusty footprints and long sweeping curves in the dirt where they'd moved furniture. Sweat pricked out on her temples. Had they kicked over their tracks?

If they hadn't, a siren would soon sound, flashing red lights would swirl over them, and a team of heavily armed guards would burst through the door—

The light moved on.

One long breath out …

How long did a drone battery last? Thea had absolutely no clue. But it couldn't last forever. That one must have used up a lot of its power playing its part in the explosion. All they had to do was wait it out. At some point it would have to go back to its … hive, or whatever, and they could make a break for it. Unless they just sent new ones. Thea told herself not to think about new drones with freshly charged batteries.

'Thea!' Rory hissed and pointed at Rosie who was shaking. No, not shaking, she was in the middle of a fit: hard, jerking shakes made her body twitch until she slipped down into a heap onto her side. Thea's heart lurched.

'Can it hear us?' she asked.

'I don't know,' Rory said, his voice low, 'but we've got to keep her still!'

The tracking light continued its orderly search of the room, each slow arc taking it just a little nearer to where they crouched.

Thea immediately knelt next to Rosie, not sure what to do, not needing a scissor stab to keep her awake anymore. A weak humming sound came from Rosie's froth-flecked lips. There was something she should be doing, Thea was sure, but all she remembered was that someone in a fit could swallow their tongue, or bite it off, and she tried to keep Rosie on her side.

'What's happening to her?' Thea's voice shook and she turned to Rory who frowned.

In the gloom, Rosie's face became Ethan's and Thea was instantly back at the lighthouse. She could feel the rough carpet under her hands. That moment when she'd known that she'd been wrong to trust Kyle, the moment she'd reached out to knock the headphones away, and Ethan's eyes turned from panicked but still his – recognisably Ethan's – to … nothing. No one's. Another person she hadn't known how to save.

'What do we do?' She looked to Rory.

The light completed another arc and swung closer.

Thea tried to work out angles. They were under the window, through which the beam of light shone. Surely it wouldn't be able to scan the small space directly under it; surely it would have to stop? Thea noted with relief that no other window provided it with a better view.

'We're going to have to keep as close to the wall as we can,' Rory whispered.

Rosie continued to shudder and jerk as the smooth swinging light kept on its path ever nearer to them. It almost hypnotized Thea. She couldn't keep her eyes from it, a frightened field mouse in the gloom. It inched closer.

And closer still.

Holding Rosie proved difficult, so in the end Rory pushed her feet down and Thea took her by the shoulders, her head on her lap, all three of them squashed so tightly against the wall, Thea could smell the mould covering it.

The light crept nearer, skimming over the floor an inch or so away from them.

Thea had never held herself this still in all her life, her heart loud in her ears and her muscles straining.

The light lazily trailed closer to them, so leisurely that Thea was sure it had slowed down on purpose.

It trailed an inch past Thea, then worked its way, so agonizingly close, past Rosie's shoulders, her hips, legs, knees ...

It stopped.

Some dogs, when they hunted, froze to something called a point while they sniffed out whatever game they were tracking, Thea thought wildly. That's what the light was doing. It was trying to sniff them out.

But her thoughts were interrupted when Rosie suddenly arched her back, kicking her feet hard and Thea jolted with her, seeing it almost in slow motion as the light started moving again and Rory's hand was kicked away. He went reeling backwards and Rosie's trainer flailed out.

Heading straight into the beam's tracking light.

It was fitting, Thea decided in a strange, floaty way, as if she was no longer a part of the room but a ghost hovering above it, looking down on them. It was fitting that a scuffed and soggy trainer would be the thing to get them caught; after all, it was what had got them all into this in the first place, her asking: *'Please, miss? May I have some shoes?'*

The light moved closer to Rosie's trainer and the floaty feeling disappeared as Thea slammed back into the room and almost scrambled over her, trying to reach her foot. She imagined the light creeping across the laces and the wall behind them being laser-beamed into smithereens as they were all killed in a blaze of heat and a shower of cuddly monk stuffing.

The light was nearly at the sole of Rosie's shoe.

Thea stretched until her sore shoulder felt ready to pop, but she knew she wouldn't be able to reach her foot in time and could only watch helplessly as the light crept closer and closer and closer ...

But then, with a grunt, Rory heaved himself up and threw himself forward, his fingers grasping on to the padded tongue of

Rosie's trainer, dragging it back with a second to spare as the light washed past them, cool and white.

They cowered in the shadows.

One long breath in … and hold the breath …

Dust flitted in the beam of light as it reached the end of its arc and halted.

Then it blinked out.

Chapter 57

Almost as soon as the light went out and the scratching stopped, Rosie flopped into a horrible stillness.

Blood seeped from her nose.

Thea gathered her up and stroked the hair away from her face. 'Rory?'

He put his finger to his lips again and carefully peered out of the window.

'I think it's gone—' he began but stopped when he turned and saw Rosie's limp body.

Rory's expression as he unclipped and unwound the padding told Thea all she needed to know. She could only manage one glance at the seeping, raw-meat mess of Rosie's eye before she had to turn away, but she couldn't escape the smell. Rosie shivered, a sick heat coming from her.

'We shouldn't have moved her,' he said, slumping next to them, his head in his hands.

'What do we do?' Thea gripped his arm.

So far, there had always been something to do, hadn't there? Run, hide, hit … *kill*. And she'd done it.

There had to be something. Rory hung his head.

'Rosie?' she said gently. She thought that maybe Rosie's eyelids flickered, but in the shadows it was hard to tell. She murmured something incoherent and new blood seeped from her nose. Thea held on tighter.

Something squeezed at Thea's throat, making her light-headed.

What happened next did not happen quickly, nor was it peaceful.

'We should get help!'

But there was no help to get, no one left but the two of them, kneeling in the dust.

Sometimes, Rosie knew what was happening, and they were the worst times. A hand like a claw, a rasping voice that tried for words but ended in a whimper.

'It will be okay,' Thea soothed over and over, that word, *okay*, said so many times that it bruised and softened until it tasted rotten in her mouth.

Thea held her the whole time.

She gave up on words. Instead, she just lay down next to Rosie and put her head close to hers, holding her hand and kissing her cheek, letting her know someone was there with her, even though it was dark, and where Rosie was going was darker still.

Eventually, words stopped and only breathing was left.

At some point, Thea moved to rest her head on Rosie's chest, listening to her weak, jumpy heartbeat.

She stayed that way for what felt like a very long time, each beat heard a relief, a rhythm and a song with only one lyric, a plea: 'Keep beating.'

Until it stopped.

She'd held Rosie the entire time, but death is a letting go and, after what could have been hours, could have been days, finally, there was no other choice …

Thea let go.

She didn't want to lift her head and see Rosie's face, still and slack, but she did because that's what the living have to do – those who survive, they have to look at death again and again, stare it in the face and then try to remember why they keep going.

There was still a little hand-drawn heart around one disc on Rosie's temple.

Words and thoughts and tears would come later. All of her grief, hot and tumbling, would pour out.

But not yet.

Thea clamped her hands over her mouth as her vision blurred. She squeezed them tight because if she let go she wasn't sure what was going to come out of her mouth, some unholy howl that would break her eggshell-thin body.

Thea half waited for the production team to call "cut" and the scene to be dismantled, chunks of set rolled away, the gift shop opening up like a doll's house. Rosie would be helped up, laughing with the crew and brushing dust from her hair. Someone would pass them coffees and give them thick coats and fur-lined boots to wear while they waited for the crew to reset.

She sat in the silent dark.

Swallowing down the lump in her throat, she concentrated on the patterns in the dust on the floor as if there might be an important message in there, one that would only be revealed when she stared hard enough.

'In the lighthouse,' – Rory's voice seemed to come from very far away even though he was right next to her – 'I didn't know what would happen to Ethan, but, so you know, even if I had, I would have tried to save you first.'

Thea closed her eyes, watched the colours pulse on the edges of the blackness. Her hand found Rory's, at first her palm lightly on top of his until their fingers intertwined. She put her head on his shoulder and he shifted to take the weight, her head fitting neatly into the side of his neck where his heartbeat pulsed. She needed to hear it thump.

'I couldn't think of him,' Rory said quietly. 'All I could think about was you.'

He slumped next to her and hearing his breathing, when Rosie's had stilled forever, was a torment and a comfort at the same time.

Thea needed a drink, something so alcoholic that one sniff would be enough to numb her and block out thought. Her head pounded and she was so empty that if someone tapped her the sound would echo. But the problem with emptiness was that it could be filled – and Thea knew what was waiting to rush in if she let it. She continued to stare at the dust.

Even though they would probably be killed before they found the boat, even though the boat itself could then be tracked easily enough, even though the chance of escape from all this was laughable … she was going to try.

For Rosie.

She was a tiny cog in a big mechanism, but sometimes tiny cogs could make a difference, couldn't they? A small wrong move from one of them could wreck the whole damn machine.

Chapter 58

Vivian stood on the clifftop, lighthouse-bright with the sheer force of her rage.

It was morning. She cursed the waves below her, stupid frothy things that were to blame because they had gnawed at the land in the first place and eventually chewed off that chunk of island. She cursed the island for not having more staying power, for not clinging on to the mainland with all of its might – for allowing itself to be eaten away.

She was cold, and her feet ached. It was intolerable: the standing, the uncertainty, the sense that she had got stuck somehow and she couldn't work out how to free herself. Was this what old and out-of-date felt like? Standing on a cliff edge knowing something important was going on around you but with no way to get to it?

Footsteps sounded behind her.

'Here.' Alastair shoved the flask at her. 'Coffee. The good stuff, not instant.'

'I thought meals weren't provided?'

'Ain't a meal. It's coffee.'

Vivian was grateful for it. Alastair helped her pour and she sipped as she considered him. She couldn't be sure but there were definitely fewer ragged edges to his clothes today and he'd tried shaving. Unsuccessfully.

'What are you waiting for?' he asked.

'Nothing, Alastair.' Vivian sighed. 'Absolutely nothing. I'm not waiting for anything because nothing is coming. I couldn't find a boat. And anyway, if I had, what was I going to do? I'm nearly seventy. Did I think I could ride in, a geriatric in a rowboat, and save the day?'

She stared at the island. 'What is happening to her over there? What are they doing? You see the smoke, don't you? You heard that sound?'

Alastair nodded. They both watched the smudge of grey as it funnelled down to a point hidden by the island's hills.

'This is like one of those awful anxiety dreams you get when you're a parent. You have to get to your child but you can't, no matter how hard you try, or how many roads you go down, and then you wake up in a cold sweat, relieved it was all a dream. Except I've been trying to wake up for bloody days.'

He poured her another cup of coffee; the wind was getting in through the gaps of her coat and making her shiver.

'I've summoned the troops of course.'

'Army?' He frowned.

'Nearly.' She smiled. 'I'm part of a … well, we jokingly call ourselves The Menopausal Army. Of course, that joke's a bit past its sell-by date, now. We're well out of the menopause. But we raise awareness on issues we think are important. People call us conspiracy theorists. I prefer the term "activist".'

'Menopausal Army …' Alastair chuckled, then said more seriously, 'But maybe we should call the police? Seems like this 'as become somethin' they should deal with …'

Vivian shrugged. 'I have a horrible feeling that it doesn't matter who comes, or how many. By that time, it'll all be over. It'll be too late.'

It felt like the day before getting sick, Vivian thought, when you weren't sick yet, but you could feel it developing: the hot rasp in the back of the throat, the thirst, the headache building behind your eyes. There was nothing to do but wait for the universe to pummel her.

So, this is where she would be when it came.

'Gotta boat, if you want it.'

Vivian's gasp hitched in her throat.

'What?' she whispered.

'Gotta boat,' Alastair repeated, not looking at her but out towards the island. 'Didn't tell you about it before, when you asked, but ... well, I've been doing some thinking since then. I'm done with this place. I likes the quiet but there's quiet and there's dead. Time to move on.'

Vivian was too scared to breathe.

'Your girl,' he said quietly, 'I remember her. I remember them all. They looked ... tired. And sad. All of 'em. I took the money because it was offered and they were a big, important business, they told me. But now? Your girl. Flames and smoke.' He paused and stared at the horizon. 'You wouldn't know because everyone's gone now but this used to be a good place once, a happy place. It shouldn't be *this*.'

He screwed the cap back on the flask and cleared his throat.

'I think I can get a boat. If you want to get there, we can try.'

Emptiness all around her: sea, sky, land for miles.

'I do,' Vivian breathed. 'I want to get there.'

'Right then.'

He stalked off and Vivian knew she would need to hurry after him. But she wanted to hold this moment in her head, this fluttering of hope once more, this feeling that she could still do something, she could still ride to the rescue of her little girl.

Two geriatrics in a rowboat.

Because that other feeling was still there, wasn't it? The sick feverish belch of something horrific lying in wait for her. It was coming. No matter what she did, how much she scurried around, how many people she roped into her cause, it was always there. She hadn't ever deserved a daughter like Thea; she'd got lucky.

And her luck was about to run out.

Chapter 59

The worst part was leaving Rosie.

They wrapped her in monk-made blankets, closed her eyes and smoothed her hair.

Another body to leave behind.

Then they dragged away the things they'd piled in front of the door as a barricade and both put their hands over the doorknob, looking at each other one final time.

'Ready?'

'No.' It was the first word she'd spoken since Rosie had died. 'Wait.' She picked up one of the cuddly monks from a nearby shelf, blew the dust from it and placed it gently in the crook of Rosie's arm.

They pushed the door open into a harsh, white world.

The air scoured Thea's eyeballs, which was good because they needed it. She took a deep breath and blinked at the snow and a sky so blue it looked like a glass bowl over them. Time had slipped away from Thea since she had left the lighthouse, but the daylight had a freshness to it that felt like morning. The gift shop had swallowed a whole evening. A day had gone past. Only a day.

They walked, quickly, to the cover provided by the copse of trees, Thea taking unsteady, drunken steps. Weirdly, she'd felt more awake in the dim light of the gift shop. Out here, the daylight seared its way through her eyes and burned a headache into her temples. A part of her wanted to slump into the snow and sleep until the white covered her up completely. She stabbed the point of the scissors into her palm and kept walking.

Despite thinking of them back at the Centre, there had been no time to get boots or warmer clothes and Thea's feet were soon soggy and freezing again. At any moment she anticipated the whine of a bullet zinging past her ear, and then another into her spine where she'd fall, like an animal tracked in the woods, bleeding out and terrified until someone came to cut her throat.

No, no, no. No thinking of things like that. Think of the plan. It was ambitious to call it a plan but it was all they had. Rory and the other sleep techs had seen a map of the island at their own orientation day where all the no-go areas had been pointed out.

'Just around from the main beach is a cove, not a beach, kind of like a rocky outcrop and a cave where a boat could, in theory, be hidden from view. Launching it would be tricky though because of the rocks.'

They would launch it. It wouldn't be the hardest thing she'd had to do over the last few days. The boat would take them to land and they would escape. They would make it. The universe owed them that.

Amongst the trees, feeling safer even though they probably weren't, they both took a second or so to look back at the Sleep Centre. Framed by arching branches, it took on a sci-fi gothic all of its own. It was a smoking husk, the two huge spheres now half destroyed, charred streaks running down their curves, their insides spilled out onto the snow where the explosions had thrown them. Thea had been here a few weeks ago. She had taken this path with Harriet, but it had been night then and she had been full of … trepidation, yes, but also excitement. Because this place had held a promise for her then, a nebulous hard-to-believe promise that she could be fixed, that she could live the kind of life she imagined others lived: bright-eyed and energetic.

'I've been hallucinating,' she confessed.

Rory turned to her.

'Twice, I think. I refused Delores's trial but … well, there was at least a week wearing those bloody discs where I was waiting for Rosie to be well enough to move … anything could have been tested on me in that time and I think, maybe, it was …'

No whirring black objects appeared in the sky, but she gazed at it anyway because it was easier than looking at Rory.

'I didn't sleep. And I felt fine.' She paused and chewed on her lip. 'And we know what happens after the hallucinating …'

Blank stare. Drool.

Rory took a moment before he said anything. 'You probably need to just get some sleep.'

And it was exactly what she'd wanted him to say. Lie, if he had to. Each time she blinked she was afraid that the blink would go on for far too long.

They trudged through the wood towards the beach, but at least they trudged together. Thea liked the way the trees closed in around them, not just because their branches blocked out much of the sky, and what could be flying in it, but because they felt friendly. Soft peeling bark and cushiony velour moss – not hard-edged concrete, glass that shattered too easily and a glossy plastic sheen that could close over a person's face.

Their steps were muffled by the snow.

They would make it, Thea thought again, even though their steps were leaving a clear and easily trackable print right from the door of the gift shop.

She was aware she should say something to Rory. He was walking beside her and hadn't said much since the gift shop where they had sat side by side, shell-shocked.

'All I could think about was you.'

That was something that needed a reply, wasn't it? The thing was, Thea couldn't even begin to think what her response to that should be. She had spent much of her sleep-deprived life a dead tree, hollowed out and brittle, the nothingness at her heart grown around by fragile, flaky layers. But she had seen pictures of fires inside those hollowed-out trees, a deep, burning orange.

It could happen.

'The beach.' Rory put an arm out to stop her. She'd been so engrossed in her own thoughts she hadn't been paying attention to her surroundings. They hid behind one of the last trees before the copse gave way to the shore.

There were people milling about on the beach, wrapped up in padded coats and thick boots that made Thea's feet throb with jealousy. A small boat, no bigger than the one that had brought Thea to the island all those weeks ago, was moored nearby.

'But, I don't think everyone is here yet. We can't leave!'

That was a voice she recognized. She peered around the tree at Harriet only a few metres away from her, tucked up in a coat that was more like a duvet and gesticulating at a man with his back to them, dressed in black outdoor gear with a crackling walkie-talkie clipped to his belt.

'Ma'am. We have orders. We only have a few people left to evacuate and we'd like to do it while we've got the weather with us.'

'But, the explosions! We all heard them—'

'Controlled explosions. The building is unsafe. Everyone will be accounted for and, anyway, that is not your concern—'

'But …' Harriet sighed and looked around her, as if searching for help in her argument, shifting her weight from foot to foot, undecidedly.

Instead of seeing help, however, what she saw in its place was Thea.

Chapter 60

The world did not freeze whilst the two women stared at each other because that is not what worlds do.

Harriet didn't gasp, or point; she didn't even raise her eyebrows. Thea held herself very still, fixed by Harriet's gaze, a pinned butterfly too exhausted to even wriggle.

Perhaps Harriet's eyes widened a little, perhaps she stared for a little too long – whatever the reason, the man with his back to them shifted and half-turned his head.

'Ms Stowe? Are you all right?'

There was only Harriet and Thea and the look stretching between them like putty, binding them. The rest of the beach, Rory, the boat – all of that was just scenery.

'I …'

Thea was aware of the cold snow she was kneeling in, how her kneecaps had numbed. She was aware of Rory breathing next to her and the wrinkled bark of the tree that had not hid her well enough.

Harriet snapped her gaze back to the black-clad man. 'I'm fine.'

Thea pressed her forehead against the crumbling bark of the tree and felt her heartbeat thud in her throat.

The man turned and peered into the trees. 'You looked as if you'd seen something,' he said suspiciously.

Thea darted out of sight.

'What? No. I didn't see anything ...'

There was a pause big enough to contain a whole life. Rory was pale, sweat beading on his forehead despite the cold.

She heard snow crunch and squeak as footsteps moved closer to them.

'Wait!' Thea could hear the panic in Harriet's voice. 'I think it was a ... a fox or ... something ...'

'This is an island, Ms Stowe. There aren't any foxes on here. Unless they swam across.'

More crunching. Closer again.

'No! No, of course not! My imagination, been here too long, probably. I should get on the boat, yes? Like you said?'

But the crunching continued, far too loud, far too close and then, suddenly, there he was, near enough for Thea to see the light blinking on his walkie-talkie and the grey in his hair, near enough to stretch out and grab his leg. He had his back to them. Harriet came floundering behind, snow puffing up around her steps.

'Over there!' She pointed in the opposite direction to Thea. 'That's where I was looking. Not that there's anything there. I'm just spooked by this place. Shouldn't we go back?'

The words tumbled from her too quickly, too loudly. Thea couldn't see the man's face, but she imagined he was eyeing her with a frown.

A few electrical signals from brain to neck muscle, a small movement of the head as it turned; that would be all it would take from this man. He would find her and Rory and that would be it. Whatever "it" turned out to be. Thea suspected it did not involve a trip back to the mainland and a warm drink.

But, miraculously, the man headed over to where Harriet pointed. Whilst he was walking the few steps away, Harriet turned to Thea, two hectic spots of red on her cheeks, her eyes huge, the panic thrumming off her as if she was a badly played theremin.

That's when Thea saw their tracks, fresh trails in the snow, leading right to them.

Harriet saw them too and, checking that the man wasn't looking, stumbled over to them, dragging her feet and taking great gouges out of the snow as the man bent to inspect something further away.

They could hit him, Thea thought wildly. She cast about for a weapon, a handy tree bough or one of Harriet's stilettos, except she was wearing snow boots with useless flat rubber soles. Thea could tell Harriet was thinking the same thing but there was just snow and the rocks on the beach were too far away.

'I should get on the boat, now, hmm?' Harriet tried again, moving to block his view of Thea and Rory's tree as they shifted around it, trying to keep out of sight.

He stood up and turned, wiping the snow from his gloved hands, leaving white patches on his trousers. Harriet moved and then Thea could only see her boots, the way that clumps of snow clung to the waterproof material, before melting. There one minute, then gone.

There was just the quiet of the trees, a gentle shushing of branches rubbing together, most of the leaves long fallen and rotted away. There was no birdsong and daylight crisscrossed the snowy forest floor in a delicate latticework design. If the man saw her, all that would be left of her would be a dent in the snow.

Above her, Harriet crossed her fingers behind her back.

The walkie-talkie at the man's waist crackled.

There was a tinny voice that Thea couldn't catch, but then the man spoke. 'What? Say that again? Over.'

Harriet shifted her feet. Crackle, crackle, a smudge of a voice. 'Copy that.'

More crunching of snow.

'I've got to go back to the Centre, Ms Stowe. But I'm getting you on this boat first.'

'Of course! Of course. Lead the way.'

Harriet's boots disappeared and the footsteps retreated. Thea wished she could have seen Harriet's face one last time, to somehow show her in a silent look that she was grateful, indescribably grateful for what she had just done and that she would remember it – and her – for as long as she lived.

However long that was to be.

'Let's go,' Rory whispered.

Chapter 61

The blank whiteness of snow on the ground started to make Thea's eyes ache. It burned through to her brain.

She felt very visible as they veered off through the trees and started to climb sharply, roughly following a coastal path. Thea's leg muscles protested at the sudden exercise. She wasn't sure if it was the brightness of the snow, or the lack of food, drink, and sleep but the world was starting to spin.

Her shoulder remained stiff from the fall she'd taken with Ethan at the lighthouse but she kind of quite liked that dull ache. In a way she didn't want it to heal because when it did, there would be nothing left to remind her of him.

Ethan was already fading.

Rosie was a body they'd left behind.

They only had ghosts for company.

The track started to level off and they found themselves on the cliff path once more, acutely aware that they could be clearly seen, two little sitting-duck silhouettes against the sky. So they crawled the final stretch, hands numb from the shock of the snow.

Thea's body took over. All she had to do was keep putting hand in front of hand, knee in front of knee; it was simple. Her brain snagged and caught in a loop that would have made no sense to anyone but her: she was a burning tree and, on each of her branches, ghosts were tied like bobbing balloons.

Burning tree, ghost balloons, burning tr—

Finally, in front of them were the rough stone steps that led down to the cove.

'Down there.' Rory pointed. 'That's where the boat could be, if it's still there.'

The steps were treacherous, the kind of stone that was lethal when wet and positively murderous when covered with ice and a smattering of snow. Though it wasn't elegant, they took the steps toddler-style, sliding down on their bottoms: more elegant than slipping and breaking a leg, or tumbling head-first into the rocks.

She was a burning tree.

With bobbing ghost balloons.

Thea couldn't shake the feeling that all of this was wrong. Why had they been allowed to get this far? Why wasn't anyone chasing them, or already waiting for them on these steps? Had they really escaped the full might of whatever was hulking behind Ing Enterprises, a shadowy beast of a corporation that could wipe out what happened here with one smack of its paw? She wanted to think she was clever enough to escape, but she couldn't quite convince herself. It was chance that had got her this far and now … something else … was taking her the rest of the way.

'Wait!' she called out to Rory.

He stopped on the step below her and swivelled awkwardly. 'What?'

Thea rubbed her hands together, trying to rub some warmth back into them. They were out of sight of the beach and below them swirled the sea, gulls diving with raucous shrieks, freewheeling in the air.

'Doesn't this feel wrong? We should have been caught by now …'

'Is this about me again? Do you think I'm leading you into a trap? God, Thea, I just want to get off this island as much as you do.' He glared at her, the hollows of his eyes a bruised grey, his jacket too thin for the cold.

'No, I—'

'How many more times do I have to tell you?'

She stood on the steps with screeching above her and swirling below.

'I believe you,' she said, her voice hoarse, not able to meet his eyes at first, but when she did she saw how his own had softened. There was a lot in the gaze that passed between them, a quiet calm binding them together on those steps at the edge of the island.

It was Rory who started moving again in their absurd, almost comical descent of the steps and Thea was left sitting where she was. Burning tree, bobbing ghost balloons – lab rat in the maze. The only difference now was that they had widened the maze, made it so big she thought it was freedom, until she came upon the inevitable dead end and sharp jolt of electricity.

It was just a matter of time.

She kept going because at least down in the cove there would be more shelter from the wind.

She didn't expect to see a boat waiting for them in the dark arch of the cove.

She expected Delores to have been lying, as she had lied about so many things before. She expected it to be somewhere else, somewhere further from the beach, somewhere more hidden; God she half expected Delores to be there waiting for her, her spike-heeled boots planted firmly on the slippery rock, her bright hair holding back the shadows.

So it was a huge surprise when she thumped down some more steps and the cove came into sight.

With a small, empty boat in it.

Chapter 62

The small boat was jauntily painted in blue and white, with a motor at the back and varnished wooden seats set into the sides.

Jaunty but no longer moored.

It had been at one time, but high waves, or faulty knot-tying, meant that now it had floated over to the other side of the cove and got itself stuck on a rock.

'We could walk across ...' Rory offered.

This was not a pleasant sunbathing cove where couples would go to jump off the cliff edge into the clear waters below, shrieking happily. If they did, they would shriek only because, as they landed, the rocks would tear them apart. Instead, this cove was a shelf of slick rock interrupted at its deepest point by a cave, guarded by huge boulder teeth so jagged and steep there was no way they could climb over them.

They could see the boat but they couldn't get to it.

Rory slithered to the edge and looked at the water that separated them from the bobbing boat.

'We could swim it.'

Rory could, perhaps – if his heart didn't seize up in the cold water.

'I can't swim.'

'What?' Rory gaped at her. 'Everyone can swim! You just can't swim very far. You can float, right?'

Her first ever swimming lesson had been when she was about six or seven. It had been centred on learning to float. She'd worn her little inflatable armbands and the rubbery swimming cap that snapped tightly on her forehead. Holding on to the edge of the pool, she'd kicked out her legs and let them float behind her, feeling that this swimming thing was going to go well … until she let go of the side as encouraged, and promptly sank. She'd never again got past the sinking stage.

'Everyone can float!' Rory said.

She started to shake. She was not a burning tree; she was a freezing woman who couldn't swim.

Rory held the tops of her arms. 'I'll help you. It's not far and it's probably not that deep either. We have to. It's our only chance.'

Thea stood and eyed the rocks at the cave mouth that were blocking their path. Maybe it wouldn't be so hard to climb them, after all? All it would take was a delicate balancing on a knife edge and a few impossible leaps …

Easy.

Her foot slithered on a patch of slime and shot out from under her. She flailed her arms ineffectually as Rory caught her around the waist and steadied her. They held on to each other like that for a few seconds, scared to move in case they slipped again.

Around them the sea slapped against the rocks and the dark cave loomed behind, taking the sound of the waves and dragging it into its depths, so it could twist and torture it. There would be bats in there, maybe, or maybe years ago smugglers had used this cave to store their loot taken from shipwrecks. Thea had read somewhere that on islands like this the whole community would come down to the shore if there was a ship floundering, not to help, but to take it apart with pickaxes and strip it of its cargo. Perhaps even beacons up on the cliff had lured unsuspecting vessels to their doom.

Thinking about smugglers and bats took her mind off how she was still clutching Rory, his bulk steadying her and also sheltering her from the wind. From far away it would look like they were caught in a fervent embrace, the cave and the rocks providing a dramatic background.

'All I could think about was you.'

The words remained between them, like static.

'I have a memory stick,' Thea blurted out, not quite sure why she was speaking but barrelling on. 'Moses gave it to me in the lighthouse. Proof of what the technology can do.'

Rory tilted his head. His face was very close to hers.

'You should take it, in case – I mean, it's got to make it out and I can't— I might …'

His expression when she finally looked him in the eye was enough to make her breath hitch. 'You will make it,' he said. 'We will make it. Okay?'

She nodded because any words were jammed tight in her throat.

'But,' he added, turning to the waves again and letting go of her arms, 'you should put it in the zip pocket of your jacket to be safe. It's waterproof.'

She felt dizzy without his support but squared her shoulders and edged closer to the flat rocks where the water swirled, trying to remember everything that swimming instructor had told her years ago.

'Should we take off our shoes?'

'They're pretty lightweight. And they're another layer against the cold water.'

'It looks quite … choppy.' She swallowed.

'But …' Rory bent to grab at a bit of frayed rope that had been tied around a cone-shaped rock. 'I think this is where the boat was moored. So if we go in here, maybe the current will just carry us straight to it.'

That "if" was so big, it dwarfed Thea. It was best not to think about it, or about anything.

282

She edged out some more and then sat on the rock, holding her feet up, ready to push herself in. Rory sat down next to her.

'It's going to be really cold. Remember to breathe. Keep hold of me.'

Experimentally she dipped her feet into the water but the iciness of it grabbed at her and she yanked her feet back.

If the past few days had taught her anything, it was that the key to bravery was not to think too much about what you were about to do. Thea pushed herself in.

Chapter 63

The air in her lungs was driven out and replaced by ice.

Thea opened her mouth to gulp and more freezing water slapped in. A huge iron bar wrapped itself around her chest and started its inexorable crushing. She couldn't feel her body, couldn't see the boat, couldn't tell if Rory still held on to her arm. The only thing she could focus on was keeping her head above water.

She was a burning tree.

Her ghost balloons would keep her afloat.

She tried to keep her eyes on Rory, but the water was a hand that batted her this way and that, twisting and turning her until all she could think about was "water" and "not water". It was a strong hand too, much stronger than she had expected and she spat out the salty water it tried to shove into her mouth.

Rory was in front of her and he had her by the arm.

Then he was gone.

A half-scream, half-strangled gulping noise came from her throat.

There was nothing to hold on to, no tiled side of the pool to grab whilst she kicked her legs behind her. She flailed but the water was now a long icy sheet. The more she struggled, the more it wound around her, a shroud, dragging her down.

'Thea!'

She couldn't see him, but she felt a tugging, something trying to pull her on, not down, but the icy sheet was stronger than either of them had imagined and it yanked her away.

It was not a rollercoaster ride, because when you sat in one of those you knew that eventually it would end and you would get out again, possibly a bit wet, possibly a bit nauseous, but free to carry on your day eating candyfloss and trying to win cuddly toys.

There was no candyfloss waiting for Thea.

Without Rory's arm there was nothing to cling to, just the water that 'wanted to help you float, you just had to let it,' according to her old instructor. But then she'd been in a calm, chlorine-scented leisure centre pool, not this twisting, churning, slamming water that didn't want anything, and it certainly didn't want to help.

Water closed over her head.

There was a horrible feeling of pressure, pushing up against her eyeballs, filling her ears, shoving fingers up her nose. A plunger had sucked itself over her face so tightly, she almost heard the pop. She breathed out.

For a second it was peaceful, dark and quiet, all sound muted to a gentle blur. A warmth came from inside her, such a beautifully delicious warmth that it made her want to curl up in it and close her eyes. She went limp.

So peaceful.

Warm like a burrow, like her mother's living room with its joss sticks and hot tea and women talking.

Then it wasn't.

She tried to take a breath in and suddenly she was sinking and choking and flailing and fighting all at once, the warmth swiped away and her heart hammering at the icy band across her chest as if it could crack. There wasn't time to think about anything apart from breathing and moving. She had to move. She kicked and pushed herself upwards, her arms reaching for a surface she knew was there; she just had to find it. And she kept kicking, she kept moving, even though her lungs were bursting and soon her eyes would follow. She kicked and pushed and eventually her hand broke through into air.

Someone grabbed it.

She reared out of the sea, coughing and gasping, expecting any second to be snatched back under again. The cold dropped over her head like a frozen wet cloth and she felt arms under her armpits, dragging her, stopping her from sinking.

When she reached out, she felt smooth, varnished wood and she tried to cling to it, her throat beginning to burn as Rory pulled at her but her hands slipped on the polish and she felt the world tilt once more, the dark, waiting depths opening its mouth for her again …

Rory hauled her up.

Chapter 64

Thea was a burning tree.

Her lungs, chest and throat were on fire. She slithered onto the boat and lay where she'd collapsed, retching and coughing until she vomited sea water. It was only when she sat up a little and wiped at her mouth, pushing her hair away from her face, that she noticed Rory sprawled next to her. His chest heaved and water seeped from him.

This time, when she began to shake, she was certain that it would never stop. It came from her very core, some tuning fork within her that had been struck hard.

Rory staggered to his feet and the boat rocked violently.

'I'll …' But his voice ended in wordless chattering.

The boat had a little covered wooden-framed front with wild-flowers painted on it. Thea wondered why the wildflower person had sold their treasured boat to Delores.

Maybe the wildflower person had been Delores. Once.

'Here.' Rory handed her a coat and a blanket. 'They were all I could find. Take off as many of your wet clothes as you can.'

With fingers that seemed to have doubled in size she wrapped herself in the dry clothes and they both huddled in the front of the boat where the covered wooden frame offered some meagre protection from the cold.

'Do you know how to work the motor?' Thea asked as she found gloves in the pocket of the coat.

'No, but how hard can it be?'

The engine actually proved harder to work out than Rory had thought. But one of the books Thea had read in her wide-awake nights at the Centre had featured just such a boat as this. The engine was an outboard motor, she told him. She lowered the propeller and plugged in the kill switch – the device that would shut off the motor if they were thrown overboard and save them from being chopped up by the propellers. She then looped the cable over her wrist.

Together, they pushed themselves away from the rock and pulled the handle of the motor for the third time, Rory's mouth a grim line of determination.

'Can you flood a boat engine?' Rory asked anxiously. 'Shouldn't we just wait a few minutes before you try again?'

He looked like he wanted to kick it, but instead stopped and let go of the handle.

A few minutes was a long time. Especially when Thea was anxiously scanning the cliffs and jumping at every scrape of the boat against the rock. It was also probably the longest time lately that she'd had to just think without reacting to whatever latest horror was unfolding around her.

She thought about her mother, perhaps at this very minute making up placards with Thea's face on them (hopefully a good shot, not one of her awful passport pictures) ready to storm the Ing Enterprises building. Not that that would do any good – it was just a building, the people within it easily removed to another location at a whim. Anyway, Ing Enterprises itself was owned by Aspire, the bigger parent company calling the actual shots. And Vivian would have no clue how to go about finding them.

Stay away from it, Mother, Thea thought, tears stinging her eyes. Stay away from this because it's too big for you. It's not your world and it will eat you up. The idea of her mother in danger because of her stupid decision to take part in the trial was too much for Thea to bear. She pushed the thought down, but her brain was a badly packed suitcase and it had had a lot stuffed into it over the last few days, much of it waiting to spring back up again.

She was a burning tree.

With bobbing ghost balloons.

In her hallucination, the boat she'd been in with her mother had been full of baby owls and this boat was full too. She was taking the dead with her. Rosie and Ethan, but also all the others: Moira, Richard, the guy with the shark-tooth necklace who'd spoken to her during yoga, and every other person who'd joined the sleep trial with her. Kyle. Even Delores and Moses. They'd be with her for the rest of her life.

'What are you going to do? If we make it?' Thea asked.

Rory considered her, both of them moving gently in time with the waves. A gull screeched and Thea couldn't help but flinch; it sounded like a warning, like panic.

'Forget this ever happened.' Rory sniffed. 'Hide. Get a normal job and change my name. Survive.'

The word was unspoken between them: *if*. *If* we get to the shore. *If* we don't capsize ourselves or get intercepted. *If* there isn't a crew waiting for us on the mainland. *If* we find a way to get from the tiny deserted ghost village to a city, any city. *If, if, if …*

And then if she got to that mythical city, before she got warm, or a shower or food, first she would have to get that memory stick out – that was still in the zip pocket of her jacket, and she would have to … do something with it.

Right now, she couldn't think what that something should be, but she knew it would be a big task. It would require someone equally big to take it on. Fearless. The thing was, despite being a

289

burning tree with bobbing ghost balloons, despite everything that had happened to her on the island and everything she had done in response (*wet, thudding sound of an axe meeting flesh*) she wasn't sure she was the *right* person.

But she was the *only* person.

Her thoughts were her own. Her own head, her own dreams or nightmares were not tampered with, taken out and held up to the light, squeezed or moulded like plasticine. What went on inside her brain – be it weird, disappointing, or depressing – was hers. Ing Enterprises, Aspire, whoever they bloody were, did not respect that.

She would do it for the dead who crowded into the boat with her. Not because she wanted to, but because if she didn't do it, no one else would. Maybe then the ghost balloons would float away.

A few minutes was up.

'What are you going to do, when we get to the shore?' Rory asked as she once again choked the engine, put the motor to neutral and grasped the handle on the pull rope, pulling it back until all the slack was gone.

What would she do?

Once the contents of the memory stick were out in the world, what would she do then?

She was a burning tree. She wouldn't let that fire go out. If they made it, she would sleep the hours she was meant to sleep whenever she was meant to sleep them. She would stop battling and instead accept it as a part of her, much like the shape of her nose or the colour of her hair. In those hours in which she was awake, she would *live* for once.

Not hollowed out anymore.

The rope tightened and Thea yanked the handle back, her eyes on Rory, both of them praying to a god in which they did not believe that the engine would splutter and start.

It coughed.

And again.

And then it chugged into life. They sat there for a second, staring at it, and then they both did something they hadn't done for what seemed like a lifetime – they smiled. But Thea realized that what she really wanted to do was scream, loud and long, until she was doubled over with no breath left, so hoarse it hurt.

They carefully edged the boat out into the sea, Thea keeping her eyes on a mainland she knew would soon start to appear out of the haze.

'What am I going to do?' she said lightly, not looking back at the island as they came out of the shadow of its cliffs.

She smiled again.

'I don't know,' she said, paused and her smile widened. 'Yet.'

Behind them, the island paled into the background, a dissolving watercolour. But Thea didn't look behind her, she gazed straight ahead, watching the white ripples of water being pushed from the boat's prow.

She kept her eyes on the mainland.

Chapter 65

The map took up one entire wall. It was a map of the world, coloured black and outlined in white; on it, little red dots shone like hellish stars.

The barefoot man, dressed in unbleached cream cotton, didn't have to have the map beamed on the wall, it was not as if he *needed* it.

He liked it.

A warm breeze billowed out the white voile that hung over the terrace doors.

The terrace led to the pool where, that morning, he had already swum his allotted lengths and, next to it, he had eaten his carefully compiled breakfast, swallowing the accompanying tablets.

He was waging a war, one that had been ongoing for years. It was a war against his body, which wanted to degrade, decay, defragment like a badly maintained computer hub. He would not let it. He had the money for nootropic supplements, exercise, nutrition, meditation and education to stop the rot. But that was the thing, as the years had gone by, he realized he didn't want to merely *stop* the rot anymore ... he wanted to *transform* it.

Aspire had been born.

'Sir?'

He had been about to begin his first micro-nap. The staff knew that. He would not get irritated by this interruption, however, as irritation led to a spike in cortisol, which was napalm for the nervous system.

He nodded.

'Sir?' The man was poorly dressed for the heat, dark blooms of sweat flowering the armpits of his shirt with its too-tight, buttoned-up collar. 'I have had an update from St Dunstan's.'

The barefoot man found the little red dot on the map. The island. It was one of his favourite trials. He'd met Moses once, many years ago, when he'd just been starting out with his shiny new sleep idea. An over-caffeinated man with bloodshot eyes and poor skin but he'd had an idea for sleep technology that made the barefoot man's heart beat faster, cortisol be damned. It started with fixing sleep issues, but the end result? Well, the end result was altogether something more interesting.

It was a technology that, eventually, became part of his arsenal.

Increasingly, as Aspire grew to take in other technology, gene therapy and medication, the barefoot man had found himself waging war not just against the body, but also against the old world, the old way of doing things, the old order. Disappointingly he discovered that governments were hardly worthy adversaries because they couldn't keep up with the pace of this change and didn't understand its scope. Even when they did, legislation then worked so slowly they were destined to lose the battle before they'd even realized they were in it.

There were plenty of others who understood the potential.

Sweat Stain edged into the room. 'St Dunstan's has been compromised, sir.'

'How?'

'The problems with the trial proved insurmountable. The full evacuation policy has been activated.'

Full evacuation policy. He knew what that meant, and he sighed. Regrettable.

As if on cue, one of the red lights on his map began to blink.

The jarring dissonance of that blinking light against all the other steady, unwavering ones was perturbing. He didn't like it.

Sweat Stain was nearly at his elbow. Too close. The barefoot man could smell his cologne, just about, under the stench of meaty perspiration. Perfumes were beautifully scented poisons. He reminded himself to issue a memo about them.

'Ms Maxwell? Mr Ing?'

'I regret to inform you of their passing, sir.'

It was inconvenient to lose Delores and Moses. The woman had been clever, in her own way, and Moses, well he was a legend. But, as they said, legends ... *never died*. Moses would have to continue, in one shape or another.

It was messier than he would have liked. But that was beta-testing for you. Unpredictable. Thankfully, it was frighteningly easy for people to be wiped away – if you chose the right people in the first place.

But still ... messy.

And exactly what Morpheus could be used for in the future: one carefully constructed dream, one perfectly balanced REM sleep, and those people would simply forget what had happened on that island. Their brains would be reprogrammed. So much *cleaner*.

He clasped his hands and tapped the two index fingers together. Sweat Stain cleared his throat nervously.

'And?'

'Well ...' The man swallowed loudly. 'We've just had a report of a boat, coming from one of the coves and heading to the mainland. It has two people in it. As yet unidentified.'

The barefoot man clenched and unclenched one fist, watching the tendons in his wrist flex and disappear.

One day those tendons might be reinforced with a biologically compatible substance that hadn't been invented yet, something that would keep his skeleton strong while his organs were replaced one by one. Then, eventually they would find a way to open up the parts of the brain currently unmapped, stimulate those dormant neurons into activity as yet unimagined.

Better human beings.

Smarter people who learned quicker and made better choices. The kind of people who would not choose to get in a silly boat and sail away. This was the ultimate purpose of the glowing map, wasn't it?

The barefoot man hadn't realized how useful sleep could be, before he discovered Moses. The world was obsessed with it, or rather the lack of it, but previously he'd thought of it as wasted time: necessary, but a waste all the same. Thanks to Moses though, sleep now held all sorts of possibilities that could be utilized by all sorts of people with different agendas.

Well … they'd *think* they had different agendas. He smiled. Soon though, they would discover they all had the same agenda: his.

The flashing light that represented St Dunstan's on the map blinked out.

That was an improvement. Now there was no irregularity to needle him as he stared at the map, all the lights glowing unwaveringly. It was like one of those magic-eye pictures, if he stared at it long enough something else would form in his vision – he could see the future in it, a future in which he was the centre and pivot.

The barefoot man tapped his fingers together a few more times. Curiosity was a sign of an active mind and he had to admit, he was curious. A boat. Delores had had a hand in that, no doubt. He had never trusted the woman. It might amuse him to find out what had happened.

The lights on his map shone unwaveringly, each of them representing a trial in some forgotten part of a country somewhere. Not just sleep, of course – that was merely one part of his arsenal in the war he was waging.

Birdsong piped up suddenly. His micro-nap was over. He wondered whether one of his telomeres was fraying slightly because of the missed rest and imagined it, the broken fronds swaying like coral under the sea. A full day and a fixed regime stretched out before him. He would be late for his LED light bathing.

Sentimentality. It would be his downfall. He got up and Sweat Stain backed away before him as if he was a god.

Not yet.

'Intercept the boat at the mainland. Discreetly.'

'Yes, sir.'

Chapter 66

It had to be a hallucination.

Thea blinked. She'd already had this one before: a boat, some owls scrabbling amongst golf balls and her mother at the prow.

She blinked again.

'Who's that?' Rory shielded his eyes with one hand.

Thea turned to him. 'You can see it too?' And then she grabbed his arm, her blanket slipping from her shoulders. 'You can see it too!'

'Umm … yes? And there is a woman waving at us?'

Thea clambered across the boat, the waves lurching as much as her heart because, without a doubt, there standing at the prow of the orange and navy lifeboat, vagina-printed scarf blowing back in the wind, waving her arms as if she was helping land a plane was …

… her mother.

No owls, no golf balls, no mushrooms, no hallucination. Real and in the flesh.

'Thea!' she heard her mother yell.

When she had been little, like all small children, she had believed that her mother could fix anything, could make anything better, that she could cry out for her and there she'd appear, ready

297

to reprimand, repair, or rescue. It seemed, even at twenty-seven years of age, that trust held true.

Burning tree, ghost balloons, lab rat in a maze.

A daughter enveloped in a hug by her mother.

Hands had helped her into the boat and now arms held her, her face pressed close to a scarf that smelled of patchouli and herb-infused tea. All those times on the island when she'd thought that this was it, this was the moment that her life ended, on a coastal path, in a lighthouse, or a white corridor, each time she had imagined these arms around her, this smell. Part of her still thought it couldn't be true, that the force of her imagination had conjured up this boat and all the people on it.

'Dear girl, dear, dear, girl,' she heard her mother whisper over and over again, felt her arms tighten. Thea wasn't sure if she said anything in return apart from meaningless sounds, the words in her brain hopelessly mangled.

Though it felt to Thea that they had only been hugging for seconds, Vivian eventually pulled away to get a good look at her, lips twitching, a glint in her bloodshot eyes.

'I told you it was a cult, didn't I?'

Thea gave a hoarse laugh and glanced around the boat, not a small inflatable thing, but big with glistening orange paint, safety rails, walkways, and people. Quite a few people, faces that she didn't know. Behind her Rory was being helped aboard. She knew that the people were made of flesh and muscle and blood, that the boat was fibreglass and plastic and rubber but to her it all felt paper thin. She could poke her finger through it all and watch it tear.

'How?' she managed before her legs wobbled and Vivian helped her into the cabin where she could sit out of the wind. She worried she would sink straight through the hard seat, puddle through its cracks and pool on the floor into a shapeless blob, but with Rory sat on one side and Vivian on the other, they kept her up and kept her whole.

She scanned the sea around them and shifted in her seat. 'Wait. I don't think it's safe. I think ... there are probably people coming for us—'

And then a familiar voice interrupted her: 'This is the coast-guard, girlie. Official now, see?'

And if she was just getting used to the idea that all the rest of it was real, then this part at least had to be a hallucination, Thea thought, as the man walked towards her. This man should have been in a pub armoured with abandoned hanging basket hooks, making tuna and dandruff sandwiches.

'But—?'

'Thea, this is Alastair,' Vivian said. 'He's been a great help.'

'Nice to see you again, Thea.' He held out his hand and she took it, her own dwarfed in his rough fingers. 'Said I was a life-boat man, didn't I?' He chuckled.

Vaguely she remembered the dust-fogged photo on the pub wall and the collection box on the reception counter. There was something different about the man stood in front of her, however. It wasn't the newly shaven chin and dandruff-free shoulders, though that was surprising enough; it was the way a new light shone in the granite of his face.

'So you see, Alastair's lovely friends at the lifeboat station were more than happy to help – after all, you did need rescuing from sea.' And when Vivian next spoke her voice was steel. 'You are safe.'

There were other people on board the boat, three men and a woman and Thea tried to see individual faces, but they blurred together into a mix of shy smiles, waterproof clothing and worried frowns.

'But what about when we get to shore?' Thea's jaw started to tremble, making it difficult to get the words out.

'The lifeboat men called the local police. They're waiting on the mainland.'

'Official now, see?' Alastair added.

Thea realized that both her mother and Alastair were waiting for the whole story, but the trembling that had begun in her jaw was now spreading, outwards through her arms and chest but also inwards, making her mind buzz and judder like a badly connected television. The whole story. It was there, inside her, but there was too much of it and too little of her.

Burning tree, ghost balloons, lab rat in a maze.

'It can wait.' Vivian tucked the blanket tighter around Thea's shoulders. 'Don't worry, it can all wait.'

Thea's fingers were so stiff that, at first, she couldn't do it, but on the third attempt she managed to unzip her coat pocket, taking out the memory stick and pressing it into Vivian's hand.

'That ... that explains a lot ... of it,' she managed.

Vivian held it between thumb and finger and studied it before giving a nod and popping it under her bra strap. 'Safest place, teapot.'

Thea cringed at the hated nickname and cringed even more when she heard her mother say, 'And who's this handsome young chap?' as Rory shifted beside her and gave a deep, throaty chuckle. But then the world went fuzzy and Thea watched colours swim lazily across her vision, the voices around her blurring into nothing but a soothing lullaby.

She felt an arm around her back and was grateful for the way it fitted perfectly behind her neck. Dragging at least some of the focus back into the world, she moved her head – which was now the size and weight of a small planet – and traced the arm back to Rory.

Rory.

The beard at her preliminary testing, chocolate smuggler extraordinaire, ally ... friend.

He smiled down on her. There was something different about him too, she realized, taking a while to work it out. Lines. The lines on his face – those of worry, fear, tension – were gone, smoothed away. It made him look younger.

She gave him some of her blanket.

This time, when he held her hand, they were no longer on their own in a dark room with Rosie's dead body in front of them. This time the island was merely a smudge on the horizon, a memory, a nightmare. She laced her fingers in his and the warmth of his palm brought a tingling into her own. She wanted to tell him about the hollow trees she had seen that time in a documentary, how the dark spaces can be filled with a fierce burning light ...

... but thoughts were beginning to slip from her like eels.

'I'll be here,' Vivian whispered. 'We'll all be here. Go to sleep.'

She knew she could no longer keep her eyes from closing. But, with her mother on one side, and Rory on the other, she was no longer afraid. She finally let the darkness take her.

And, that night, in a city far away, in a tiny flat in the bedroom of someone who had been awake for hours, a phone beeped. A message popped up on the screen:

Morpheus. Dream your way to a better you – one sleep at a time.

Acknowledgements

A book is very much like the performance of a play. What you hold in your hands is the well-rehearsed performance, shining under the stage lights. But behind the scenes there are many people in the shadows making sure it all happens: moving the set, finding the costumes, swiping the gin bottle out of the main actor's hands …

To those people.

Thanks to Kate, my marvellous agent, who found my story in her slush pile and has championed it ever since. Her support has meant the world to me and I know she is always there: willing me on, cheering me on, and occasionally giving me a gentle shove in the right direction.

To my HQ family. Thank you to my fairy godmother Lisa Milton, who took the time to not only read the whole of my manuscript but also help me shape it. She is truly one of the most generous and supportive women in publishing. And Abi, my editor extraordinaire, who has so carefully dug through my words to help me bring out what I *actually* meant to say. She is the kindest, bestest editor I could wish for. With eagle eyes.

Thank you though to everyone at HQ who has worked on this

book: copyediting, proofreading, cover design and marketing. Their expertise and professionalism is invaluable.

Huge thanks to the Primadonna Festival. There are many literary festivals out there, but this one really is special: warm, friendly, inclusive and truly life-changing, not just for me but for others too. That sunny weekend in Suffolk in the summer of 2019 was where my adventure began.

Thank you to Gillian who read my manuscript in its rawest state. Her lovely feedback gave me the confidence to continue working on it and her insight helped me see what the story could actually be.

As an insomniac myself, I didn't have to go far for most of my research for this story, but there were two books upon which I relied. Matthew Walker's *Why We Sleep* and Guy Leschziner's *The Secret World of Sleep* both provided inspiration, knowledge and an insight into what the brain does while we sleep. Any flights of fancy or misinterpretations are, of course, my own.

Thanks to The Coven – we have been meeting in thunder, lightning and in rain for a very long time now. Where would I be without you? (No, really, where? I'm terrible with directions!) Em: the woman who knows where all the bodies are, helped bury them and brought nibbles and drinks for afterwards. Fi: the first reader of many books and stories, grammar queen, hot dog legs, 'I'm not being funny but …' Oh yes, and Chris: I have been waiting a long time for the right opportunity to introduce him as 'my friend's husband.'

Thanks Ian for reading the book when I was still trying to understand what worked and what didn't – and for your enthusiasm. 'There's a book in that!'

Also thank you to the writing community, on Twitter and Facebook, all of them so generous with encouragement and help – far too many to name individually, but you know who you are.

Thanks to my family. To Cath, for her super-quick emergency read when I desperately needed a fresh set of eyes, Martin, Aidan,

Ffion and Gwen. Auntie Irene who brought Christmas every year when we were little and braved all of our caravan holidays. To my sister Caroline who always dressed my Barbie first when we were little. And to my mother, who worked so hard to make the best life for us and who gave us our love of reading in the first place.

Finally, thanks to my husband Jason, the best partner-in-crime, cheerleader, sympathy-giver, chef, beta-reader and friend. I cannot imagine my life without you.

And to all the sleepless, those who know about darkness, reading this so late at night that, after what seems like years, it eventually becomes morning.

Dear Reader,

We hope you enjoyed reading this book. If you did, we'd be so appreciative if you left a review. It really helps us and the author to bring more books like this to you.

Here at HQ Digital we are dedicated to publishing fiction that will keep you turning the pages into the early hours. Don't want to miss a thing? To find out more about our books, promotions, discover exclusive content and enter competitions you can keep in touch in the following ways:

JOIN OUR COMMUNITY:
Sign up to our new email newsletter: hyperurl.co/hqnewsletter
Read our new blog www.hqstories.co.uk
🐦 : https://twitter.com/HQStories
📘 : www.facebook.com/HQStories

BUDDING WRITER?
We're also looking for authors to join the HQ Digital family!
Find out more here:
https://www.hqstories.co.uk/want-to-write-for-us/
Thanks for reading, from the HQ Digital team

ONE PLACE. MANY STORIES

If you enjoyed *Sleepless*,
then why not try another gripping
thriller from HQ Digital?